AUTHOR'S NOTE

Historically, Romanes, the Romani language was used
only by the Romani between themselves, or as a way of
communicating with each other amongst non-Gypsy people;
the odd comment, for example, when dealing or at
a market. It was spoken, not written.

It was first written down about 150 years ago and the
spellings and pronunciation vary from region to region. For
example: there are several words for a non-Gypsy person.

I have used the term more commonly found in Wales:
gajo – ga'jō, (singular), gaje – ga'jē, (plural). *See glossary.*
The Gypsy characters in this novel speak a mixture of Anglo
Romani jib (speech). As they cross the Welsh border to pick
hops and fruit in the Welsh Marches they use both English
and Welsh words in conversation with the 'gaje'.

Nb: 'Gypsy' is used with a capital letter as in Welsh, English,
not as a pejorative term. The Romani consultant for this
book advised me that this is both acceptable and correct.

ELI'S SECRET

To Dulcie

with best wishes

DMLewis

D. M. Lewis

Published by Dolman Scott

ISBN 978-1-905553-61-7

Book design by Maggie Aldred

Dolman Scott Ltd
www.dolmanscott.com

For my father and my children,
Nicholas, Samantha and Howard

Part One
1913

ONE

The Church of St Michael and All Angels stood surrounded by yew trees, hollow with age, and six centuries of forgotten graves. It was empty and locked, abandoned long before the Revival across the border that had swelled Chapel congregations, and all but emptied the pubs. The backwash had even reached this quiet corner of the Welsh Marches. In summer nature spread its own tribute in memory of lost souls. A haze of pollen drifted above the mantle of Queen Anne's lace, past clustered hawthorn blossoms exuding their sickly-sweet odour of death, to the lower branches of chestnut trees around the perimeter.

It was a silent place, and a secret playground for the villagers who could not relate their homespun beliefs to this ancient wilderness of stone sepulchres. At the least disturbance, a jay would flash and swoop through the air, its klaxon cry fading into the distance, and all would be still again. But the headstones bore witness to many a tryst for the living.

The Reverend ApIvor had reorganised his timetable to drop Arthur at the railway station. There were only two private cars in the district apart from those at the manor. The more opulent belonged to Doctor Bevan. Couldn't wait to get rid of his horses, could the Doc'. He was the first to adopt this new mode of transport. His Prince Henry Vauxhall was the grandest car for miles, but it was the appearance of ApIvor's more modest Austin model T that was the real source of wonder. For a man as small in stature as their Reverend to master such a machine, and at his time of life too, caused many an open mouth. Folk marvelled that a man of the cloth should buy a car at all, but soon recovered from this show of eccentricity when his 'Tin Lizzie' became the open-handed, unpaid 'means' of 'transport' for those with neither.

Arthur was looking forward to the journey in; a chance to chat and share his hopes, wanting the minister's blessing, his almost parental approval. He had a couple of stories too (admittedly a bit second-hand), but different, sharpened by the salty tang of the bustling port he now called home. Dear old Pompey, he couldn't wait to get back there.

But instead of heading for the main Hereford road, ApIvor turned the car around.

"Now don't you worry, Arthur," he said. "There'll be plenty of time."

He took a run at the steep gradient of the Devil's Lip, crouched over the wheel as if the effort was his own and not the engine's. Cresting the top, he pulled in by the gateway to the old churchyard – much to Arthur's relief.

"I'll just stop by here. I must drop off a copy of the Parish News at Old Eli's. Don't trust myself trying to negotiate this girl of mine on that steep driveway." He gave an apologetic smile. "I know! How many years is it since he left? The tenancy has changed hands several times, but I can't help it. It will always be 'Old Eli's' place, as far as I'm concerned, and I'm sure I'm not alone in that. 'High Fields Farm' its proper name, I believe. The new people there are pleasant enough, though not as regular to Chapel as one might hope. Going to farm peas and strawberries, so I'm told. Now there's progress for you. Shan't be a tick."

Without waiting for any comment, he hurried away.

Arthur opened the car door, and sat for a moment deciding whether or not to climb out. He knew ApIvor's minutes of old. Time for a cigarette, at least. He took his tobacco tin from his coat pocket, and leant against the wall overlooking the churchyard, twirling a thin roll up with practised fingers.

His forty eight hours compassionate leave was almost over. Every winter, these past seven years, he had been expecting his older sister Louise to write: 'Our mother is dead'. But every winter their mother clung on, as if reluctant, at the last, to face the Maker she had worshipped with such fervour. Others, falling victim to the same disease, were diagnosed later, and died sooner. His brother-in-law Jack claimed he'd read it in her face, and had given her twelve months. As predictions go it was long overdue.

Her funeral was unusually well attended considering she had never been the most sociable of women. It felt odd being valued so late. Boys he had scrapped with in the school yard were now ruddy-faced, and uncomfortable in their formal attire. Most were labourers on the estate. Resignation had set in their shoulders: the mark of country men. One by one they came forward to shake his hand, commenting on his uniform with a mixture of envy and respect.

The eyes of near enough the entire village bored into their backs as the service began. Every latecomer caused a momentary silence followed by a rustle of disappointment. There was an air of expectation more befitting a wedding.

Mary Prosser and her mother had positioned themselves in a side pew with a better view of the aisle.

Don't hold your breath, Mary. There's one Pritchard you'll never see again. He isn't coming back, and it wouldn't be for you if he did.

Plain, lumpy Mary, the butt of all their schoolboy jokes, who made herself a laughing stock over his big brother. All these years on surely she was over it, or maybe she and her mother were there to gloat?

Howell would never return. Twelve years had passed without a word. None of them had broken their silence about his sudden disappearance, nor would they. He knew it was out of respect for his sister, who lived on here, and the will of the Reverend, that nothing was said to stir up that particular memory. For Howell had been the favourite; unashamedly preferred by the woman lying in that wooden casket. He alone had been conceived with love. The rest of them had followed in due season, destined to come a poor second along with their father.

Half way through the last verse of 'Abide with me', as the assembled voices swelled in a triumphant finish, the Chapel door creaked open and shut. The brisk tap-tap of a woman's heels advanced towards their pew. Nancy slid in next to Jack, but kept her gaze fixed upon the coffin. Arthur felt the air vibrate when the singing stopped, but the Reverend ApIvor's voice boomed above them allowing no opportunity for comment.

There were three old favourites left on the board. None of his family needed a hymn book. They were word perfect – drilled into them from childhood. He could hear Eddie and Will's rich bass voices behind him, and to his right, Nancy's soprano, pitch perfect, soaring above the others. Their Mum would have been proud to hear it.

"Should have had her voice trained..." she would say, while Nancy pulled a face behind her back, "...it's a gift from God."

He supposed God could appreciate her singing in a music hall. At least she used her talent.

Louise, and the two younger sisters, Ruby, and May, wore their Sunday best clothes in shades of grey, and brown, with mourning bands fixed to their sleeves. Each had bought a suitable hat for the occasion. Nancy's outfit must have cost a packet. It flattered her pale skin and auburn curls. Even in black she made her sisters look dowdy.

The Reverend had volunteered the back of the Chapel for the wake. True, he hadn't expected such a turnout, but the village hall had yet to be repaired following the floods. The Pritchards' old home remained uninhabitable, and the lane to Louise and Jack's cottage was too much of a climb for most.

In the centre of the refreshment table, someone had placed a large fruit cake of the sort usually found in hotels. It dwarfed the plates of delicate scones and sandwiches his sisters had prepared that morning.

Nancy bustled forward to kiss Louise.

"I brought that, Lou', didn't have time to make anything." She glanced disdainfully at the chattering congregation. "Should be more than enough for this lot."

Gwyneth Prosser nudged her daughter. He could imagine the comments over the Post Office counter. "Shop-bought cake, and at her mother's wake too. Agnes would have had a fit."

Without waiting for a formal invitation to start, Nancy helped herself from the tea urn. She sat down a little apart from the others, lifting her cup with exaggerated delicacy – little finger extended.

Jack brought a cup of tea for Arthur, and one for himself.

"All right, our kid?" His hands shook with the effort of holding such delicate china. It was his wife's best service. "I still prefers pouring mine into a saucer, cools it down quicker." He winked at Arthur. "D'you 'spose our Nancy'd mind if I sat next to her while I sup mine up?"

Arthur smothered a grin. Not so long ago he would have been embarrassed by his sister's behaviour. Now he had no illusions.

Jack, mindful of his duty, moved away to join Louise, leaving him standing alone at the back. From there he had a good view of the assembly. He sensed a change in the atmosphere. A circle was tightening around Nancy.

Their token cups of tea discarded, Gwyneth and Mary were homing in on their prey. The two younger Prosser sisters had joined them, along with Jim Evans. One of them was married to him now,

14

or engaged, he couldn't remember which, Louise had written. That Evans always was a nosey devil, couldn't wait to stir up trouble even as a boy. Well, Nancy might not be his favourite sister, but she was still family. He moved in front of her, effectively blocking their view. His brothers, who must have been watching him for a signal to disperse, detached themselves from the main group and formed a line by the door. Those remaining mourners took the hint. This was all. No one else would arrive. There was no more to see, and nothing left to eat.

❧

Louise and Jack, with Nancy hanging on to her sister's elbow, walked ahead to their cottage. They were followed by the others, relaxed now the wake had disbanded; even enjoying a joke or two. Arthur strolled along behind them keeping pace with May's shorter steps, her arm linked through his. Another hour and all this would be over. Eddie would take his girl back home to the next village; Will, smiling and apologetic, would cycle back to his digs; Joe, heavyset and belligerent, would hold his peace and follow him. At least, that was his hope.

They went in through the back door without ceremony. Nancy pushed ahead into the front parlour. They heard her gasp, and found her standing in front of the mantelpiece, arms folded, jaw set, her cheeks flushed. With all that paint on her face she looked like an angry doll. She came straight to the point.

"You didn't waste any time, did you, Louise? I wondered who got the bronzes. All those years I dusted them for our Mum. Said

I was the only one she trusted to do it properly. Good as promised them to me, she did."

Before Arthur or the others could protest, Joe stepped forward, and placed himself squarely in front her.

"The Reverend gave those bronzes to Mum and Dad as a wedding present. And in front of witnesses our Mum gave them back – during one of her clearer moments – no doubt to stop any of your nonsense."

"Joe..."

Louise, close to tears, began to plead with him, but Joe was in full spate now.

"Last week he returned them to our Lou', in recognition of all her hard work." It wasn't true. Louise had spoken to him about the bronzes wondering what to do. She'd rescued them from their old home, 'but only to keep them safe' as she'd put it. Listening to Joe's strategy, Arthur hoped the others would fall in. "There's no argument about it. We all agree." His other siblings were nodding vigorously. "So, if you don't like it you can do the other thing. Take it up with the Reverend. See what he has to say." Knowing full well she wouldn't. "But," he added, looking her up and down, "you and Mum were about the same size, I'm sure no one will mind if you want to pick through what's left of her wardrobe."

The shaft went home. Nancy narrowed her eyes at him, oblivious to the hostility she had roused. Turning to her eldest sister, she tried a different tactic.

"Louise, how could you let him say such things to me, today of all days?"

16

She even produced a tear or two. Funny watching her mind working; growing up, everyone gave her the benefit of the doubt, unwilling to believe she could be devious. Everyone except Howell, that is; yet he had been Nancy's hero.

As if on cue, they heard a car pull up outside the gate. The driver left the engine running, and honked his horn. It fractured the peaceful country air sending Jack's hens cackling round their enclosure, and setting off next doors' dog. Someone hurried down the path, knocked twice, and retreated as quickly. Joe ducked his head to look through the front room window.

"Your fancy man's come for you – and not before time."

"He's my fiancé."

"If you say so."

Nancy looked ready to spit.

"Goodbye Louise. Goodbye Jack, Arthur."

Snatching up her bag, she ignored everyone else. Joe swept open the door, stood in mock salute as she slipped through, then shut it none too gently behind her. In the silence that followed he cleared his throat and looked hesitantly at his sister and brother-in-law.

"I'm sorry for speaking out of turn, but she makes me that angry, always did. Got away with everything, scheming little baggage. I'm sorry about that story too," (he baulked at the word 'lie') "but you know the Reverend *would* have done just what I said. The rest of it is true enough. We're all of an accord. Those bronzes belong to you – no argument. And don't you go soft, our Lou', and tell her otherwise, or she'll have them away, and sold, and be wearing the profit." His brothers and sisters murmured their assent. "And now I've gone and said too much again."

Jack patted his shoulder.

"Consider it forgotten. We're all a bit upset today, Joe."

Louise twisted her handkerchief in her fingers.

"It still dussen seem right, Jack."

"That's enough now. Everyone's agreed. Here they stay." He tried to give her a little hug. She didn't respond. "Come on, love, this won't do, let's forget about all this nonsense, or I'll take the bronzes down to the Reverend myself – and we'll have to go through the whole performance again when he sends them back."

Outside, in his eagerness to be gone, Nancy's beau tried to turn his motor car on the steep road junction. The wheels churned up enough sticky red mud to spatter most of the gleaming exterior, windscreen included, before it roared away. They crowded at the window to watch. Will spoke up for the first time.

"He'll need to be a bit careful on that slope."

Joe agreed with him.

"It's a wonder he can see over the steering wheel. Perhaps he has blocks to reach the pedals!" They both laughed. "Must be doing all right for a jockey, having a car like that. They'll be chewing it over for weeks in the village."

Perhaps Nancy's visit was welcome after all. It had provided a diversion from their unspoken hope. A false hope as it turned out. They could go their separate ways now: no more harm done.

"We'll be off too, Arthur." Joe gave his older brother an affectionate wallop on the arm. "You'll see the rest of us in uniform before long, though it'll be sommat a bit more becoming than Navy blue!"

While the others busied themselves with coats and hats, Arthur moved nearer the mantelpiece to examine the imposing, and controversial, bronzes. He'd never paid them much attention before. 'The sower', and 'the reaper' were Italian, or French maybe, and had occupied recesses either side of the chimney breast in their old cottage for as long as he could remember. They were 'exquisite', as the Reverend might say. Every detail was sharp and beautifully crafted. They must be worth a few bob. Now he had all of Nancy's motive.

The only other thing of value he remembered was the lectern their father had carved for his new bride to support her family Bible. It had been made at the height of his skill and was much admired. He wondered what became of it. Back then it held pride of place by the front window.

Her face still troubled, Louise came over to the fireplace.

"There's something else I should have mentioned – went clean out of my head earlier. We gave ApIvor the lectern. It seemed only proper. Said he'd keep it at the Chapel. The wood dried out after the flood, but Mum's Bible was damaged beyond repair. Jack did try, but it was hopeless. You don't mind, Arthur, do you?"

"No," he said. "The Reverend will be pleased to have it. Remind him of Dad, and their long friendship."

As for his mother's precious Bible, he wouldn't upset his sister by saying so, but picturing its watery end gave him immense satisfaction. There had been many occasions when he wanted to hurl the unwieldy tome into the river and dance upon the bank awaiting damnation or else tear out fistfuls of its slippery pages and thrust them into the range while her back was turned.

'The Almighty sees into the blackest hearts. He'll strike you dead...'

That was a favourite line while she chased them round the kitchen, or down the garden, in pursuit of a confession. You can only beat so much religion into a child.

There was a pleasing, if warped, justice in that Bible's destruction. Maybe such thoughts were risky. But here he stood – not struck dead yet.

He drew on his cigarette only to discover that it had gone out. He relit the dog end, narrowing his eyes against the acrid smoke, and glanced at the scene in front of him. Their local post office kept cards of a painting made in an earlier century, a romantic depiction of St Michael's that didn't sit well with Arthur's memories of boyhood escapades and conker tournaments. He preferred the photographs ApIvor had arranged in the village for Queen Victoria's diamond jubilee celebrations in 1897, when he and Howell were in the choir.

There, he'd thought of him again, his eldest brother long gone from the place. Grinding his cigarette stub under his heel, he climbed into the passenger seat, not wanting to dwell on anything else that held sad memories. It seemed that everywhere he looked something half-forgotten surfaced to remind him.

Turning back to the lane, he saw ApIvor puffing up the hill towards him and leant across to open the driver's door.

"All done now?"

ApIvor's face was a deep crimson from his exertions. It was several minutes before he could reply. He obliged him by cranking the car into life again. It was all the old chap could do to nod his thanks.

"Yes, sorry about that, but if I don't do these things when I think of them, I forget."

He released the handbrake gently, allowing the car to creep forward until his breathing and the engine's shuddering rhythm were in harmony again.

ApIvor looked older. His hair was thinner. Each strand stood out from the shining scalp as if sewn on individually, although there was still no trace of grey. His face was rounder than ever, and gold-rimmed spectacles – a recent addition – emphasised the small, almost delicate features gathered in the middle. Curiously, the gap in his front teeth looked wider. It increased the benign effect. If a cherub could age, he would resemble ApIvor.

He smiled at the man who had been their family friend through many a crisis, and generous in ways not measured by money. Arthur had known him all his life, and loved him. If he missed anyone, it was ApIvor. Settling back in the seat, he knew it might be years before he saw him again.

"Come... on... now... my... lovely." Punctuating each word with a grunt as he wrestled the wheel, ApIvor turned the vehicle round. "Now, Arthur, a chance for us to chat uninterrupted, for once, but you first while I catch my breath. What were you going to tell me about this new posting?"

It would be all right this last journey together. There was no need for platitudes, or sentiment. Now their mother lay at rest with their father, a curious peace had enveloped the family. It affected ApIvor too. He read as much in his eyes. Like his companion, he felt the need to change the subject and fill the silence with something life-renewing. Not too many laughs though. He wanted to keep both ApIvor's hands on the wheel, for when laughing, tears would stream down the good Reverend's cheeks, and he would have to wipe his eyes. No doubt the old fellow had some personal news he wanted to tell. There would be plenty of time to chat on this last trip, but nothing too animated or emotional. Now they were leaving, Arthur didn't want any more diversions or unexpected stops.

No, keep it all simple, and they might just arrive in one piece.

TWO

ApIvor served the Chapel, and the Chapel those who were God-fearing for miles around. Whenever there was a service, it was packed. His flock preferred simple rituals, polished boards, and plain prayer. Like their minister, they could all sing. They loved to sing. The walls reverberated with ApIvor's trained baritone and their enthusiastic harmonies. They left elated, and much closer to God.

Anyone wishing to visit ApIvor at home faced a half mile walk uphill to the manor gates. Set in the wall was a brass bell-pull, but the amiable cleric would open the side door to the lodge long before his visitor recovered breath enough to ring it.

ApIvor liked the elevated position of his 'abode', as he called it, claiming the exercise to and fro kept him fit. He had been to public school with the present incumbent of the manor, Godfrey Chalfont. It was one of his reasons for applying to such an out-of-the-way place to practise a ministry. His other reason, well hidden from all save his friend, was more prosaic. He had built and furnished the Chapel with his own money. Every brick and board a penance for the vast fortune his father, and grandfather before him, had accumulated at the height of the copper industry boom in South Wales. His conscience drew him away from the ornate mansion on the Gower where his only sister Gertrude still presided. It spared him her disappointment. She never recovered from the shock that once ordained he eschewed 'High Church' for Chapel.

Godfrey had been more enthusiastic.

"They're a Godless bunch in these parts since the old church fell into decay." He told ApIvor, by way of encouragement. "Altogether too much nonsense from the past. Too close to nature by half. Could benefit from a little fire and brimstone."

Godfrey's comments were only half-serious. They agreed a 999 year lease for a plot of land owned by the Chalfont estate on the edge of the village.

"After all," the 'squire' had reasoned, "a God-fearing workforce will be advantageous to all."

Over the years they developed a truce on the subject of alcohol. ApIvor would have had them all teetotal, but Godfrey was adamant.

"My success (and patronage) is founded on the cider and brewing industries. Discourage drunkenness by all means, but you know I still pay half my casuals in cider. Take away their life blood, and you, my friend, will have no congregation!"

ApIvor chose to rent the smallest of five houses within the manor grounds, a single-storey arrangement of three and a half elegant rooms behind rose-coloured stone, with deep windows.

The gillie lived in a matching lodge on the far side of the estate, nearer the river. Though married, he had no children, and for many months of the year, one salmon after another occupied the bath. It amused ApIvor, who had listened to his cleaning lady's outrage on the subject more than once.

"It's shocking, just shocking. A proper bath to themselves, and he keeps fish in it. I blame her, mind, dirty madam. More than half a Gyppo, if you ask me. Water strictly for drinking with her."

"Come on now, Gwyneth, that's not a particularly charitable thing to say, is it? And it's not every week he has a salmon."

He smiled to himself, prepared to overlook the gillie's laxity towards personal hygiene in favour of the few choice cuts of salmon that came his way. But Mrs Prosser had warmed to her theme.

"Oh, I'm sorry I'm sure. But most of us have to put child after child in our tin baths of a Saturday night. Well, you wouldn't know how inconvenient it is, of course, or the time it takes filling it up and baling out again afterwards, and water spilt everywhere. Seems such a waste for a couple like that."

"Ah, but 'Judge not', the Lord said."

He attempted to look stern, but the image of salmon cutlets with a side boat of delicate hollandaise sauce (his particular favourite)... new potatoes... early garden peas... maybe even a few broad beans... wouldn't leave him.

He shook himself out of such inappropriate musings, aware that Mrs Prosser, having ignored his admonition, was polishing with renewed vigour, and muttering.

"And you're wrong about the Gypsies, Gwyneth. They think we're the dirty ones, so I'm told."

Mrs Prosser snorted her contempt. Long-ingrained prejudice was hard to shift amongst the village women, even though their community was closer to the Gypsies than most. They worked along side them for six months of the year, and he knew they enjoyed the fortune-telling behind his back. Little escaped his notice, or if it did there was always someone willing to enlighten him.

He turned away to study his fine book collection. Mrs Prosser took the hint and retreated, leaving a trail of lavender-scented disapproval in her wake.

ApIvor appreciated the scaled down aesthetics of his accommodation. He was comfortable there, felt 'at home', and relished his bathroom, despite the chill that seeped through the lime-wash, summer or winter. He propped his shaving mirror on a little shelf that had been installed just for the purpose. It was one of his late friend's, (Wilf Pritchard's) many well-constructed niceties.

That morning, as he prepared for the day ahead, he thought about the Pritchards. He'd volunteered to take young Arthur back to the station after the funeral, and reminded himself that he must speak to him about the family. It was high time. He'd been sworn to secrecy while Arthur's parents, Agnes and Wilf, were still alive, but now, well, Arthur was a man, full-grown and responsible. He needed to know the whole truth. He owed him that. It had been so difficult to talk to any of them after Howell left. There was a complicit silence amongst them. Now, despite Arthur's maturity and good nature, he knew it would be difficult to instigate any discussion on the subject. He felt awkward compromising him in such a way, but springing it on him in the car was his last chance.

Young Howell, where are you now?

He doubted he'd recognise him so many years on. Millions had left from all over Europe for the New World. He prayed he'd used the brains God gave him, and made a decent life for himself.

The wardrobe door swung open, and he glimpsed the elderly man he knew to be himself from an unexpected angle. The thought depressed him, and he pushed the offending reminder out of the way with uncustomary irritation.

Where had his life gone? Three score of his allotted span were already used up, yet the interim years seemed to have passed almost without him noticing. So many looked to him as the arbiter of their problems, or for advice, but on days like this he felt convinced that he was the least qualified to solve the dilemmas of others. Nothing had worked out as he intended.

It had been his suggestion to send Howell away; his money that funded the voyage. Yet, truth be told, there were moments of regret. Moments when his heart raced remembering the enormity of such a choice, banishing the one young man he had truly loved (he would say like a son) for no one in their quiet backwater would repudiate such a statement.

The events of
1901

THREE

Mahalia sheltered behind the skirt of hawthorn separating their encampment from the neighbouring fields. This sudden squall had caught her unawares. Rain began beating a tattoo on the stiff piece of canvas that served as a makeshift cape.

She carried a small hurricane lamp, but feared its light would betray her. Hooked over her arm was a new enamel night-pail from the collection stowed beneath the steps of her grandmother's waggon. Struggling with two objects in this weather was foolish, and might prove her undoing. She set down the lamp. It would be easy to retrieve in the morning. The pail had another purpose.

Their waggons, six vardos of differing sizes, had been grouped together for protection. In the spaces between, several bender tents wobbled uncertainly as the wind tested their stability. Tiny plumes of smoke wavered as each family's fire sputtered and went out.

Farther away, in a more sheltered spot, a larger yog had been lit.

A group of men were tending it, arranging overlapping corrugated iron sheets, already slick with water and blackened by soot, at angles to protect the blaze. Their figures cast large shadows on the remaining stone wall of a derelict barn.

Wood smoke stung in her nostrils as it spiralled along the ground towards the thicket. Rain gleamed on nearby branches. Their mesh of thorns captured the firelight in a display of brittle lustres that trembled, and betrayed the slightest movement. Although her hair hid most of her face, she was careful not to stay too long in one position, or turn fully towards the light.

Mahalia counted the men. Caleb, her older brother, stood nearest the fire. She blinked away the rain and the picture cleared. Yes, and next to him a slighter version, her other, younger brother Job. Caleb was holding forth as usual.

She watched their gestures. They must be discussing the move across the border. It couldn't come soon enough. She hated this place. Within days, the few families accompanying them would take to the drom, splitting off in search of better sites. She would remain with her old grandmother, her Puro Dai – widowed only a year ago, Caleb, and Job – neither of them wed, and their cousins and families, less than twenty counting all her cousins' chavvis. It would be a time when tensions rose and the main topic of conversation would be her proposed marriage to Reuben. She felt like one of her Puro Dai's songbirds trapped in a cage.

The wind was mountain-cold, and relentless. She began to shiver, but concentrated on the group of men in the firelight. Two had their backs to her. It was harder to identify them. One must be

32

Noah, her cousin-in-law, but the other... She couldn't be sure, even now, that it was wise to move.

She had slipped away again, desperate to be alone before being closeted for the night in the stifling heat of her Puro Dai's vardo. The old grandmother felt the cold too much and no longer slept outside in the bender tents. She kept Mahalia close, as much to keep the men at bay as for her own comfort. But most evenings, if only for ten minutes before she was missed, Mahalia crept off. It was becoming a habit – anything to get away from all the noise.

There was no privacy anywhere. Someone was always watching. Now, in the darkness, her pleasure at being alone evaporated. Far from the others she was vulnerable. Ordinarily, she need stay only a few minutes longer before one of the women, Kezia probably, would worry enough to call out. Tonight, in these conditions, her reply would be snatched away on the wind.

The smoke pothered through the branches making her eyes smart. She would have to move or risk coughing. Gathering her skirt into a knot in front of her, she covered the joint between the handle and pail to prevent it clanking. If careful, she could slip past the tethered horses unnoticed and from there to safety.

She could see her Puro Dai's vardo now, the custom-made, smaller Ledge that had replaced her grandfather's ornate Burton show waggon.

When her Puro Dadus died they had left the familiar faces and places of their show folkendi. Her grandmother was anxious to get back to her roots, back to the old ways; the more elderly she became, the more difficult and demanding. Coming here to the Beacons was like an obsession with her: it made no sense. She claimed the openness improved her health, but Mahalia saw only her age and frailty. There was no spare money for medicine, and they avoided gaje doctors. Just the mention of one would make Puro Dai curse and spit.

There were few opportunities now to play her harp. Cash work was getting scarce, and she feared that one day Caleb would make good his threat to chop it in, if only to have enough wonga to keep them fed. How had it come to this so soon? As the memory of her beloved Puro Dadus faded like winter grass, so had their fortunes, but for now, her grandmother was 'queenie', their acting leader until the family could agree on another chief. Her word was law. Mahalia had no choice but stay; no say at all in her own future.

Twenty yards to go. She paused to catch her breath. Edging along in the dark needed all her concentration. There were so many unseen obstacles waiting to trip her up. Every few feet she stopped to listen. The rain struck each surface with a different note, rising in a crescendo and drowning out familiar noises. Ahead were two bender tents; one for Lymena's numerous chavvis – tangled together like a mound of sleeping puppies; the other for the single men.

The wind had been savage these past few days, driving most of the family into their vardos earlier than usual. Only the sturdiest tents remained. She was spared the usual catcalls. Three more yards to go. More confident now, she emerged from the shadows.

Reuben stepped in front of her, barring the way. With one swift movement he grabbed her upper arms in a pincer grip, lifted her off the ground, and pushed her against the wooden panels. She had enough presence of mind to hold on to the bucket, concealing it behind the fullness of her skirt. Using it as a weapon was no longer an option. Another idea occurred to her – it would get her into trouble of a different sort, but was worth the risk.

Crushed by his strength, she managed to wrench her face away from him. Undeterred he laughed, slurring his words.

"Dikka for sommat, are yer, Mally? Think ya'd give me the slip? I've been waitin'. What yer after in the dark, eh?"

He breathed beer fumes over her. These days, it seemed, he never lost the smell. She shuddered, fearing his strength and nearness.

"Cold eh? I'll soon warm yer up." He pressed closer. "Can't put me off much longer, our Puro Dai agreed, remember? Yer mine, or soon will be..." His breath was hot on her cheek, "...no use struggling, though I likes a mort with fight in 'er."

Not caring if it angered him, she shook her head until all her loose, dark hair completely obscured her face. Summoning all her remaining strength, she yelled,

"Caleb!"

It came out as more of a squeak. Through her hair she saw him grin in triumph. He took no notice of this gesture of refusal, amused by her helplessness. Pinned in this position, it was difficult to kick him – he'd made sure of that – being too well-practised at subduing people. He had beaten her brothers before now, though never in a clean fight.

In the distance she recognised Caleb's voice, and hoped he was coming towards them, though she risked his temper being out here alone. He'd say she asked for it. Give her a thrashing most likely if she upset him. But she had come prepared.

Reuben heard him too, and released his hold a fraction. It was all she needed to half-throw the bucket, letting it clatter against the wooden steps. If that didn't put him off at least the noise might bring someone... anyone. Seeing the night-pail roll towards his feet, he dropped her with a grunt of disgust, and lurched backwards.

Caleb hurried round the side of the vardo, his anxiety giving way to anger at the scene in front of him. He looked from one to the other, then down at the bucket. Mahalia sprang forward, snatched up the offending item and returned it to the hook beneath the steps. Reuben swayed on his feet. Her brother glared at her, jabbing his finger towards the ground.

Pushing past him, she hissed,

"It was empty. I took it to protect myself, since my prala don't think I'm worth the effort."

With that she ran up the steps, and out of reach. Balancing on the narrow top step, she slipped off her boots and jerked open the doors, leaving him to cope with their cousin, the man to whom she had been promised, with little regard for her feelings, since childhood.

❦

"Dordi! Dordi! Shut the door quick, Mally, we're losin' the warm."

There were already three women inside the vardo. They had been playing cards while they waited for her return. Lymena, her cousin Paoli's wife, sat on the rug directly in front of the entrance, with her back to it. Without getting up, she hitched over to make room.

"Look at yer, soaking wet. Yer been out so long I reckoned yer found a mush to keep yer dry!" She rolled her eyes at her sister Kezia, sitting next to her, and dug her in the ribs. "Don't know what 'er's missin', does 'er, penna? Don't know what it's like to 'ave a mush keep 'er warm. Wait 'til yer wed, then'll see." She turned towards the old lady sitting in a small upholstered seat fixed to the side of the waggon. "Shoulda put 'er on a lower stool when 'er was fourteen, Beebi Rae, to see if 'er was ready, 'er being such a kusi thing! My Zilla now, 'er toes reach the ground at eleven. Be ready next year, that one, and look at yer, twenty this summer – an old woman nearly – and still not rommed. I had three by that age. Folk'll think there's sommat wrong wi' ya." She nudged her sister, who was more concerned with helping Mahalia remove her muddy outdoor clothes, and gave a lewd wink. "...and I wouldn't keep a mush like Reuben waitin'."

Kezia took the towel she had been warming by the small stove, and wrapped it around Mahalia's hair.

"Leave 'er be. Let 'er enjoy a bit o' freedom while 'er can. There'll be no time for day-dreaming, or playing that harp once 'er's rommed and 'as 'er first tikni in 'er arms."

"Aye, true enough." Lymena laughed, "That mush'll give 'er a drom full of chavvis."

Mahalia hung her wet clothes on the hooks above the door next to those of the other women, and joined them where they sat on the floor, clad in just their bodices and petticoats. It was stifling: an over ripe mixture of stale pipe smoke, sweat, and damp, unwashed clothes. Even though it was a good size vardo and they were small women, she didn't know how long she could stand the atmosphere. Hated being shut in, but to be shut in with Lymena – a proper ferret that one, always spite behind everything. She hoped her Puro Dai would soon feel drowsy and send the sisters away.

Lymena was fixed on the subject, worrying at it like a snappy jukel. They'd heard it all before, yap, yap, yap. On and on about being wed, but when she had laughed Mahalia noticed that another of her teeth was missing. There were those who said she talked too much, looking the other way when her mush used the only method he knew of shutting her up.

As for Reuben, he and Paoli were from the same stock. Despite the fact that he boasted of her to other men, as if she was a prize mare ready for breeding, she knew it wouldn't be long before her youth and dreams were knocked out of her.

There was a different atmosphere these days. She sensed the unrest between the men. Who would become chief? If she married Reuben, he would have a stronger claim to the title. The drinking worried her too, and the way Job seemed to be shifting his loyalty from Caleb, to Reuben, the cousin he admired and copied.

When their Puro Dadus was alive he had made such a fuss of her, relishing the gift (his words) of a granddaughter in a familia where the men outnumbered the women of her generation. He insisted that she should marry only when she was ready, preferring instead to encourage her music, even buying her a harp, a cause of great resentment at the time.

Music was her only love. From the first notes she plucked, it had bewitched her. While other girls accepted their future role, this enchantment took her to a different place. She had the gift, her grandfather said, and no one could deny that. The harp had been an unusual indulgence. Now he was dead, her Puro Dai was anxious to resolve matters. But in her dreams she played in different places, halls like those the gaje built for their singing and dancing, where sound bounced off the walls and encircled her. Locked in this imaginary world, she accompanied songs she composed for ears that could no longer hear them. But although the dimensions of her dream shifted and changed, one thing remained constant: it contained no cousin to ensnare her.

Lymena had been watching her face closely.

"Look at 'er, sulkin' now that 'arp of 'ers bin stowed away." When her teasing went unanswered, she nudged her sister again. "I'll read the leaves. That'll tell us, eh, penna?"

Kezia removed the first towel, and put another around Mahalia's shoulders.

"Set by 'ere," she said, moving from her position near the stove. She fanned out her friend's luxuriant hair to catch the heat. "It'll soon dry." She checked the amount of water in the kettle. It had been simmering on the hotplate. Satisfied, she reached for the teapot and caddy. "Let's see what the leaves say, Mally. I wants another readin'."

The wind shook the vardo making everything rattle. There was no sitting outside in this squall.

Mahalia relaxed. This was a chance to get her own back. Lymena was hopeless at the leaves, though no one dared tell her. It was a skill that needed patience and imagination to interpret correctly. Her cousin's wife had neither virtue. She snatched at the first image she saw, and invariably made a hash of it.

Mahalia understood Kezia's eagerness for a new reading. She wanted another baby. Fate had left her with two children. The eldest, a boy of nine, spent most of his time with the men and the other lads, while her remaining son, little more than a toddler, slept in the bender tent outside amongst Lymena's brood. Kezia had lost almost as many babies as her pen had carried. Some trick of the blood, their outsider's ratti, her grandmother thought. Such a shame; she was the better mother.

The sisters sat together, knees touching. Lamplight softened the reality of life on the drom so clearly etched on their features in daylight. Lymena was twenty-eight, Kezia a year younger, yet their bloom had faded early. Their fingers bore permanent stains from years of hop-picking, and the hand-rolled cigarettes they smoked incessantly.

'Strong and limber' with 'flying fingers and feet' that was the measure of a Romani chi, so her Puro Dadus had said, not 'bone and string' nor 'soft and whey-faced' like the gaje.

How she missed him. There were moments, sitting in the vardo like this, when she sensed his presence. He had been a rare mush – a 'one-off', she realised too late, believing everyone was blessed with such a grandparent.

'A regular peacock' her Puro Dai called him. Nothing, and nobody got the better of him. And no one could miss him. He wore an old-fashioned frock coat with a silk dikalo knotted at his neck in the traditional way; the brighter the better. But it was his headgear people noticed most. His favourite was what the gaje called a 'topper', bound with coloured bands and pierced by jay feathers.

"Dikka that mush!" her grandmother used to say, "Why 'e 'as more hats than one of them fancy Paris ladies!" half in pride at his appearance, half in mockery at such vanity.

The topper exaggerated his height, and he enjoyed causing a sensation. A showman he had been when her grandparents first met – and a showman he remained in his heart. 'Swanky Jessel' people called him. No one remembered his other name. Yet despite the hostility between the show folk and the travellers theirs had been a remarkable marriage with a temporary truce between families.

It had all been so different when he was alive. He had shown her what it meant to be Romani, taking pains to explain their traditions. From the moment she could talk, he had taken her hand explaining every small detail.

"The gaje are dirty," he said. "Use the same bowls for washing their clothes as they do for their dishes – and all their crockery is mixed up. No one has their own special things. No wonder when sickness visits one of their houses they all get it. We can't afford to be ill, not on the drom."

And it all made sense to her. Later, when she railed against the inequalities of women's lives compared with the men, the taboos surrounding her femaleness – the restrictions all the women had to endure, her grandmother had been exasperated with her. Unusually, for this was always considered 'women's business', his had been the logical explanation.

"Women are vulnerable," he said, "too much familiarity raises the temperature, fires the blood – and Romani men are ever prey to that. Modesty is your protection, that and honour, which binds the Romani chal. At least for most...", he had seemed displeased when he spoke of this, as if a name occurred to him that rankled. "There will always be those who break it."

He left the rest of his thoughts unsaid. She realised he meant his grandson. For while Reuben could charm (and fool) most people, she had heard her grandfather admonish his wife many times for spoiling him. Maybe he delayed the marriage deliberately, hoping Reuben would change his ways?

The relationship her grandparents enjoyed would be hard to match. It was his favourite topic.

"As for romipen..." There had been a gleam in his eyes as he turned to this subject, "a Romani chi should be proud to have a mush approved by her elders. It was good enough for us."

He had looked over at his wife, but catching the expression on their faces, Mahalia hadn't believed him. As she thought about her beloved grandparents, she knew a kinder fate had joined them together. She glimpsed something exceptional, real love, and she wanted that for herself.

Her head had been too full of music, too bound up in her grandfather's view of the world to dwell on her future. Now he was dead she had no choice in the matter.

Rachael, her Puro Dai, was tiny, smaller even than Mahalia who was barely five feet tall; a brittle kusi bird wrapped in layers of shawls secured by jewelled brooches. Each fragile wrist seemed too insubstantial to support her bangles. Rings slipped up and down her fingers when she moved her hands. Only the swollen knuckles prevented her from losing them.

All this gave a false impression. She was indomitable. The family had been rich, in Romani terms, making her a woman of importance. The lamps caught a glint of gold amongst her possessions, for there were still a few reminders left of their former status.

Mahalia remembered her grandfather boasting.

"A *two hundred and fifty* book vardo, this beauty!" referring to the booklets of genuine gold leaf decorating his home. "Ordered it special. Done by the best – that gajo, Jones of Hereford."

Well, that was long ago when he'd had a show waggon that was the talk of the fairs. Now, that old vardo was chopped away, and all the bright display of wealth with it. No one could bear to burn it when he died.

Her grandmother's pride persisted though, despite her loss. Amongst the dozens of ornaments she stored with such care, and set out each time they stopped, was a miniature of her as a young woman. She had been black-haired and smooth-skinned once, considered a rare beauty. Now her face was criss-crossed with wrinkles like the last withered apple left over at the end of winter, but the eyes which surveyed them were shrewd and all-knowing. They gleamed in the lamplight.

Mahalia smiled at her, and the old lady gave her a ghost of a wink in return.

"You first, Mally."

Kezia looked at her expectantly.

Mahalia swirled the dregs in the cup, inverted it over the saucer, righted it again quickly, and held it out to Lymena, who made a great show of peering at it. Without warning she let out a loud crow and thrust the cup under Mahalia's nose.

"There! See for yourself. A chavi, a pretty chi, and *soon*." Before Mahalia could take it and make her own interpretation, she passed it to her sister. "I don't know that shape, what d'yer reckon, Kiz'? Maybe an *old* mush?" She sniggered unkindly.

Kezia studied the patterns in the leaves. She handed it to her friend, but with a look of longing.

"Looks plain enough to me. Show Beebi Rae."

Mahalia passed the cup to her grandmother.

Several minutes elapsed before Rachael spoke. She turned to Lymena, who was beginning to fidget.

"Well, you're doin' better. I see a chavi, and to me it looks like a pretty chi. But an old mush? It must mean sommat else, Reuben's only three summers more'n Mally."

There was a note of approval in her voice. That, in itself, was unusual. It was no secret she still considered the sisters outsiders, despite all the years travelling together.

"It's enough. Plain as the nose on my face." Lymena grinned at her sister. "Now we wait out the summer. See if I'm right. Maybe she's already started courtin', eh, penna? Jallin' off in the dark, whether it's rainin' or no, and didn't I hear a certain mush outside?" Laughing loudly, she poked Mahalia's knee, giving her an arch, knowing look. "Sommat to tell us, Mally?"

Mahalia ignored her. It made her hot with anger to think others believed she encouraged Reuben. She squeezed Kezia's hand.

"You now, Kizzy. Let's hope she does better."

Lymena frowned, but took her sister's cup without a word. Before she could start there was a thump on the lower door, and her husband shouted for her. Mahalia glimpsed a moment of panic on her face as she pulled on her overdress and gathered her belongings.

Kezia stood up.

"I betta jal' an' all."

She moved aside to let her sister through. Lymena scuttled down the steps. As the door shut behind her, the two younger women exchanged looks of resignation. Kezia put her arm around Mahalia, and hugged her.

"It'll be all right, Mally. Leaves don't lie."

Will it?

She forced a smile. Dukkerin' for the gaje was something they did for wonga, talked up into a worthwhile performance. There were only so many predictions you told strangers. But amongst themselves they took each image seriously. It never occurred to Mahalia to question her fate.

Once Kezia was down the steps into the light of her own vardo, Mahalia began to close the doors.

"Leave 'em, Mally. I wants one last draw on this ol' swiggler afore settling."

Rachael unlocked her stiff joints, and sat in the open doorway, despite the cold, blowing pipe smoke out into the rain. A shout came from Lymena's vardo followed by a muffled yelp. The old lady shook her head in disapproval, spat in the direction of the noise and hobbled back inside.

Before clearing away, Mahalia stared at her discarded cup. The image disturbed her. To cover her reaction she began locking up for the night, conscious that her grandmother watched her throughout.

"Come here a minute, luvvie."

Rachael was careful not to favour her in front of the others, as if to compensate for the past. Now they had gone, her voice grew softer, and she looked at her with open affection.

Mahalia knelt at her feet. The old lady took both her hands in her own and stared at her so intently she was unable to withdraw her gaze. Kneeling on the hard floor made her dizzy, unravelled, as if all the secrets she kept buried were being drawn into the light and examined.

"You shall have this last summer, kusi one, then you must wed. It can't atch no longer. We've the family honour to think of."

She sighed, and released Mahalia, looking beyond her into dark memory. Without warning she shook her hands above her head, and called out to one of her dead children. Her voice rose in a thin, reedy chant. Silver bracelets clattered down her arms.

"Sar shan, Elvida! Miro dir. (How are you, Elvida, my dear.) How could you lay such a curse upon us?"

Mahalia put her hands over her ears. Dordi! This was terrible. Even though she often remembered her Dai and Beebi, for one of their names to be mentioned at all was unthinkable. Worse, it was wafado bokt – such bad luck. It made the hairs on the back of her neck prickle. The older her grandmother became, the more she brooded on the loss of her jealous daughters.

In the ensuing silence Rachael stroked the glossy head bowed in front of her. The gesture seemed to restore her humour, but Mahalia sensed this was her final warning. There was no way out.

"We gotta make it right, Mally. It's a kushti match. There's folki who'd be glad of it. Reuben's my grandchild too, remember."

Mahalia kept her eyes lowered to prevent tears from spilling down her cheeks and betraying her. It was hard to conceal such thoughts, but she must never reveal her longing to leave, to find someone like her Puro Dadus maybe, who would love and respect her. Such a one would not be found among their folkendi. The heart had gone from it. When her grandfather died he had taken more than laughter with him.

Throughout the winter there had been moments of despair when she felt tempted to walk up the frozen mountainside and find a place to hide. Somewhere remote, allowing her to slide into cold sleep and never wake. It had seemed preferable to life with Reuben.

She busied herself with their nightly routine. Before extinguishing the lamp, she helped her grandmother up onto the bunk, and tucked the blankets around her. She liked Mahalia to sleep with her, she said,

"Better'n a hot stone in winter."

They slept in the top extendible bunk at the back of the vardo. She chose the side nearest the window. Her grandmother burrowed closer, and soon Mahalia recognised the change in breathing that signified sleep.

Caleb had closed the sliding shutters earlier, all bar the two at the back. Raising the curtain a fraction, she stared through the gap at the wild sky. Dark masses of cloud threatened to blot out the moonlight. The moon's kindly face appeared to darken and crumple, as if weeping.

From beyond the thicket came the distant screech of an owl. It made her jump, but Rachael didn't stir. Mahalia touched the glass with her index finger, and breathed a prayer to the Holy Mother for protection against such omens.

She was trapped then. Her courage faltered at the prospect of openly defying her family. She buried her face in the pillow, unable to stop her tears.

There was one, meagre, consolation – something else she had seen in the leaves – one thing they were all too superstitious to say. It *had* been there though, along with the clearer symbols of a daughter and an old man. She had read it in her mother's leaves before her death. There was no mistake.

Mahalia pulled the covers over her face, like a shroud, excluding every last chink of light. With no hope, at least her life would be mercifully short.

FOUR

Howell had gone out early. Had a plan up his sleeve, so he said, to enlist the Reverend ApIvor (the only person their mother respected) and convince her that Louise must be allowed to marry Jack. The whole family liked Jack – with one exception. He had an easy way with him, and adored their sister. They would have encouraged him on that count alone. She was eighteen now, and although Jack had vowed to marry her ever since they were sixteen it had drawn nothing but barbed retorts, accusations of wrong-doing (unfounded) and finally vehement opposition from their mother.

"Only one generation away from Gyppos!" Agnes had shouted. It was the worst insult she could muster. "It'll be over my dead body you marry the likes of him."

Howell had bitten his lip to suppress a smile, and winked at Louise and Arthur behind her back. They had a pact, the three of them, negotiating the tricky business of Lou' and Jack courting without incurring their mother's wrath. If the Reverend ApIvor agreed to help, they hoped to present such a strong case that Agnes would lose face in the village if she opposed them any longer. They'd given up on Wilf, knowing their father avoided any confrontation with his wife, lost in his own world of imagined ailments and self-pity. But if ApIvor persuaded her, they would have a wedding yet.

Howell found the Reverend standing on the Chapel steps. He was watching the approaching caravan of Gypsies like a child entranced. Every year he encouraged a mixing of cultures at the summer festival, believing that through a universal love of music they would put aside their differences and prejudice – at least for a day or two. The sound of a well-played harp had been known to reduce him to tears, but he reacted in much the same way to music of any kind.

Howell took the Chapel steps two at a time. Perhaps, while ApIvor was in such a receptive mood, he would agree to the proposal. He grinned down at him but was taken aback when the Reverend didn't bother with any opening pleasantries.

"I know what it is you are here to suggest, Howell. I've given it a lot of thought, but I cannot interfere in the way your parents raise you, or their expectations for any of you, particularly Louise, as the eldest daughter." The smile died from Howell's face. "I know you all want her to be happy, but she's barely eighteen. Too young, you all are, and you're making these judgements from a position of inexperienced youth..." Howell stirred, impatient to interrupt, but knew better than to stop ApIvor mid-flow. An autocratic note would creep into that voice; the classic education revealed beneath Welsh overtones. He could not be gainsaid. "...I know this isn't what you want to hear, but early marriages cannot be undone without great shame and recrimination, and most important of all, going against God's teachings. Some people have to live with their rashness for the rest of their lives."

He meant their parents, of course, who else? He had married them.

"But it wouldn't be like that for Louise."

He heard his own voice, like a child protesting 'It's not fair', and looking down into the familiar red face saw ApIvor's resolve. It was pointless to argue with him.

"This is not the place to discuss it." ApIvor's tone was dismissive. "Let us enjoy this delightful spectacle for the moment. Oh, now there's old Gypsy Rachael. She's in charge. Forgive me, I must go and pay my respects. She was widowed last year."

He hurried away.

Howell had no interest in the Gypsies, and no intention of wasting time watching their procession. Mary Prosser would be loitering, with her sisters, on the lookout for him as usual. He was in no mood for her reproachful glances, or to bandy inanities with the village girls. There was not one amongst them with spark, nor one pretty face to tempt him.

His mind was set on Louise. Maybe she and Jack could elope? It would be a solution, though it might lose Jack his position. ApIvor, as a family friend of their employer would have plenty to say about it.

He strode down the street oblivious to the noise and bustle until a group of onlookers prevented him from moving forward. Sprinting across the road between the lumbering waggons put him fifty yards behind Mary Prosser. She was peering in the opposite direction, but he couldn't escape detection for long. He was about to retreat again when he noticed one of the Gypsy women watching him, with a grin on her face. She nudged her companion, and called to him.

"Well, my 'andsome, ain't they pretty enough for yer the local rakklis..." she looked pointedly at the knot of villagers farther down the street, "them local gals? Won't I do instead?"

Her friend chuckled, and said something in her own language. This made the first woman laugh so much that she started to cough, and waved him on, tears in her eyes.

"You want to watch those Gypsy women," the foreman had warned while they were working out estimates for temporary labour. "They'll flirt with you, outrageous some of the things they say, then coax the money right out of your pocket."

It was a harsh judgement, but here was this brazen piece flirting with him in the street. They were making fun of him, he knew, and had to be ten years older than him, at least. Ahead of them, a third, and younger woman, from the set of her head, kept her back turned throughout all this. She walked away without looking at him. He decided to give as good as he got.

"Well, at least let me have the best of three, or don't I get a choice?"

This set the first woman off again, and she flashed her eyes at him in a mock come-hither look. Hearing him speak, the girl looked back over her shoulder – and he forgot his purpose.

His tormentor hadn't finished with him yet.

"Watch 'im, Mally, 'e's an eye for you now, I'm too much for 'im!"

He barely listened to the teasing words except to store away the name, 'Mally'. The young woman called Mally began to walk away. He wanted to talk to her, make her stay, touch her. She didn't belong amidst the overpowering smell of horse, the rumbling waggons, or the noisy, barefoot children. It was as if he had been blinded by dust, and when his vision cleared found a rare woodland orchid in his path.

"Mister..." The banter stopped. The first woman's none too clean hand plucked at his sleeve, nervous suddenly. He was puzzled by the change in her voice. "Yer'll 'ave to find one of yer own kind. She's spoke for."

"Howell!"

The Reverend ApIvor called to him from across the street. He turned back to look for Mally, but she had disappeared into the crowd. ApIvor frowned at him.

"Don't stare at their women, lad. Whatever has possessed you? They don't like it."

Howell turned an unrepentant face towards him.

"*They* flirted with me, although I think it was only to have fun at my expense."

"Nevertheless, I've warned you. She's a beauty, young Mahalia Jessel. You can be sure her brothers don't miss a thing."

Howell put an affectionate arm around ApIvor's shoulders.

"You worry too much, she's only a Gypsy." And ApIvor's face relaxed, as he knew it would.

'*Only* a Gypsy'? His mind could see little else but her face. There had been a look of recognition in her eyes, as if... no, he was being fanciful, but it gave him hope. He had her name now. 'Mally' her friends called her, and ApIvor had inadvertently supplied him with the rest. 'Mahalia Jessel'. It was as if by repeating her name to himself he already owned a part of her.

He set off for the manor knowing the estate manager would still be there. If he volunteered for extra hours he might see her again soon. It would take careful planning, but in his role as wages clerk he would have a legitimate reason to talk to her. He would contrive it somehow.

His pulse was racing. This time, as with no other girl before, there was a definite charge in the air. It felt... He struggled to think of an appropriate word. With it came the realisation that this particular element had been missing from his life until now. It was dangerous.

The question of Louise completely slipped his mind.

FIVE

Everyone agreed that Nancy was a dear child, 'such a sweet little thing, with those great grey eyes', always following her eldest brother Howell around like a little pet. Louise was good with her too. No, to all appearances, she was not a bit of trouble. And Nancy preferred it that way.

Few people remembered she had been Christened plain 'Anne'. Wilf had chosen 'Louise' for his eldest; Agnes picked something modest for her second daughter. But when Wilf indulged little red-haired 'Nan', calling her 'fancy Nancy' after the lacy pink flowers growing out of the garden wall, gradually the name stuck.

Agnes could only 'tut' and mutter, but wound Nancy's hair with rags every night to encourage the curls.

"What's wrong with her given name, I should like to know?" she would say. "It's straight from the Bible. Good and honest."

But 'good' and 'honest' were not part of Nancy's make-up. She learnt early in life that it didn't pay to be pert or too bright around her mother. If there was a case to answer, she had a knack for directing blame towards her two younger brothers, Will and Joe, so close in age they had been born at opposite ends of the same year. They brushed these deflections aside, impervious to nagging or the occasional slap, priding themselves on their growing toughness.

Nancy was small in build, and most adults assumed she was younger than her age. Yet she could run faster than Will and Joe, and climb higher, careful to apply the patience of a mountaineer to her ascent thus avoiding the tell-tale rips and scrapes of her pastime. Her brothers would lose interest in this long-winded approach. It suited Nancy when they left.

Their favourite playground was the old graveyard at the top of the hill – banned by their mother for obvious reason of safety, but more so on religious grounds since she despised all show of popery. It was a paradise for hide-and-seek, and surrounded by the oldest chestnut trees in the district.

In summer she liked to climb so far into the upper branches she was hidden from below. There she could spy on all sorts of activities, squirrelling away her knowledge for an appropriate occasion when she could be sure it would get her favourable attention.

Nancy started her descent later than usual, one Friday afternoon at the end of June. She usually counted time by the chimes of the Chapel clock down in the village, but had been enjoying herself too much to pay close attention. The half-hour struck. She did a swift mental calculation: it must be half-past five. The realisation made her hurry.

Her skirt snagged on a twig, pulling a thread. She stopped to release it, teasing the strand back through to the underside with careful fingers. Wedged high in a fork off the main trunk, she was hard to detect unless someone looked straight up into the canopy.

Voices approached from the direction of the lychgate. Two people, she thought. A girl laughed, then came a beseeching, feminine giggle. Transfixed, she heard:

"No, Howell, not here. Wait!"

And her brother's laugh, unmistakeable, coming nearer, heading towards her hiding place, and the concealment of the trees.

Nancy froze, hardly daring to breathe in case she should give herself away, and edged round the trunk an inch or two. She didn't know her brother was walking out with anyone special. The top of his head came into view, a flash of blonde hair in the dappled sunlight. He moved towards someone, but the broad-fingered leaves of high summer concealed his sweetheart.

Fear of discovery; self-preservation; curiosity, all combined to keep her still and silent above them, not daring to lean out, but fascinated by the unidentifiable sounds and murmurings. Then she heard her brother panting rhythmically (like their spaniel after a run), and both of them cried out, one after the other. There followed more giggling and 'shushing' each other. Finally, she heard her brother saying, over and over again, "I love you."

She was desperate to know who it was.

"All the girls in our village have a crush on him." her older sister

57

said, and, "Boys will often tell you they love you, but it doesn't mean anything."

Louise had told her that too, though she'd put her hand to her mouth, as if to take it back, remembering how young her sister was.

Nancy was getting pins and needles in her leg, and a numb bottom. She guessed all this 'spooning', as her Dad called it whenever courting couples were mentioned, couldn't go on for much longer. Howell would have to be in for his tea, and she couldn't remain there or she would have some explaining to do.

In the distance, away to her right beyond the church wall, came the sound of men's voices shouting. It had a sudden, dramatic effect on the couple below. She heard Howell say,

"I must see you tomorrow, but earlier, when they're all at the market."

Her brother continued talking as they moved away, but Nancy couldn't catch the girl's reply.

She began climbing down despite the stiffness in her legs, no longer bothering to be quiet. Back on the ground, she hastily brushed dust off her clothes. Dry twigs cracked under her feet.

A hand caught her roughly, and swung her round. She looked into the angry face of a Gypsy woman, and her heart nearly stopped beating. She didn't register anything else, not the age of the woman, nor her appearance. Her only thought was 'a Gyppo, a Gyppo', and how she would be in serious trouble if anyone found out. It was a term they bandied about in the village, and being a child who latched on to cat-calls and forbidden words first, she had been reproved for it, more than once, by ApIvor. But at home it was the term of censure their mother used most. She hated the Gypsies with a passion, though Nancy could never discover why.

"What yer doin' 'ere?"

The woman's voice was husky and fierce. Before Nancy could reply there were heavy footsteps behind them. Two young men ran up. They were Gypsies too, and they looked from her, to the woman, and back again, puzzled. She pushed Nancy away in the direction of the lychgate, and said something to them in an unfamiliar language before turning back to her.

"This ol' place ain't safe, not for a chavi like you, on yer own."

One of the men took a step forward. Nancy backed away. He found that funny, and barked at her, stamping his foot. Nancy fled.

He shouted after her,

"Don't come aspyin' on us again, girlie. You know what yer ma told yer!"

And he laughed at her retreating figure.

Her heart was still in her mouth. She must warn Howell and his girl somehow. Maybe if she hurried she'd catch up with them. But even though she ran as if pursued by a pack of mongrels there was no sign of the couple in the lane.

Arriving home, less than five minutes later, she saw that Howell had reached the gate ahead of her, his face flushed.

"Hello." he said, "You afraid of being late too?"

He tweaked her hair ribbon, and strode round to the back door. Nancy opened her mouth to say something, but thought better of it: the windows were open.

She didn't know what to do. All through tea she was quiet, turning the problem over in her mind. She couldn't tell Louise. There'd be trouble if she did, for Louise had no secrets from Howell. She couldn't risk her parents finding out on any account, yet she had to share it with someone, or burst. It gnawed at her all night, until her younger sister Ruby woke up crying, complaining that she kept kicking her.

It rained the next day giving her no opportunity to go out, even though Howell had done so, brushing aside his mother's remonstrations about the weather. When he came back he was quiet, and went out into the garden with Louise. Nancy could see them talking together all the way down to the far end of the path, and back.

❦

The following day, being Sunday, they prepared for morning Chapel. Louise chivvied her up more than usual so that she was ready before the others. That, in itself, was unsettling. Her older sister usually preferred her to go at her own pace while she attended to the little girls, both incapable of buttoning, lacing or tying. She seemed anxious to have her out of the way.

"Nan, are you there?" Howell rapped on their bedroom door. "I could do with your help this morning, little sis'. Come on, we'll be first for a change."

Nancy felt surprised and pleased, though there was something odd about this invitation.

Without waiting for her response, Howell went downstairs

again, and out through the back door. Agnes ignored them, busy with her final preparations for their midday meal when they returned. Breakfast was no more than a drink and a piece of bread standing before worship.

Nancy slipped through the kitchen. Behind her came the approaching din of her two younger brothers jostling each other down the stairs. She ran outside, only to see Howell fifty yards ahead, and hurried after him wondering why he hadn't waited.

They passed several people they knew. Each time his smile was polite as he exchanged pleasantries, but he didn't speak to her until they were inside the Chapel.

Her first task was always to sort piles of hymn and prayer books ready for distribution.

"Come over here, Nan." He patted the pew beside him, "I want to talk to you."

She put down the handful of books. So this was what the change to their routine was about. His first words were those she had been dreading.

"You were seen in the old churchyard on Friday."

At this she jumped up in panic, and blurted,

"I didn't talk to the Gyppos, honest, Howell. They frightened me. I didn't know they were there." She began pleading, "Don't tell our Mum, will you? I tried to catch up with you and your girl, but you'd gone."

Howell didn't respond immediately, but stared at her, a strange expression on his face. When he spoke his voice was cold.

"What do you mean, Nancy, 'my girl'?" She started to cry,

genuine tears for a change, but Howell's expression didn't alter. "Well?"

She snivelled, and wiped her nose on the sleeve of her dress.

"I didn't see her, I just heard you laughing. I was up a tree and when I got down this Gyppo woman grabbed me," (he started at this) "there were three of them, two men as well. They thought I was spying on them."

Howell gripped her arms, squeezing them to her sides so that she couldn't wriggle away.

"I'll let you off this time. I think they frightened you enough. It wouldn't be fair if you got the strap as well, though if our Mum ever finds out..."

He left the warning unfinished. She stopped crying, sucking in great gulps of air, relieved to get it off her chest, grateful to her brother for saving her skin this time.

"One last thing," he said, "you don't tell anyone about me courting, not even Louise. I want to do it in my own time. That'll make us quits, eh?" He smiled, and Nancy, relieved at being let off, smiled back, drinking in his benevolence, agreeing. She would have agreed to anything, and keeping it from Louise – that was unexpected, special, a secret between them. He handed her a large, white handkerchief. "Come on, dry those tears or they'll think something's up. Go on, have a good blow." Nancy took it, and blew noisily. He put his arm around her shoulders and gave her a reassuring little hug. "I should stay out of the churchyard for a while, just in case. Don't want any harm coming to my little sister, do I?"

As she concentrated on her Sunday duty, Nancy's fear subsided. She placed herself at an angle inside the doorway, the better to observe her brother in his role as 'Greeter'. Each new arrival received a hymn book from her hands in a show of modest good manners (including the sulky Prosser sisters) allowing her to monitor his reactions. She knew every girl in their village, and most from the surrounding district. Anyone of a suitable age came under close scrutiny. But as the last people arrived, and the opening hymn began, she was disappointed. No one in the present congregation, from his lack of reaction, could be the girl in the churchyard, and there were no newcomers.

There was only one conclusion to be drawn; it must someone from a different church. That would explain all the secrecy. She shivered with excitement at the possibility.

Supposing his girlfriend was Catholic? Their mother would have a fit. She hugged her secret knowledge to herself. Whoever it was, she had but one mission now: to find out. And she wouldn't tell anyone, of course, providing his sweetheart was nice. No, she wouldn't tell a soul, not until the last possible moment

SIX

Reuben, Paoli, and Kezia's husband, Noah, left at dawn. They took fifteen horses to trade, and an open cart for supplies. Mahalia waited in the darkened vardo, and watched them disappear into the early mist; it promised to be another humid day.

Rachael slept on. Throughout early summer, she had complained of being tired, couldn't get comfortable unless she slept alone, so Mahalia had moved to the floor space beneath the sliding bunk. She would have preferred the open night sky, but such was her fear of Reuben she endured the hot stuffy interior, and her grandmother's snoring. It was as well the old lady was much preoccupied, and inclined to fixate on each of her ailments in the way of the elderly. Mahalia had missed her lunar time. Her body seemed strange now beneath her clothes. Her white swelling had begun.

She was scared. It was too soon to tell Howell. And yet, though terrified, it meant the prediction had proved right. She was carrying.

But it was becoming a struggle to control her sickness. The last thing she wanted was her grandmother's attention.

Anxious not to wake anyone, she walked barefoot through the dew until far enough away from the site. No other footprints marked the silver-grey grass. Just out of hearing, she gave in to the nausea. It was becoming worse as the days progressed. Doubled over behind a clump of foxgloves, she retched until her ribs ached. When the feeling passed, she laved her face with dew, and picked her way through high bracken to the stream. There she knelt, resting her forehead against a cold, moss-covered boulder at the water's edge.

"Mally?"

Kezia's soft voice made her jump. Her cousin-in-law stood silhouetted against the watery, early-morning sun. Mahalia steadied herself, fingers clutching moss, still giddy.

"It's the gripe, that's all..."

"Garn! You're carryin', ain't yer? Did yer think I wouldn' notice? It's come true, ain't it, the leaves? Lymena'll be so full of 'erself, gettin' that right!"

"Kek! Yer can't rokra nothin', Kizzy."

Mahalia scrambled to her feet, overbalancing on the slippery surface. Kezia's smile faded. She came over to her friend and stared into her face, pleasure giving way to disbelief.

"What yer askin', Mally? Ain't it Reuben's?"

Mahalia trembled from the shock of discovery.

"Reuben? How could it be Reuben's? I'd as soon be dead as let 'im touch me."

It was out now. She'd said it – voiced her dislike. What a relief to share it with someone, though she was dismayed by the pain in her friend's eyes.

"Who is it?" In the ensuing silence Kezia put her hand to her mouth in horror. "Not that gajo? Not the fair haired one from the gav?" Mahalia's face gave her away. Kezia began to cry. Real fear underscored her next words. "What 'ave yer done? We'll all be for it now. They'll think I 'elped yer, an' when Lymena finds out there'll be such trouble."

"No one'll blame you, Kizzy. I'm jallin' with my Howell soon. It's what we planned." She was panting, both from the effort of spilling her secret, and fear. "Swear you won't give me away."

But Kezia was angry now.

"I don't want to 'ear none of this. The shame of it. A gajo. Wafado!" She spat into the ferns. "Reuben will kill 'im. And Caleb, Job, when they get 'old of you... Caleb won't 'ave no gaje ratti in this familia. He'll turn yer out. Remember what was done afore, to that other juval? Your Dai, an' Lymena, and two others, gone since, tied 'er to a wheel by 'er earrings and cut 'er hair. Starin' Billy, 'er Dadus, flayed 'er raw – near enough killed 'er afore 'e threw 'er out on the drom."

Mahalia went cold at the image. They'd been made to watch, every young juval, every mort, so they'd know what would happen if they strayed. She had half-expected Kezia's reaction, but was surprised and hurt that the only one she trusted could turn on her.

"We're friends. Don't give me away, I'm beggin' you, Kiz'."

Kezia looked past her. Lymena was hurrying towards them.

"Too late for that." She was breathing heavily, as if dreading the approaching figure. "She's got a nose for it, that one. You better jal now. You know what she's like when she's carryin'? The least thing starts her off. She'll be wild."

"Don't tell 'er."

"How can I not? She's my pen. And she'll do anything to stop yer. She reckons Reuben's wasted on yer, as it is."

Lymena came towards them like a questing dog, scenting disaster.

"Why yer out early? Yer ain't carryin', Kiz." There was a pause. She looked Mahalia up and down, staring at her with growing awareness. "What yer bin doin', Mally?"

Mahalia glared back at her.

"Mind yer business."

The sun's strength was growing. They could hear noises from the encampment as others stirred. She was beginning to feel dizzy. Another bout of nausea would be her undoing. She backed towards the path leading down to the village.

Lymena rounded on her sister.

"It's 'er ain't it? She's carrying, ain't she?" She caught her sister's arm, and pinched it. "Eh? Answer me, Kiz."

The grass had dried out in the time they stood there. Mahalia had only seconds to escape. If she ran now she might not slip. What a dinilo she was leaving her boots off, but she had wanted to feel the dew on her feet.

"Atch! Where you jallin'?" There was malice written all over Lymena's face, thrilled at the prospect of seeing the favourite suffer.

"Yer Puro Dai don't know yet, do she? Yer'll be for it, though she'll go soft on Reuben."

Her face must have betrayed her. Lymena's eyes widened. She stepped in the way instinctively to cut off escape. "Who is it?" She turned to her sister, "Who? Is it that gajo? Is it?" Mahalia ducked to one side as Lymena tried to grab her hair. "Grab 'old of 'er, Kiz."

But Kezia turned away, put her hands over her ears, and wailed.

There was nothing for it but to run. Mahalia was younger, faster, and her cousin-in-law was handicapped by ill-fitting boots. She heard the sound of a slap as Lymena set about her sister, but didn't hesitate, or look back. Lifting her skirts above her knees, she leapt away down the hill. It was not so many summers since she had been barefoot all the time. With each stride, she became more confident. Lymena screamed abuse after her. She would badger Kizzy for the truth.

She'll raise the others – they'll come after me – bring me back – punish me. Jallin' with a gajo – couldn't get no worse.

Her life, her unborn child's life depended upon Howell now. He would hide her, but she must find him without the villagers knowing.

A natural barrier stopped her. She had reached the ancient ditch at the top of Old Eli's fields and clambered across. Below, in the distance, she saw the cob stallion raise its head. The animal could sense her condition. She must get through the hedge and into the lane out of danger. The horse started up the field towards her. Driven on by one final surge of fear, she squeezed between the thinner branches of hawthorn near the base, and scrambled over the wire fence on the far side. The stallion, though aware of her presence, couldn't see her. It began running up and down looking for a place to break through.

Trampled by a grai, or beaten by Caleb: it didn't seem much of a choice. She had one chance, to shelter inside Old Eli's barn. He was a good mush, for a gajo. He had been a friend of her Puro Dadus. At least he wouldn't send for the gavvers. But Reuben... Reuben traded with him. That might be a bigger problem. If only she could talk to Old Eli first. She gathered up her skirt for one final effort, and ran.

❦

Their plans had centred upon the New World. A family belonged in the future. She couldn't be sure of Howell's reaction.

The previous afternoon they had held each other tightly, hidden beneath the broom thicket on the ridge. Everything was still. No breath of wind disturbed the arch of dark green branches above them. They kept their voices low, mindful of how sounds carried in the unnatural quiet.

Howell was distracted by the amount of work he'd been given now the hop-picking season was about to start. Gypsies had settled in their time honoured encampment on the common above the hop yards. Other folk were arriving too, from as far afield as Birmingham, carrying makeshift tents, cook pots, bedrolls.

They planned to make their escape when picking was well in hand. By then everyone would be too busy to look for them.

"It's going to be difficult for us meet so often over the next few weeks," Howell said, "but my bonus will be worth it. We've nearly enough money for our tickets, and six month's keep."

"For me too. Lymena's carryin' again. We all try and help 'er with the chavvis."

"Again?" He shook his head in exasperation. "How old is she? God in Heaven! But now I think of it, my parents could almost match her total and at much the same age." He smiled down at Mahalia, and her heart turned over at his next words. "Let's not think about children until we've settled somewhere. When we're ready, let's have just two, a boy and a girl, and give them a better start in life. I couldn't bear any child of mine growing up in the conditions we have at home. There are five of us in our bedroom. Imagine, five boys, three of us grown." He grinned at her. "No, first we're going to explore, see something of the world. Won't stop until we fall in love with a place."

Mahalia kept her eyes on the horizon. Yes, she could travel carrying their baby. She had hoped they would put down roots sooner rather than later, from his earlier talk, somewhere in that far country of his imagination.

There was laughter in Howell's voice as he enthused about their future.

"All I heard growing up was, 'Find a girl, settle down.' but with you I can travel. It must be in my blood, Mally, way back, like it is in yours. The first thing I'll buy is one of those modern motorised vehicles, even one that's basic. It'll be essential out there."

Out where, Howell?

For even though convinced this was part of the prediction, she couldn't be sure how he would react to her secret. She glanced back at him trying to study his face. There had been no ocean in the leaves: no ship.

Howell laughed, that full uninhibited laugh she loved, so reminiscent of her Puro Dadus, and her fear evaporated.

"Listen to me," he said, "getting ahead of myself, and all our plans. I must go. If you can be at the old church tomorrow, around five, say – I'll try and be there within half an hour. "

He kissed her then, in an abstracted, unsatisfactory fashion, and ran off in the direction of the manor. She watched to see if he would turn and blow her extravagant kisses as usual, but he was intent on the path downhill and didn't falter.

It was enough to convince Mahalia of her next move. This wasn't meant to be, she told herself. She must hope to get rid of it somehow. This was an accident, a mistake, not the daughter foretold. If she failed, there would be time enough to tell Howell when they were on their way to a new life. Nothing must spoil their plans. But Romani women were hardy. They gave birth all the time in barns, if needs be, or beneath vardos. She would manage.

There was still no rain as she walked back avoiding the village. The silence was oppressive, like the heat. Twice, she stopped, imagining thunder. Occasionally, a large drop of water splashed her face, but when she looked up clouds parted to reveal the sun. It unsettled her. A good downpour would clear the air, dampen the dust, lift her spirits.

There had been something evil watching her that day, maybe even the Beng himself. But the feeling came too late. Here she was with nothing but the torn clothes she stood up in, and her gold earrings.

She reached the barn and crawled into the darkest corner to recover. Her heart pounded so fiercely it dulled the rest of her senses. She must plan her explanation to Old Eli, but the baby within her had other needs. Mahalia stretched out on the makeshift bed of straw, and gave in to exhaustion.

Voices woke her. Two men. They were outside, nearing the barn door. Sitting up in panic, she realised several hours must have passed while she slept. It made her skin prickle. There was nowhere to hide. The barn was empty save for a few bales of straw from last year's harvest, and a collection of harness.

No wild creature cornered by a fox ever felt so helpless, for there was no escape: one of the men was Reuben.

SEVEN

People called him 'Old' Eli. It had become a habit, yet he was the same age as ApIvor. Like his friend, Celtic forebears had ensured him a fine head of black hair, but whereas ApIvor's had thinned and retained its colour, his had turned grey prematurely. By the time he settled into farming, his hair was white with mutton-chop whiskers and a moustache to match. He topped his other friend Wilf by at least four inches. This extra height caused him to stoop. He certainly didn't feel 'old', but the moniker stuck.

His farm lay outside the village, on the Gloucester side, under the lee of the Devil's Lip. The hop yards belonging to the manor estate started below his barn and cowsheds. For most of the year, he had an uninterrupted view over the valley.

He managed well enough with part-time help, employing labour as the seasons demanded, teaching the better lads amongst the local children how to ride, milk, cut and bale the hay, in particular the older Pritchard boys.

Eli guessed Howell was courting. Saw him striding about at odd hours in the direction of the copse on the ridge, or down to the abandoned oast house near the main Hereford road, or else walking along the little-used back lane towards the old cemetery. They were the usual meeting places for sweethearts. Never saw her though, and imagined it was a girl from a neighbouring village. He didn't pay it much heed. Howell was like his father in that respect: there would always be a maid or two sighing after him.

Over the past week Eli had seen him more often. They had obviously found a quiet spot, and although he wasn't unduly concerned, his curiosity was piqued. He kept his eyes sharp for a glimpse of her. Howell went up there after work a couple of days each week, just for an hour, often returning home at a run, no doubt to appease his exacting mother.

Eli sighed, and shook his head. That Agnes! He'd been sweet on her himself – the only one he'd ever noticed. Missed his opportunity there, but if he was honest, he often asked himself, was he ever in the running?

It all went back to the night of that village dance; the final one as it turned out. Geraint, as he still called his boyhood friend ApIvor, had insisted he accompany him, though he was unsure about the real motive. The new Reverend had mentioned his difference of opinion with Godfrey Chalfont on the subject of local dances.

"I want to turn their minds from temptations of the flesh. Encourage them to express their Faith through hymns and prayer.

When they sing their spirits will soar – lifted up above the meanness of their existence. I firmly believe that it's *Godfrey* who is stuck in the past, not the parishioners, by letting them indulge in such wild festivities. All they need is guidance, and an example. And how can I possibly encourage them to take the pledge when *he* makes no secret of his fine cellar, *and*, to make matters worse, all the local pubs serve cider produced on *his* estate?" He paused, wheezing slightly in the November chill. "Don't you agree, Eli? You haven't said much so far." He looked around, a reforming zeal in his eyes. "Doesn't this place have promise?"

"I confess it was difficult for me to imagine you here, Geraint, though there are attractions, I grant you. Thinking of settling down yourself?"

He smothered a grin, remembering the imposing Gertrude's scathing assessment of her brother's potential as a minister, let alone a husband. He could picture her reaction should Geraint 'demean' himself by consorting with a local woman.

"Me? Out of the question. No, I hoped to pair you with the inestimable Agnes. Everything you could want in a wife: devout, sensible, hard working."

"It didn't occur to you to ask my opinion before embarking on this course of match-making? It's an odd role for you."

"Hah, yes I take your point. Best left to the women, I grant you. But I confess young Agnes has made a favourable impression. Do you know she can almost equal me in quoting from the Scriptures? Such dedication – and from a woman!"

They had walked about half-way to the village hall. The thunder of wooden clogs, pounding out the rhythm of a traditional dance, echoed down the street.

As they opened the main door, the heat hit them, and with it the unmistakeable mingled odours of sweat and cologne. There was something else unnamed in the atmosphere too. It caught his breath. Glancing sideways he saw Geraint flush with anger, then disgust. He knew that look. It didn't bode well for the flock of this parish. The first thing to go would be these overt displays of masculine prowess in clog dancing, and its obvious effect on the local girls. Every young woman's face was pink with pleasure.

A ripple went round the room, a murmur of curiosity as many stared at the late comers. Wilf grinned, and mouthed a welcome from the makeshift stage. He began to play a gentler air on the squeeze box. The clog dancers sat down. Many removed their footwear in favour of newer, hard-earned boots. Couples took to the floor in a more sedate fashion, still casting covert glances in their direction. ApIvor appeared not to notice, intent on his mental inventory of sin. Eli recognised that determined look of old.

Wilf and his small band (two of them his brothers) came from a village nearer Hereford, some twenty miles away. Each could play several instruments: fiddle, penny whistle, squeeze box, and, in Wilf's case, the pianoforte.

Eli stood at the back, reserved and silent above the heads of whispering girls who ignored him, all eyes fixed upon the band leader.

"Their singer smiled at me," giggled one. He felt mildly embarrassed to hear his friend discussed in this fashion.

"Pah! 'A dimple in his chin, then his love you will win, a dimple in his cheek, then his love you will seek' that's what my Mam says about the likes of him." It was Gwyneth Thomas, newly engaged to Prosser the Post. "He'll never make any woman happy, that one, too much of a wandering eye."

He was surprised by the venom in her words.

As she turned away, Eli saw one of the girls pull a face behind her back. Realising he'd overheard they rushed away in a swirl of skirts and squealing laughter.

Wilf was taller than the others in his band. There were few girls who didn't watch when he sang, or blush when he caught their look and winked at them.

Agnes stood a little way in front of Eli, her back straight, her dress modest, unadorned save for a string of rose-pink glass beads. ApIvor had been right in his assessment, knowing his friend to be shy with the pretty or talkative ones. Eli watched her discreetly, summoning up his courage. He was about to walk over and talk to her when the music changed yet again to a more vigorous jig. Agnes moved nearer the stage, looked up at Wilf long enough to catch his attention, then turned on her heel. Her eyes were shining. There was a look of resolve on her face as she threaded her way back towards them, heading for the exit. When she passed Eli, some instinct made him glance up at the stage. Wilf was playing mechanically as he watched her disappear into the crowd.

That was long ago now. It surprised everyone when Wilf and Agnes began courting. No one believed it would last, him being so full of fun, and Agnes, homely Agnes, not noted for her sense of humour. There were those unkind enough to count, but they were disappointed. The Pritchard's first baby was born nine months, more or less to the day, after their wedding.

Too many babies; they never gave themselves a chance. It was Wilf who took to his bed the most though. Eli suspected he was a disappointed man. The squeeze box hung from a hook in the below stairs cupboard until the leather pleats stiffened and cracked, and Wilf forgot it was there.

Agnes worked and worked, pride and discipline keeping her tethered to a malingering husband. Like many a woman before her, she had fallen for good looks. Wilf was drawn to her purity and passion. It was the inevitable attraction of opposites that would end, at best, in puzzlement and exasperation. It also put paid to Eli's daydreams.

He knuckled down, concentrated on his work, but never quite forgot his feelings. They had nice kids though, he couldn't deny that. She turned them out well. He'd enjoyed having Howell help him when the lad was growing up. Both the older Pritchard boys spent many of their free hours with him over the years. Howell, with his unaffected charm and wild dreams, and Arthur, the quiet responsible one, happy to stay in his brother's shadow. But inevitably it was Howell who had spent the most time at Eli's, sharing his hopes and anxieties, sometimes straying into family matters that should have been kept to himself for want of a man's opinion. Eli knew the lad trusted him. In a perverse way it was as if he was his son, not Wilf's.

Eli returned late from inspecting his herd to find the cob stallion lathered up and pacing the fence opposite his barn. If he didn't get it under control and into a stable it was sure to do itself a mischief, or worse, get out and rampage around the yard.

He was expecting one of the Gypsies to call. Reuben said he had a couple of good mares. They could come to an arrangement.

"Got yer 'ands full there, mister."

Reuben stood a few yards behind him watching the commotion. His shirt sleeves were rolled up, a jacket draped over one shoulder. He nodded towards the stallion.

"What's up with that grai? You got a mare in heat nearby?"

"No, I can't think what's upset him. Help me put him into the back stable, will you? He won't kick his way out of there so easily."

It took ten minutes of dangerous dancing and manoeuvring before they managed to hook a twitch around the stallion's top lip, and rope the beast well enough to control it.

When they released the horse into the stall, its broad hooves skidded on the stone floor. It pawed the ground, scoring bright grooves into the surface. Reuben looked it over from a safe distance.

"Thank you." Eli said, once the stallion subsided and began investigating the manger. "I couldn't have managed him on my own. One more thing, while I fetch straw for this fellow, I've several pieces of harness that might be of interest to you."

They walked towards the barn. As he opened the door, a sound within made him stop. He raised his hand in warning to Reuben.

The barn seemed empty, yet he sensed someone else there. For several seconds he was unable to adjust to the darkness until a slight movement drew his attention. A young Gypsy woman was hiding in the corner next to his heavy horse equipment. He recognised her face, for the whole village had remarked upon it. She was Swanky Jessel's grandaughter. He and ApIvor had listened to her play the harp at the summer festival two years ago, when the old Gypsy chief was still alive. Swanky Jessel was friendlier than most, and had traded with him throughout the years. It was all right then; he could trust her. There must be a good reason for her to hide up here.

Reuben came to the entrance and peered in. With an angry cry, he pushed Eli aside and rushed at her. The girl screamed, and he looked on in disbelief as the young man grabbed her hair and smashed her, like a rag doll, into the barn wall. She slumped to the ground. Coming out from his stunned inertia his own anger boiled up.

"Stop that, there's no call for that."

He caught Reuben by his collar and upper arm, outmatching him in strength and experience, despite a thirty-year age difference, pulling him away as he aimed kick after kick at the whimpering girl. She curled into a ball to protect herself.

Reuben struggled, yelling abuse. Breaking free, he gripped her arm again, hauling her up. Eli reacted instinctively. Seizing the largest of his driving whips, he lashed him across the forearm. Reuben dropped her. He reeled round to face him, nursing his wound. The thin weal oozed red.

"You don't understand! She was promised to me, but now…"

He glared at Eli. "You know what upset that stallion. A grai can sense it a mile away." He shouted at Eli. "She's carrying – carrying some other man's tikni." He rounded on Mahalia, "Who is it, you whore?"

Eli had to act. He couldn't in all conscience allow Reuben to drag her away. He looked at the cowering little figure on the ground and was moved to pity.

"That's enough," he said. "It seems to me she's made a different choice."

"It wasn't 'er place."

"Even so, you'll not touch her again, not while she's on my property. You'd better leave."

Reuben scowled at Eli, eyeing the whip. He pointed at Mahalia, shouting again, but in Romani this time. His words scythed through the air making her flinch. He snatched up his jacket, spat on the ground in front of them, and slammed out of the barn.

Eli looked down at her small frame, angry with himself for not acting sooner.

"What did he say?"

But he'd already caught the gist of it: a threat sounds the same in any language. Ignoring his outstretched hand she stood up, still trembling, and steadied herself against the barn wall.

"Said he'd find out who it was, that he'd be back to get me. Said I'd pay for this."

She's so slender and lovely, he thought, *like a little wild flower, and should never have been promised to a brute like Reuben in the first place.*

Mahalia turned towards him revealing the ugly graze down the side of her face, and the reality of her situation struck him. If Reuben intended coming back for her, perhaps with others, he would have to do something – fast.

"Perhaps if I can get a message to?" He looked at her for encouragement, but saw her retreat into wariness. "...to the father." He said, putting it rather more bluntly than he intended. Mahalia began to cry, and Eli, being a man who believed that women were tender creatures no matter what their origin, was moved to comfort her. "Come on now", he said, resisting the urge to touch her, "tell me his name, and we can put this right."

She shook her head. Her words had an unexpected vehemence,

"No, mister, you don't understand. He's from the gav. Your village. He's a gajo – one of you."

The pieces fell into place. He looked at her in dismay, his mind running through all that he'd seen. The jumbled images assembled themselves into the right order. Now he understood the reason for all the secrecy. Howell was only weeks away from his twentieth birthday, but Eli already knew what his parents' reaction would be. They would never let them marry. And how old was she, the same age perhaps? It could be even more of a problem with Reuben out for blood.

"There's no hope." She said, her voice little more than a whisper, "No hope at all. His mother..." she began.

"Yes, lassie, I know all about his mother. Your young man's Howell, isn't he? Howell Pritchard." Her expression slipped from bewildered to desolate, confirming his guess. "You'd better come

82

into the house. You'll be safe there, and we can decide what to do."

She followed him into the kitchen, and sat at the table while he made tea for them both. He looked at her anxiously.

"You're sure you're all right?"

Mahalia nodded, avoiding his eyes, uneasy in the strange surroundings.

The yard gate clanked open, and she clutched the table spilling the cup of hot sweet tea he'd put in front of her.

"Steady now," he peered down into the yard from the high window over the sink. "Ah, well, if that isn't a coincidence," he said, as if pleased by what he saw. He turned back to her. "It's nothing to worry about, just one of Howell's younger sisters, and a brother, come for their eggs." Her eyes widened in alarm. "No, this is perfect. I can get a message to him without arousing suspicion. Go through there, along the passage into the front parlour, and don't make a sound."

He ushered her into the other room, then unlatched the back door, calling out to Nancy,

"Come for your eggs, little maid?" Nancy skipped over to him. Her brother trailed behind, reluctant, and heavy-legged. "Got your baskets?" Joe released the strap which held them on his back. He'd been relegated to the role of porter that afternoon. Eli smiled at them. They were such bonny kiddies. "Good, well I'm a bit behind, so I want you to give Howell a letter – about a job that needs doing."

Two sets of solemn eyes stared up at him. They weren't usually trusted with delivering messages. "You pick out your eggs. Use some loose straw to pack them," (they'd had catastrophes before now on the way home) "and I'll sort out this note for your brother."

Nancy whirled on her heels, and raced to the shed by the side of the barn where the eggs were kept. Eli gave Joe a brief smile and went back into the kitchen. He decided against too clear a message. It would be better dealt with in person.

'Dear Howell', he wrote,
'Something has come up on the farm. Can't manage
on my own, I'd consider it a favour if you would call in
tonight. It is <u>urgent</u> or I wouldn't trouble you.
Your friend, Eli'

He wasn't prone to dramatic statements. On this occasion he hoped the underlined word would have the desired effect. He sealed it in an envelope addressed to:

'Mr Howell Pritchard – private' and put an additional little blob of sealing wax on the flap. That should stop any prying fingers from prizing it open.

❧

Out in the shed, he found the children admiring the Bantam eggs he'd collected that morning.

"Are you done yet, Nancy? Oh, you've found those have you? Here you are." He selected six, brown-speckled, perfect specimens, and placed them into a small enamel bowl lined with straw. "These are for you little ones. Just the right size for you, eh? As a treat, tell your Mum." They beamed at him. "Now, Nancy," he said seriously, "it's important that Howell gets this as soon as possible. Do you understand?"

Nancy snatched the letter from his hand before her brother could respond, shouting,

"Straight away, I'll do it straight away, don't worry."

And she ran up the lane, leaving Joe the task of carrying the eggs home unassisted.

❦

Nancy saw Howell, in the distance, coming from the direction of the village; his hair blowing about as he hurried. He was obviously preoccupied, and hadn't noticed her. She decided to wait by the lychgate to surprise him.

A bird whistled from the hawthorn hedge opposite, or so she supposed, and was answered by another farther away. It made a curious two-note whooping noise rather like a cuckoo. She contemplated the little rhyme she'd learnt in school.

'The cuckoo comes in April
Sings its song in May
Changes its tune in the middle of June
In July it flies away'

"It's the wrong time of the year, silly birds. Haha, silly cuckoos! You're cuckoo, cuckoos."

It was becoming a habit talking to herself. She giggled aloud at her own joke. Her brothers could have told her maybe, but there was something else of interest here. The wooden seat had many hearts carved on it by lovers. She tried to identify people from the rough hewn initials, but there was no 'H. L. P.', 'H. P.', or even an 'H'.

The most prominent declaration read:

'J. M.'

L

'L. P.'

and had been enclosed in a heart.

That was obvious, 'Jack Millward loves Louise Pritchard'. Everybody knew that. The letters had been cut years ago. The edges were soft and weathered. No, her eldest brother had left no clue to his sweetheart.

Howell's footsteps drew nearer, and she rushed out to meet him. His startled expression turned to anger, but before he could say anything she thrust the note into his hand.

"Old Eli said I was to give you this. It's important."

"Mr Jenkins to you. Show some respect for your elders."

Nancy met his glare with perfect innocence, and said,

"Me and Joe went for the eggs, and ...Mr Jenkins," she pulled herself up hastily, "asked me to give you that note straight away. We're on our way back now. I was only waiting for Joe to catch up."

At that moment, as if timed to back up her story, Joe appeared over the brow of the hill, walking slowly as he concentrated on his burden.

Howell tucked the note in his pocket.

"Joe and I went," he continued, frowning at her, "not me and

Joe. And you're twelve, Nan', not six, so don't simper at me in that stupid fashion." He looked beyond her, and gave Joe a sympathetic smile as he plodded up, adding, in his usual voice, "Thank you, Nancy. You'd better help young Joe with those eggs."

His frown faded, and he smiled at them both. She grinned back now harmony was restored and, for once, did as she was told.

Howell stood in the lane, and watched his brother and sister round the corner to the village before opening the envelope. The message, though intriguing, would have to keep. He had another, more important appointment before visiting Old Eli.

He wandered into the churchyard. They had arranged to meet there again. It was the closest spot, though he felt uneasy about their recent near-discovery. Today there was no sign of Mahalia, which was odd. She was usually there long before him. She didn't hide in order to tease him, the way other girls might have done. Their feelings were too intense, too serious for such games; their time too precious.

He lit a cigarette, and leant against one of the raised stone tombs. Ivy covered the top in a dense, dusty mantle. It rustled beneath him as he tried to find a comfortable position. His movement caused the resident jay to burst from its sentry post nearby. It swooped away towards the chestnut trees shrieking its annoyance.

Someone tapped him on the shoulder. Howell looked round, the name 'Mally' dying on his lips when he realised his mistake.

EIGHT

At first ApIvor was puzzled by Wilf's anxiety over his eldest son. If any of them had been allowed freedom over the years, it was Howell.

ApIvor could picture him as a boy, leading his brothers and sisters in the hymns, wholly given up to the ecstasy of the music. That unblemished young face haloed by blonde curls, 'Like an angel in a renaissance painting' as he was fond of saying. At nineteen Howell was taller than his father, and set the hearts of village girls for miles around aflutter. But he was easily bored, and his eyes strayed farther afield in search of someone more exciting.

For the lad to be late for his tea seemed a minor matter, but when Wilf stepped into the light, he altered his opinion. His friend's face was drawn. There was more to this disappearance than he would admit.

"What's the matter, Wilf? Why do you think something has happened to him?"

"There's a girl involved. I'm not sure who, but I have my suspicions. I was frightened there'd been a..." He stopped what he was about to say, "...an accident, something of that sort." His voice trailed off. "I've looked everywhere – everywhere, that is, except the old churchyard and Eli's place."

"I'll come with you." He placed a comforting hand on his friend's arm. "We can cut over the fields from here, across the estate, and come out by the old church wall."

Wilf glanced at the sky.

"The light's going. I know he's a grown lad and can take care of himself, but I can't help it. Something's wrong. He promised, see, promised Agnes and me he'd be back early and tell us what was going on."

ApIvor took charge, more to soothe his friend's anxiety than resolve matters.

"Ah well, chances are you're worrying unnecessarily. We'll visit Eli last, and if there's still no sign, I'm sure he'll bring his dogs and join in the search."

They crossed the stubble on the top field behind the churchyard. Wilf strode forward, but ApIvor paused, half-way across, to listen. There was something odd about the air, and the stillness. Biddy snuffled on ahead, yelped, and disappeared in the direction of the lychgate. When they caught up she was whining next to an unidentifiable shape beneath the seat.

"Oh, dear God, no..." Wilf stumbled in his anxiety, and knelt next to the body. He ran his hands over his son's limp form, muttering, "Not this, not my boy..."

ApIvor raised his lantern. They were stunned into silence. Whoever had done this meant to finish him. Biddy whiffled with fear, distressed by the damage to her young master. She licked his hand, and Howell groaned. They both sighed with relief.

"Thank God, Wilf. For a moment I feared the worst."

Wilf grasped the dog's collar and pulled her away.

"I must get the Doc. Will you stay with him? You can keep Biddy with you."

"He's not there – went over to the next village – complications with a birth so I understand. I'll send one of Godfrey's lads from the estate, but discreetly. Now listen, I think it's best if we take him straight to my place. It's the nearest. We can manage him between us, if we take it slow and careful. And I'll send for Constable Roberts."

"No!" Wilf almost shouted the word at him. "No, not the police, not over a fight."

"A fight? Why do you say that? Surely this was unprovoked – a robbery, perhaps?"

"Look at his knuckles. No, he fought someone. This was no random attack, I'm sure. Dear God, how am I going to break this to Agnes?"

"We'll worry about that later. The important thing is to get him indoors, out of harm's way – and out of sight. That'll prevent a lot of gossip, and maybe trouble of a different sort."

"Who could have done this to him?"

"Come on now, Wilf, be honest with me. You must have an idea. Didn't you notice on the way over here? The Gypsies have gone. There was no smoke. No horses, no noise at all, in fact. I

90

think you guessed who he was involved with – even though he did his best to keep it all a secret."

Wilf didn't reply, his eyes fixed on his son's battered face. There was little left of the bloody, swollen features recognisable as Howell.

Back at the lodge, they lowered him on to ApIvor's bed. Though they tried to be careful, he cried out, dislodging the loose flap of skin that was once his left cheek. One of his front teeth had gone, another was broken. They were both helpless to alleviate his suffering.

"We'd better wait for the Doc, Wilf. I fear we may do more harm than good. This assault is clearly the work of more than one man." ApIvor frowned, an image of something earlier stirring his memory. "I'd lay odds, if I were a gambler, that the girl is Mahalia Jessel, and *this* the handiwork of her brothers."

Wilf wiped his eyes on the back of his hand. He seemed confused, unable to grasp what ApIvor was saying.

"You mean that Gyppo girl, don't you, the pretty one they talk about in the pub? Dear God, this will kill Agnes. She won't be able to hold up her head again in this village. You know how she is?"

It had angered ApIvor, not normally given to impassioned outbursts outside the pulpit. He had shouted at him, managing, after the first words, to reclaim his self control.

"By all that's Holy, that's the least of... No, right now, I want to prevent this son of yours from suffering any more than he has already. Your wife's standing in the community is of little importance. And they're Gypsies, Wilf, not 'Gyppos'. Small wonder I have to correct your children so often from using pejorative terms."

91

He let his anger blow over Wilf, though the man appeared to be neither listening nor capable of coherent speech. If anything he looked near to tears again. Why was he lecturing him now, maybe to mask his own culpability? He had known something was amiss, guessed the object of Howell's interest. Guessed, and done nothing. Well, they could keep it from Agnes, for the present, but while they were in the middle of tending Howell's wounds, she came to the back door, letting herself in, as was her habit, and surprised them.

ApIvor would never forget those few minutes; they would haunt him for life. Agnes recoiled, as if from a blow. Her face registered a sequence of emotions: shock, concern, distaste, and finally naked anger. She would have struck the lad's senseless body too, but he caught her uplifted arm, and restrained her. She rounded on him, angry that he should interfere, forgetting her place – that it was his house. Fading from his grasp, she sank into a chair and stared at the wall, refusing to look at her son. There were no tears. Wilf remained silent. He had looked at his wife's face when she came into the room, and the unspoken dialogue between them gave ApIvor pause. He was dismayed by the bleakness he read there.

Howell swam in and out of consciousness. When he came round, croaking what sounded like her name, she was the first to speak. She kept her head averted, trembling with the effort of self control.

"You've disgraced our family – shamed us all. You and that..." She struggled for a word, "that creature – " Howell stretched his hand towards her, but seeing it out of the corner of her eye, she flinched away, raising her voice. "God may forgive you, but I never will." ApIvor felt bound to remonstrate with her at this. He opened his mouth to speak, but she flashed him such a furious look his words stopped in his throat. She half turned back towards her son, her eyes fixed on a point several feet above him. "You're not to set foot in our home again, Howell Pritchard, never. Do you mind me?" It was an order, not a question, her voice tremulous with echoes of her Welsh forbears. "I won't have you taint the rest of my children."

She stood then and walked to the door; a woman who had aged visibly in a matter of minutes, and would never be the same again.

Throughout all this Wilf said nothing. He seemed to be waiting for his friend to take the initiative.

Conflicting loyalties held ApIvor balanced between two difficult choices. He had the greatest admiration for Agnes, on an everyday basis. She worked harder than any woman he knew. She had such Faith too, but there were limits to her understanding and compassion. Ultimately, he knew it was not his place to go against her decision, right or wrong. One thing he understood, so painful in its simplicity, she would never forgive this son, ever.

It wasn't just that she had such hopes for him. It went deeper than that. As Howell grew up, he'd replaced his father in her affections. She saw him as the embodiment of how Wilf should have been. Now, with this 'sin of all sins', as she put it, he had sunk lower than anything her erstwhile fun-loving husband could ever have done.

Wilf left him to supervise Howell while he returned to the cottage for a few essentials his son would need. The lad's breathing was laboured and fitful. ApIvor hoped it wouldn't be too long before

Doc Bevan arrived. He feared the worst; that there were internal injuries too serious for recovery.

As he sat watching the uneven rise and fall of Howell's chest beneath the covers, he recalled the day the young people met, chiding himself for not doing more the minute he saw it – that half-glance towards her when the caravan of painted, horse-drawn waggons took its traditional route through the village.

He understood perfectly how it had been: two young people intoxicated with each other's beauty, her vivid petals distracting Howell from paler, more familiar flowers; clandestine meetings outside the village hidden by the dense foliage of high summer; both of them enticed by the danger and fascination of each other's world, avoiding his family, and hers, knowing each side was filled with loathing and suspicion for the other.

Her brothers must have found out about them. Who knew what pressure they'd put on her, or what fate she'd suffered?

When Wilf returned later with his son's belongings, there was no going back. It was left to ApIvor to explain Howell's few remaining options. He must leave the village, that much was certain, but as for choices, it seemed better to go as far away as possible. Join up, and trust fate to get posted abroad, or take a cheap passage bound for the New World, and start again.

"Either way," he told him, "you must stay here until we can be sure you're in a fit state to travel." Howell raised himself on one elbow and started to protest. ApIvor cut him short. "No, there's no chance of following her, they've gone." He tried to speak again, but his mouth was swollen and split. ApIvor continued, "The girl's Mahalia Jessel, isn't she? After all I said to you – the warning about her brothers – and you took no notice." Howell stopped moving, both eyes sealed shut, unseeing slits above a broken nose; his stillness an admission. "There's not much escapes my notice, Howell, or others, I'm sure."

Wilf sighed and stared at the floor. He nodded in agreement, and spoke for the first time.

"She suspected something, Agnes did. I did too." He raised disappointed eyes to his son. "I should have warned you. Should have stopped you."

ApIvor reached out and placed his hand on Wilf's bowed shoulder.

"He's a man now, not a boy. You can't blame yourselves. He knew the rules." He returned his attention to Howell. "Didn't you?" His eyes brimmed with tears at the futility of it all. What future was there left for this young man now, the one who'd shown so much promise? "Look at what they've done." His voice was robbed of its customary vitality. "They thought they'd finished you, and if you try to find her, the next time they'll make sure they do."

He kept him hidden there for nearly a fortnight, relying on Doc Bevan's discretion and an oath as firm as his own to protect their secret. The doctor, dismayed by the injuries, debated taking Howell to the nearest hospital in his horse-drawn break.

"I can stitch his face, but his nose will have to mend before being re-broken and set later. There's not much can be done about those teeth. Those either side will blacken and fall out eventually, or I'm no judge. But there are wonderful improvements in false ones, these days. They'll hardly show, unless he laughs, and I've a feeling that's going to be difficult for him in the future. I'll see how he is after twenty-four hours, but I fear any journey might exacerbate his condition."

They all agreed it was better to let him rest and heal out of sight.

❦

ApIvor paid for Howell's ticket. Wilf came to see him at Chapel one evening during that first week.

"I've got a bit saved up, 'rainy day' money I suppose you might call it." He held out a battered tin to ApIvor. "It's not enough, but it's all I have. I was hoping..."

ApIvor raised a hand, silencing him.

"Don't worry about that now, Wilf. I'll make up the rest." He read the distress in his friend's face. "I keep funds for emergencies such as this. Consider it settled."

"I'll pay you back, I insist. This is a loan, though it may take me a while. Only one thing, I beg of you. Don't let anyone know, least of all Howell. He might try and see me – to make amends. It'd be too much for Agnes. You understand that, don't you?"

ApIvor patted the heaving shoulders, for in his friend's face he perceived the truth behind the words. It would be Wilf who would break.

ApIvor spelt it all out for Howell in the days that followed.

"You have to understand, my boy. The Gypsies have a strict tribal law. You both broke it."

"It wasn't meant to be like this. We love each other. We were planning to leave."

"Don't you understand why they did this to you? Your mother assessed the situation correctly, I believe. She was convinced the girl must be expecting."

"Expecting? You mean pregnant?"

ApIvor cleared his throat, uncomfortable with so blunt a response.

"Yes, Howell, can you look me in the eye and tell me there's no cause for that accusation?" Howell remained silent. "No, I thought not."

"But I love her. If they've hurt her..."

"They'll not abuse her, I'm sure of that. Old Rachael Jessel's a wise woman, but you must remember their ways are not like ours. She'll be looked after, and the child."

"No, you're wrong. Wrong. You don't..." he struggled to finish. "She told me once, talking about another woman, a cousin, I think. They'll horse whip her for going with me. Cast her out and the child too. It'd be different if it was one of their men, and a village girl."

Howell tried again to raise himself, but pain got the better of him. His words choked off, and ApIvor worried about the fresh blood staining the flannel he held to his mouth.

Despite his contract with God for the ministry, he couldn't help his own ambivalence towards the Gypsies. Although his policy was more liberal than that of his flock, and for all he was fascinated by their music, the vivid spectacle at festivals, and the like – he felt people should stick with their own kind. It prevented trouble of this sort.

He certainly didn't hold with violence; if anything it reinforced his view. But he was a kind man, and worried about Mahalia too. For if they'd done this to the lad – but what more could he do? He felt sure Howell's concern for her safety was unfounded. They had gone, and must have taken her with them. That was an end to it.

His immediate problem lay with this young man, and a new future, somewhere, away from the district. Out of the country altogether perhaps? He had read of good prospects in the New World. Canada seemed the best option, more familiar than the wild reports they heard about Australia. More affordable too.

The days passed. Howell improved, mending with the speed and resilience of youth. The gossip died for lack of fuel. ApIvor's secret guest remained hidden; the inquisitive Mrs Prosser being out of the district visiting her sister, by merest good fortune. All this time they'd had no word from Agnes or Wilf. ApIvor told him bluntly,

"It's pointless to hope, or write to them. You must move on." When Howell began to protest, he put it as plainly as he could. "They'll never forgive you, at least, not your Mum," then added, out of kindness, not having much faith that he would. "But write to me, won't you?"

Doc Bevan took Howell to the nearest railway station, smuggling him out while supposedly on his rounds. They had to wait until the once-handsome face resumed normal proportions, and he could walk unaided managing his injuries. Howell's head was partially bandaged.

"If any one asks, you were trampled in a riding accident. The good Lord knows there are enough of those." The doctor said, helping him onto the floor of the break, and covering him up with a tartan rug. "Keep out of sight until we are clear of the village. Tell me if it's too painful for you in this position."

Howell grabbed the Doc's sleeve.

"Can you stop, just for a few minutes, by the old oast house? There's something I want to check. There maybe a message for me."

The doctor helped him down, fully prepared to accompany him, but Howell refused his arm. From the lane he watched his patient limp to the door. After a few minutes Howell re-emerged, his pallor increased, and passed the rest of the journey in silence, retreating once more beneath the rug. Doc Bevan looked back over his shoulder at his passenger. No, whatever remaining hope young Howell had rekindled before they stopped at the oast house had gone.

The doctor recounted the incident to his old friend, and ApIvor's sadness deepened. With no hope, how would the lad survive?

His self-doubt began on that day. Perhaps he should have done more, and not given in to accepted attitudes. But how could one hope to make the right choice, when every solution held nothing but pain and recrimination?

NINE

Nancy burned with curiosity about Old Eli's message, but despite her best endeavours to ease open the sealed flap or decipher any of the writing inside by holding it to the light she was forced to give up. Howell was already in sight.

As soon as they had rounded the corner from the cemetery, she tried to persuade Joe to take the rest of the eggs, pleading all sorts of excuses about needing to tell their eldest brother something important, but Joe was stubborn, uncooperative, and threatened to tell. She had been tempted to dump her eggs on the side of the lane, and go back anyway, determined to get a glimpse of Howell with his girl – for she was sure that's who he intended meeting – but Joe wasn't having any of it.

"I'm telling our Mum if you do. Next time you can get the eggs by yourself."

She stuck her tongue out at him, but his threat was real enough. If anyone had the nerve to tell on her it would be Joe.

When they entered the cottage kitchen, both read the warning signs and retreated into silence. They were sent to bed early, but it was hard to sleep with the ruckus downstairs.

Around nine o'clock there had been a loud 'crack' and they heard their mother shouting, "You knew, you must have. I'll have you both out of here as God is my witness!" followed by a door banging.

Both her little sisters whimpered in fright so that she missed the last bit while she settled them down again. Later still she heard the rumble of her father's voice but couldn't make out the words. She'd heard her parents rowing before, though to be fair it was usually her mother's voice that dominated, but nothing as dramatic as this.

Louise turned her face away when she came to bed, and sobbed into her pillow, but when Nancy reached over to pat her shoulder in sympathy her hand had been shaken off in a gesture wholly out of character. She was crushed into silence.

In daylight she could see why. Their mother's hand print marked her sister's cheek. When she attempted to speak, Louise turned swollen eyes towards her, and placed a hand over her Nancy's mouth in warning. She pulled her close, breathing into her hair.

"Don't say anything, Nan'. I'll tell you tonight."

When she came downstairs later than usual, there was no sign of her brothers, or her father. Louise was helping their younger sisters fold their clothes. Propped against one of the chairs, Wilf's old suitcase gaped open revealing two neat piles of small garments. Various other items were stacked on the table in preparation for packing.

Nancy was brimming with questions, but her elder sister gestured towards the parlour door, and held her finger to her lips. Their mother was in there and must not be disturbed. The two little girls, overawed by all the mysterious changes taking place around them, were unusually quiet, and started, round-eyed, at each new noise.

She went outside, and loitered in the communal back yard undecided about where to go. Eventually, she wandered towards the footbridge. Baking temperatures throughout August had lowered the river level, and that Prosser girl she despised so much was seated in the middle, on the planks, with two of her friends, elbows sticking out over the middle rail, their legs dangling above the water. They sniggered together when they saw her, and began to jeer,

"Gyppo lover!"

Nancy's face went red. She stormed onto the bridge and kicked the youngest Prosser girl in the centre of her back. Howling at the unexpected venom behind such an attack, she struggled to her feet.

"You just wait, Nancy Pritchard, I'm telling on you. We don't want to be seen with your sort! My sister said your brother's gone off with the Gyppos."

Nancy took a step forward, causing the three girls to move closer to one another and back away.

"Liar!" She shouted to cover her confusion. "My brother's got a girl, and it's not your fat sister, Mary, always making cow eyes at him."

"Where's he gone then? My Dad said all the Gyppos disappeared in the night."

"What's that got to do with Howell?"

"You know! You're the liar! Jimmy Evans said he saw your brother down by the old oast house with a Gyppo girl, just last week, so there!"

With this last triumphant sally, they ran away, giving Nancy no further opportunity to retaliate. Her heart thumped loudly in her chest. It disconcerted her not knowing as much about her own brother's whereabouts as a bunch of stupid village girls.

Behind her came the metallic ring of horse shoes on the road. Old Eli was riding down the street towards the bridge. He called her over, but she didn't want to talk to him, and answered his questions reluctantly. Whatever he wanted was of little interest to her now. Only one thought filled her mind – the old oast house. Maybe there she would find a clue to her brother's disappearance. Risking a reprimand for outright rudeness, she skedaddled across the bridge, and along the footpath, knowing Old Eli couldn't follow her on horseback.

She didn't want to think about her beloved Howell with a Gyppo. That was a lie. It had to be. Just wait 'til she saw Louise. Lou' would know for sure. She'd show that stupid Prosser girl.

But the oast house? Was that Evans tyke making mischief again, or had he really seen Howell with someone? It was supposed to be a spot for courting couples. She'd heard her mother threaten Louise if she ever went there with Jack. Well, she'd check anyway, no harm in that, and taking the lane that went over the hill to the derelict building, hastened towards the Devil's Lip lowering above the village. Looking back towards the river, she wished she'd kicked her enemy harder, or better still shoved her into the water. That would have washed her nasty mouth out.

In front of the Chapel she paused, and considered her next move. No one must notice. It would be better to take the more roundabout route, away from vigilant neighbours. Stealth was something she practised to perfection in a home too small for secrets. Now, she summoned all her cunning, and courage, for to stray beyond the boundary her mother had set invited punishment.

There was no one in the lane, or the surrounding fields. The only person who regularly used this route was Old Eli, but she was confident he was still down in the village.

彩

The oast house roof had collapsed long ago, and was considered dangerous. Faded notices hung on the walls warning intruders of the risk. It was surrounded by a yard full of rusting machinery, shoulder-high nettles, and rank elderberry bushes that cast deep pools of shadow for concealment.

Hidden from the lane, Nancy stood in the shade to recover her breath, and studied the ground. Her eyes followed the tracks beaten through the surrounding weeds until she saw the most likely path. An overgrown area around the door to an outbuilding had been flattened from recent comings and goings. A small and obviously new padlock secured the entrance. It was not what she had expected to find in such a tumbledown place. She jiggled it for a moment, but the mechanism showed no sign of coming apart.

Another trail led round the side of the building into a bank of older, dustier nettles. The sun seldom reached this area, and the lower walls were green and slimy to the touch. There were no windows at ground level. Those above showed signs of the local boys' marksmanship, but in one the glass was missing completely. She tracked footsteps into the weeds and found a ladder with several broken rungs. Judging by the caked mud on those remaining, it had been used in recent months.

Nancy stopped to listen. There was no noise, and hardly any breeze.

Lifting the ladder was easy. Despite her height, she was strong and agile. Reaching the window and clambering through proved a simple task. Inside, below the windowsill, crates had been stacked up in a double row sturdy enough to support a man. She reached the floor easily without damaging her clothes. Several different sized footprints tracked, back-and-forth, through the dust into what must have been the office. It was darker in there. Light through the doorway reflected on a row of empty beer bottles lining the opposite wall. On the floor, next to a pile of hop sacks, she found blobs of candle-wax, but there was little sign of any other activity.

Fallen soot clogged the grate. On one side of the chimney breast, a foot above the skirting, the paintwork surrounding the air-vent looked smudged and dirty, but the knob that operated the slats shone with use. Gingerly, she tried to slide the vent open, almost dropping it when the whole plate came away in her hand. An oilcloth roll, about the size of her father's tobacco pouch, fell at her feet. It felt heavy and had a lump in the middle.

Squatting on the floor, she opened it out and examined the

contents, drawing in her breath at the sight of three large white five pound bank notes. They were the first she had seen. Forgetting her mission, she smoothed them open. The lump proved to be an embroidered kerchief containing coins. They were mainly florins and shillings. There was no copper change of smaller denomination she could legitimately spend in the village shop. The total came to nearly twenty pounds, a small fortune to her young eyes.

She leant back on her heels, and considered. Clearly it had been hidden there by someone up to no good. It didn't take her long to decide. 'Finders keepers' her younger brothers would say. The hoard was asking to be stolen. The problem now was how, and where, to conceal it at home.

Nancy returned the money to the pouch, pushed it under the waistband of her frock on the inside, and bound it securely in place with her sash. She had been gone rather a long time. Not that it mattered to her now; she would worry about her excuses later. Uppermost in her mind was the money. The crates wobbled ominously as she clambered up. Nancy stopped and checked herself, careful not to overbalance. Now was not the moment to stumble. She took a deep breath before tackling the ladder.

Safely back on the ground, she heard, for the second time that morning, the sound of approaching hoof beats, and hid amongst the elderberry bushes. If it was Old Eli he might have his dogs with him. That could be a problem, but when she saw him dismount he was alone and clearly in a hurry. Something glinted in his hand. Nancy's mind worked fast. It must be the key to the padlock. As soon as she heard the door scrape open she moved from her hiding place, quietly to begin with, then ran as fast as her legs could work up the steep gradient, clutching the pouch to her body with one hand.

Once on top of the hill, she looked back at the buildings. Eli's horse remained tied to the gate, but he was nowhere to be seen. Perhaps, she reasoned, he had farm-type business inside, though she couldn't think what it might be. Not for one moment did she imagine he had come to look for the money.

❧

Louise was alone in the kitchen, surrounded by fewer pots and pans than usual. She seemed distracted and warned her to silence with a glance towards the parlour door. Nancy breathed more easily. Still clutching her waist, she muttered an excuse about stitch in her side from running home.

Louise put down her cloth, and mimed that they should go outside. The garden was empty, but despite this she seemed to be taking extra precautions about being overheard. Well away from the cottage she spoke at last, her voice still hoarse from crying.

"Now you listen to me, our Nancy, and don't interrupt for once. Howell has left home, gone to enlist. I don't care what you've heard." Her voice rose as Nancy opened her mouth to cut in. "He's gone. ApIvor confirmed it when I saw him this morning. Dad's taken Ruby and May to stay with Uncle Cecil in Hereford, so you can have a bed all to yourself for a while. Mum's not speaking or seeing anyone, so be warned. And don't you go talking in the village. He's gone, and that's the end of it. If you know what's good for you won't mention him at all indoors."

She moved into the light, and Nancy saw the full impact of their mother's rage upon her sister's face. Despite her preoccupation with her immediate problems, it made her eyes water in sympathy. Louise opened her arms to comfort her. Just in time, she remembered the pouch, and pulled away.

"That Prosser girl said he'd run off with the Gyppos... um, the Gypsies," she corrected herself, "said he'd been courting a Gypsy girl, if you can believe that?"

Louise looked stricken, but didn't answer. When she spoke again the words were stilted, almost as if she didn't believe her own explanation.

"That's rubbish. You know what those Prossers are like for gossip. He's gone to enlist. Dad told us last night when you were all in bed. There was no girl, Gypsy or otherwise, that I know of."

Nancy felt a quiver of pleasure at this news. So Howell hadn't mentioned the girlfriend to Louise, after all. Nevertheless, she couldn't have been a Gyppo. But even as she relished her secret knowledge, a picture of the young Gypsy woman in the churchyard sprang to mind. Reaching up on impulse, she kissed her sister's other, unblemished cheek.

"I won't say a word, Lulu, I promise. I'll go and tidy my things from under your bed and put them under mine."

Louise smiled at the use of her pet name, a legacy from when Nancy was small and found 'Louise' difficult to pronounce.

It was no more than a diversionary tactic. She wanted to get away and think. There was so much racing around in her head – and she must hide the money. But whose was it? An unwelcome thought began to take shape. What if this was her brother's money, his and some girl's? But never a Gyppo, no, not that. She shook the notion away.

She crept upstairs to their shared room, and pulled out her box of belongings from beneath what was now Louise's bed.

They each had a box expertly made by their father with their names engraved on the lid. Her younger brothers were no respecters of property, but they despised dolls, and that was to her advantage, especially as her little sisters had been sent away. There would be no one interested in her few bits and pieces.

She raised the lid and looked inside. The doll her father had made for her when she was small occupied most of the space. She loved it, despite the ugliness of its repaired limbs. Her Dad had shown her how to put it back together by pulling out the rubber bands suspended from a hook at the base of its head. The limbs had smaller hooks that caught around the bands, forcing them into place. It required nimble fingers, and a firm grip, but Nancy had pulled it apart and reassembled it countless times until she had the knack. The hollowed out body was the perfect place to hide her spoils.

She stared at the original cloth for a long time. In the light, the wrapping, though dusty, was covered in bright patterns with an embroidered edge. The realisation of its origin made her feel sick, then angry. That Gyppo woman had worn one just like it to hold back her hair.

How could Howell have gone with one of them? How could he?

In a corner of her mind there festered a mean satisfaction that she had their money. Maybe without it he would come back. She didn't believe that story about enlisting. Her big brother had always wanted the world in his daydreams, but never in a soldier's uniform. Despite all Louise had told her second-hand from both their Dad *and* ApIvor, she would never believe a word of it. As she sat on the bedroom floor, her anger burst from her. Gripping the doll, she stared into its painted eyes.

"I'd rather he was dead. Yes, dead. Not gone off with one of them!" She looked around the cramped bedroom, at the darned bedlinen, and the faded, much-washed curtains, the hand-me-down clothes from Louise draped over the chair-back ready for alteration. "Not for much longer, do you hear me?" She shook the doll, glaring at its unresponsive face. "I'm going too. Just as soon as I'm grown, I'll be off, and this money will be the start. I'll show them. I'll show everyone!"

TEN

During the forty eight hours that followed, Eli was at first confused, then disappointed, and finally saddened. He didn't know all of it, and if the conclusions he drew were at fault, together with his subsequent actions, then others were to blame by their omission of the truth.

He and Mahalia sat in the kitchen, starting at every sound, until well past midnight. At last, as fatigue overtook her, he persuaded her to sleep in one of the guest bedrooms. He placed the old fashioned key on the table to reassure her that she would be safe under the roof of a 'gajo'. There was nothing he could do to prevent her leaving, but he prayed she'd wait until he could find Howell, and offer them both the sort of help Agnes would deny.

Mahalia said little the next morning. He could see the full extent of her injury. Her face had swollen under the graze.

He urged her to eat, knowing she'd accepted nothing but tea since the previous day.

"You must trust me," he insisted, seeing the look of doubt returning. "Do you believe I want to witness another incident like yesterday?" She began to cry. Tears flowed down her cheeks unchecked. "Please, rest while I'm gone," he said. He placed his hand on her shoulder. The gesture was spontaneous, but gentle, and she didn't flinch. "I'll lock the door from the outside. Keep away from the windows. You'll be safe enough. I'll leave all my dogs, save old Betsy here, on loose chains in the back yard. She'll look after you. No one will come near while I'm out."

The border collie, part blind, grey muzzled and relegated to the status of house dog, half-raised her head from the hearthrug on hearing her name. But as her master prepared to leave, she positioned herself between Mahalia and the door, ears cocked, knowing her duty.

Eli left, hoping his guest would still be there when he returned, but sure in the knowledge that if she wanted to stay, no one could break in and harm her.

He decided to go to the manor first, and met an angry estate manager on his way out of the drive. Howell had gone off suddenly, he said, everything was in an uproar. The man was puzzled. It wasn't like him, but there you are, you can't tell what these young lads will do. But he hadn't thought Howell the sort to enlist, he said. Neither did Eli. It was all very odd.

"If that's not enough, most of the Gypsies have gone, at least the Jessels and their families. Never known them go so early with the work half done. I just hope the weather holds..." and still grumbling to himself, he hurried away.

Eli saw Nancy loitering by the footbridge. She looked indignant when asked if she had delivered his message. Her 'yes, of course' bordered on rudeness, but he let that go.

Eventually he decided to go round to the Pritchards' cottage and find out for himself. He knocked several times until a tired and reluctant Wilf answered.

Wilf was short with him. Yes, it was true, Howell had gone off. Sorry if he'd let Eli down in some way. Agnes didn't want to talk about it, and neither did he. And shut the door in his face.

He returned late morning. The tall pink-and-grey stone house stood undisturbed in bright sunlight. No sound could be heard save welcoming barks from the yard. He unlocked the door and found Mahalia sitting at the table more or less where he had left her. She blinked as daylight streamed through the doorway behind him illuminating her face.

"I'm sorry, mister, I fell asleep."

The embroidery on her sleeve had left an imprint on her undamaged cheek. Resting her head on her arms, exhaustion must have won out over fear. He doubted she had slept much the previous night.

Eli felt stirred by emotions he had all but forgotten. He wanted to comfort her, protect her. To be so young and desolate – she should not suffer, or be treated this badly by the young men in her life. When he looked at her face he saw her bewilderment change to regret.

Mahalia sighed,

"I never told Howell about..." she searched for words he would understand, "...the babby. Wanted to be sure there was nothing else I could do. He must have guessed." She crossed the room to where he was standing. Her eyes searched his, absolute certainty in her voice. "He's gone, ain't 'e? They found out and sent him away, didn't they, those parents of his?" And, as if resigned to it, she added, "and 'e did what they wanted."

"Your people have gone too." He told her. She frowned at this.

"They wouldn't, not now. The pickin's just started. Sommat must've 'appened. They ain't jallin 'cause o' me."

"Let's not give up yet. I know Howell. He wouldn't have ignored my note, unless I've seriously misjudged him. Can you think of anywhere else I could look, perhaps for a message?"

He saw doubt on her face again, and waited.

"There is one place." She reached under her hair, and undid the clip to a silver chain around her neck. Removing a small key, she placed it in his hands. He expressed no surprise at the location, only at the risk they took of discovery, and concealing their secrets.

"Howell has the other," she said, "maybe he left sommat for me there?"

But there was disbelief in her voice. When he returned empty-handed, her desolation was complete.

"Don't lose hope, Mahalia. There's something else I must do this evening – a meeting up at the manor with the Reverend ApIvor, and one or two others. It's Parish business, and shouldn't take long.

I don't like leaving you alone again so soon, but if I'm not there it could be awkward. One of them might call to find out why. It's best I go. I may learn more about Howell."

She went upstairs, and he heard the key turn in the bedroom lock. Above the slow tick from the hall clock came the sound of her distant sobbing. It made him wretched, but there was nothing else he could say, or do. She had to cry it out.

ELEVEN

Eli shaved with precision, trimmed his whiskers according to military guidelines, and brushed his hair into obedience either side of a central parting. A stiff new collar glowed white above his waistcoat. His best boots and gaiters shone.

It was important to give the impression he took the business seriously. If this extraordinary change in his circumstances hadn't happened, he would be preparing to argue, at length, with Geraint. It vexed him that his friend could be enchanted by the Gypsies at the music festival, and yet, as the Reverend, be vehemently opposed to them overwintering up here on the farm.

Eli's intention had been to let them stay on one of the lower fields. Though too small for his dairy herd, and steep in places, there was room enough for at least three waggons to rest on level ground. Now it was the last thing he wanted. Whatever the cause of their leaving, he guessed Reuben would not show his face in the village for a season or two.

If possible he must not appear to change his mind too quickly. Nothing should arouse their suspicions concerning his unexpected house guest. No doubt Geraint would have plenty to say. He would let him talk.

The evening was fine and clear. Having double checked all was secure, he called Betsy to his side. Though founded on old money, Godfrey's manor was sustained and enhanced with the new. The man had an eye for the latest improvements, kept his staff up to the mark, but indulged his wife's passion for décor and gardening. The result was well-maintained and pleasing whatever the season. In the mellow light of early evening, framed by dark, late summer leaf, the house and surroundings looked their best; a credit to all those who provided the necessary elbow grease – and the Chalfonts' deep pockets.

As he entered the side gate to the manor yards, he saw the estate manager emerge from his office. Eli asked for news of Howell.

"I should leave that subject well alone, if I were you, Mr Jenkins. His name's mud around here."

And excusing himself, he hurried away.

❧

Eli was shown into Godfrey's study. Doc Bevan was already there, glass in hand, and, much to his surprise, Geraint – early for once, but looking flustered as if the effort had upset him.

They must all be keen to get this over with.

His host shook hands, and gestured towards a tray of refreshments.

"Ah, Eli, welcome. Come, try cook's excellent lemon barley water – so good in this warm weather. I can't get enough of it."

He poured pale cloudy liquid from a silver bound pitcher into a crystal tumbler. It was in deference to his teetotal pledge that such a beverage had been offered. Eli knew full well that usually both Doc Bevan and Godfrey would have chosen whisky.

Geraint was not at all his usual, confident self. In contrast, the doctor was cool and watchful. Despite the gracious surroundings there was a growing tension in the air. As they sat down, Godfrey invited ApIvor to speak first.

"If you don't mind, gentlemen, I have urgent Parish business later this evening. I'll keep this brief. Others may finish. I begin by offering not just my opinion, but views held by most of the district." He drew himself up straight in the chair, his voice more powerful now he had their attention. "Whilst no one here would begin to question your motives and kindness in wanting to offer the Gypsies a more comfortable overwinter site, Eli, we three are agreed that it would have a most detrimental effect on the parish. Having them here for such a long period is bound to cause animosity. There has been trouble in the past. They are not churchgoers. They live outside the community. They would be a most pernicious influence."

His voice rose as he recounted prejudices of old. Doc Bevan shifted uncomfortably in his seat. Eli frowned. This was not an argument but a litany of time-worn, narrow-minded excuses. He had been prepared for one of Geraint's more skilful deliveries. The words were out of his mouth before he could check himself.

"Let me see if I understand you correctly, Geraint. You, as a representative of the Church, are sitting in judgement and actively supporting local prejudice. I was under the impression that you encouraged the villagers to get on with them, or are the Gypsies just part of our summer entertainment? Cheap labour, perhaps, but only as the seasons demand? Tolerated as long as they move on, and don't stay on *our* doorstep, is that it?"

He looked at Godfrey whose face gave nothing away. By comparison, ApIvor's was turning a dangerous shade of crimson. Doc Bevan raised his hands in appeasement.

"Let's try to concern ourselves with the facts, shall we? I think, Eli, that you should not underestimate local reaction, especially to the Jessels. There have been numerous incidents concerning one of them, that heavyset fellow who likes the drink – I forget his name. He seems to take a delight in causing trouble. And if you invite one group onto your land, well, you know how word travels? Soon there will be others. This village is too small."

"There's one other consideration." Godfrey broke in, unruffled by the argument. "This winter I plan to invest in more machinery for processes like ploughing, planting and, next year, harvesting. As you know, I have many tied cottages attached to this manor, and the upkeep is expensive. I intend reducing my casual labour force. If we encourage the Gypsies to stay it will cause resentment amongst the majority who rely upon the manor for their livelihood."

"And what of small farmers like me? How are we supposed to manage when you employ all available help?"

"Oh, come now, Eli. You know perfectly well that's hardly an issue." ApIvor's voice had more than a hint of pettishness. "Farming has never been your main source of income. You're a typical gentleman hobby farmer. And you can't let these eccentric liberal views of yours influence the rest of us. We need a sense of realism here."

There was a flash of arrogance in this last remark.

Eli stared at his friend appalled by the personal nature of this attack. It was crossing a line, but he bit back his retort. If Geraint wanted to ease his social conscience by playing minister in a village backwater, so be it. He drew the line at him playing God. He had anticipated opposition from his friend, but expected more in the way of reasoning, not that backhanded swipe at their shared background.

There was an awkwardness now that put him out of his reckoning. The others were clearly uncomfortable. For several minutes, no one spoke. Each sipped his drink as if waiting for one of the others to respond. ApIvor sat on the edge of his chair, poised to leave.

There was little point in continuing now Eli understood their position. There was nothing that needed a tactical about-face for they had made no concessions whatsoever. It suited his purpose well. This was a moment to withdraw and consider his next move. But first he must talk to Godfrey alone. He sighed, and replaced his glass on the table.

"You will have your way in this, as in all things hereabouts, Geraint. I have no wish to create trouble. Under these circumstances there's nothing left to say."

"Well, it is resolved then, good." ApIvor glanced at Godfrey, and stared hard at the doctor for a few seconds. He rose from his seat. "Now I must take my leave, gentlemen." He bustled out of the room with a curt nod to those present, but avoided looking at Eli. Once the door had closed, the doctor turned to him.

"You are a bit out of touch with general opinion up there, Eli. It's an uncomfortable truth that the Gypsies wouldn't be welcome. There might even be repercussions for your dairy. I know you're keen on horses and have, of necessity, had close dealings with the Jessels. But I agree with Godfrey: mechanisation is the way forward. For my part, most of the accidents I deal with are horse-related. As far as I'm concerned, change can't come too soon. 'An ill wind' as they say. But it's a change that will affect us all, Gypsies included. And now, if you both will excuse me, I doubtless have patients waiting."

Eli offered no comment and bade him a polite 'Goodbye'. He made no move to follow him out.

"This has altered things for you, hasn't it, Eli? What are your plans now?"

Not too quickly, not yet.

Nevertheless he didn't think it would hurt to sow a few seeds.

"I confess I'm disappointed, but witnessing how strongly you all feel about this subject has crystallised certain ideas I have for the future. There are business arrangements of a different nature I should like to discuss with you, perhaps tomorrow, once I've had time to think about all that has been said here, and the implications for my farm."

"Ah, tomorrow I leave for the north, could be there several weeks. Will you join me for dinner? Perhaps we could discuss it further?"

"Kind of you to offer, but no, I have animals that need my attention. My farm doesn't run itself. This issue of labour has been troubling me for months. I hoped the Gypsies might be a solution if they overwintered, but I understand your opposition, even if I can't concur. However, as Geraint inferred, I have property elsewhere, and increasingly it demands more of my time. I'm not a young man any more, and find it harder to manage alone. I have been considering renting out part of the land first and later perhaps the house, if I find it more convenient to relocate nearer Swansea. Though you must understand I could never sell. It was my mother's family home."

Godfrey, he noted was having difficulty disguising his enthusiasm. He had approached Eli often, throughout the years, hoping to lease fields adjacent to the manor. "Suppose, once I firm up my plans, I offer you first refusal, on the strict understanding that the arrangement remains confidential, at least until I move away?"

Godfrey crossed the room and shook his hand.

"Splendid, excellent, that will suit me very well, Eli. You know I've had my eye on those lower fields of yours with a view to increasing my yield. But enough for now, I have no wish to delay you. We can discuss more formal arrangements upon my return." His smile bordered on triumphant.

Eli took his leave. It struck him as remarkable how the prospect of expansion contradicted all Godfrey's previous concerns about rising costs and limiting the workforce. As if hop yards of ten thousand poles or thereabouts were not enough. But if he knew anything about Godfrey Chalfont, when any future change occurred causing even that traditional industry to become mechanised, he'd have no qualms about dispensing with his workers.

No matter. His retreat could be accomplished without comment. All he had to do was convince Mahalia.

❦

When he returned home, there was no sound upstairs. His immediate problem lay in how to phrase his suggestions without scaring her away. He turned to the Scriptures for solace. When Mahalia came down later, she found him asleep with his head laid on the open Bible. He woke as she crossed the room.

"I gotta jal now, mister," she said, composed at last, and determined. "If I stay people will find out, make trouble for you, and I don't want that. You've been so kind to me."

Eli rubbed the sleep from his eyes, pulled out the chair next to him, and gestured for her to sit.

"I want you to hear me out, Mahalia. I've been thinking about all this, and I have an idea. No...," he held up his hand as she opened her mouth to speak. "No, please listen, at least for the sake of the child you're carrying." He sensed her reluctance, but she sat down. "You say you can't stay here, and I agree with you. It's too small a village. You're well aware of how nasty villagers can be, especially where your people are concerned." He felt a brief flash of anger glance off him before she lowered her eyes again. "No, I don't say that for my own sake, but for yours, and the baby's. I have a solution that might help us all." She waited for him to continue. "I come from Swansea originally," he said, gently closing the Bible in front of him. "My parents sent me away to school in England, and from there I went into the army. My life took me on different paths, into foreign countries. There were not many in our family, and now they're all gone. I've no one else to worry about, you see. No one."

His voice lowered as he said this, and he appeared lost in memory. Betsy stretched and yawned. She wandered over from her basket by the range and thrust her muzzle under his hand. The movement brought him back to the present. He continued.

"This was my mother's childhood home. She wanted to return here after my father's untimely death. As the only child it was my responsibility to take care of her when she became frail. When she died I was reluctant to sell up. That was twenty years ago. I never intended staying this long." He looked around the kitchen as if seeing the old fashioned shabbiness for the first time. "Our family had its roots near Swansea. We owned property there, and land. They were left to me, but I've given no thought to what will happen after I'm gone. Now it's as if I have been given a purpose. You must understand that Howell was like a son to me. He spent so much of his free time here, over the years. I'd like to take responsibility for his child, since he won't, for whatever reason. I've none of my own, nor are there likely to be."

Before continuing, he took a deep breath. If he frightened her away with his next words, all would be lost.

"I am willing to give you my name, but rest assured I ask nothing else of you. I offer this protection for your sake, after witnessing what Reuben did to you – and there I blame myself for not acting sooner. It'll mean leaving here, and a life far removed from the one you're used to, but where I have in mind will be a good place to raise a kiddie."

It was a long speech. He'd been awake for most of the evening thinking about it, if only she would agree.

Mahalia frowned, and the wary look returned.

"Why?" She shook her head in disbelief at this unexpected generosity. "Why would you do this for me... for a Gypsy? People will make trouble."

"We can avoid gossip if I take you there in secret, and stay on here by myself for a while. I have good, kind, reliable friends who are to be trusted, and will be a comfort to you. Even if you are only prepared to stay until the baby is born, and you feel strong enough to cope. But think, Mahalia. I am offering this baby a different future, one of safety, away from Reuben." He gave her a minute to digest this second speech. "...I don't expect you to make up your mind straight away, but please believe me when I say it's a genuine offer. I want to help. You have my word on that. Your family has always trusted me."

For a long while, she didn't say anything. Eli resisted the temptation to speak, or move, not wanting to break in on her thoughts. Eventually she sighed, and her face broke into a soft smile, the first he'd seen since she sheltered in his barn. He knew why Howell had been captivated. Men would fight one another over a beckoning glance from such eyes. He had not seen their like since his youth. He blew his nose as a distraction to cover his own confusion, mindful that his own expression might betray him

"You're a kushti mush, Eli," she said, using his name for the first time. She struggled with unfamiliar words to make herself understood, "...a good man. I don't deserve it. My people would punish me, yours too, if I know anything about the gaje. And Howell." He looked at the angry mark on her face, and caught the underlying bitterness in her voice.

"You mustn't think like that," he broke in, "never think like that. No one has the right to judge you, not on this earth. Believe you me, everyone has something to hide, something they'd rather the world didn't see, so let's hear no more about punishment."

She shook her head, her eyes bright with tears.

"There's not much choice for me outside my family, but I can't go back to them, ever. Reuben would kill me. And if I stay the villagers will make my life a misery. It'd bring shame on everyone. Even the workhouse would refuse the likes of me. They would take my chavi though, and turn me out. I won't 'ave that." She stared into the darkness outside. Eli was disturbed by the despair in her voice. But her next words gave him hope. "I believe you're a man of honour, Eli. We *have* always respected you...and I trust you, after yesterday. You saved my life. I was willin' to leave the Romani way behind for Howell, now I'll do it for this tikni, my babby." She looked into his eyes, holding his gaze, "If you mean what you say?"

Eli sat back in his chair with a sigh of relief.

"Good, good! Wait 'til you have your fine strong son in your arms. The world will not seem so bad then."

"And what if I have a fine strong daughter?"

He smiled at the challenge in her voice.

"A daughter would be an equal blessing." He could see she was still wrestling with doubt and needed time to think it all through. "This has been a lot for you to consider, and you'll have your own ideas, I'm sure, on how we can manage it. But I won't prevent you going if you change your mind."

Then, leaving her staring into the darkness beyond the window, lost in thought, he bade her 'Goodnight'.

TWELVE

Mahalia awoke to sunlight streaming through a gap in the curtains, the smell of frying bacon wafting up the stairs, and Eli's deep voice singing 'David of the White Rock'.

She settled back on the pillows and contemplated this strange change in fortune. She had been sick before it was light, but now felt refreshed, stronger, even hungry. Above all else, for the first time in this tense, eventful year, she felt safe. In Eli's keeping no one could get at her. The bleakness of the previous forty eight hours receded. She had but one clear agenda: the protection of her unborn child. Her anger at Howell prevented her from weakening. But there was no longer any doubt in her mind; Eli's assistance had been foretold. It gave her heart, and hope. Whatever was coming over the next few years, she could face. If the love she had lost was the price, so be it.

When she opened the bedroom door, a trunk had been placed outside on the landing. Eli evidently heard her stir, and stuck his head round the stairwell.

"Good morning, I hope you slept well?"

"Yes, though it seems late to me, the sun has been up a while, hasn't it?"

Eli laughed,

"Well past your usual hour for rising, I'm sure. It's after ten." His good humour was infectious. How easy it was, laughing with this kushti, kindly mush, all her fear of him evaporated.

"Um," Eli rarely stumbled for a word. His habitual, considered conversation deserted him momentarily. "I know they won't be fashionable, and they will need a bit of cutting to size, but in that trunk is an assortment of clothing and material. Since you've lost everything until we buy you new clothes, you might be able to make something from them."

Mahalia pulled the trunk into the bedroom and rummaged through the contents. It was a relief to see clean petticoats – even a high-necked nightdress. Picking through the blouses she realised that these were the remnants of a lady's wardrobe. The lace was expensive, handmade, not the sort pedlars bought in bulk and sold door to door. A length of silk, a folded remnant of wool, several unused linen collars, a button box and full sewing basket completed the contents. It was time to put superstition aside for the sake of her soon-to-be daughter. Selecting a length of the lighter fabric, she began.

❧

The immediate threat of Reuben passed. There was plenty to occupy her while Eli went down to Swansea. Her new overdress was now in the style of the village women; severe and plain. In order to assess the correct sizes, Eli had suggested she drew around the outline of her feet and hands, and measured her height from collar to floor. She felt like a child trying on the old fashioned, over-large hats, as if parading in front of her Puro Dadus again in one of his wilder creations.

In the paper she found illustrations for Ladies fashions, and chose a style that didn't swamp her completely. It amused her that Eli had entered into the spirit of the transformation. Now she anticipated his return eagerly, wanting to see herself in this new persona.

It had been her decision to abandon her traditional dress. From that first morning, she had been determined.

"No one must recognise me, or remember me as Romani. I can't take the risk. I'll do whatever I must to protect my... child."

Mahalia stopped herself from saying, 'daughter' even though convinced the baby would be a girl. She sensed that with Eli's great faith in his bible teachings he might disapprove of dukkering. She cautioned herself against using words like 'chavi' that might give her away, going over her Welsh in her head, and the English she used infrequently since her Pura Dadus died.

The disguise – which was how she thought of it, a new district, unfamiliar faces, all would serve to distance her from the past. Whatever it took to prevent Reuben or her brothers finding her, she would do. She had agreed to the proposal; happy to give in to Eli's wider knowledge and natural authority. But her thoughts were her own. She knew how to survive in the wild. If, following the birth, she felt strong enough to leave, she would. For the moment, she would do what every woman would in order to ease the safe delivery of her child, to protect it during those first few vulnerable months.

She handed over her immediate future to Eli's keeping. When he returned from Swansea he was accompanied by his friends, Owen, and Margaret. A new world opened up before her, one of kindness and trust she had not believed possible amongst the gaje.

Margaret had bought clothes and shoes in her correct size, a hat with a veil. Although the whole exercise was full of uncertainties, they entered into the managing of her disappearance with a sense of adventure. There was no judgement in the eyes of Owen or Margaret. She was accepted. Her baby eagerly anticipated; a subject now of joy.

"It's going to be difficult," Eli said. "I won't deny that, but I think between us we can manage it for the sake of the little one. I shall do what ever I can to protect you. At the first sign of nastiness, you know what people are like, you must tell me."

When they accompanied her by train to what would become her new home, porters and doormen deferred to her with many a 'Mrs Jenkins' or even 'Madam'. It amused, rather than angered her, this complete about-face in attitude. She was used to suspicion, cat-calls from village people, particularly their children, even open hostility in places like shops. On reflection it made her sad to think that just a change of clothes and hairstyle could alter people's opinion. Mahalia was confident she could manage. Eli made her promise to write while he was away, but she'd been embarrassed by this.

"I don't know hand talkin'. Never went to school. I can read some. My grandfather showed me, though it made my grandmother shout at him. It would put ideas into my head, she said. Didn't want the gaje black talk anywhere near us. My grandfather disagreed. Said we should know what was happening. That our world was getting smaller. My brother Caleb can read a bit. Reuben too. He has more to do with outsiders." She was silent for a moment, then added, "Howell promised to teach me my letters properly."

These last words were barely audible, as if she was reluctant to say his name.

❧

Eli sorted everything out, going over there nearly every week, regardless of the expense. Eating into the reserves he'd kept against… well against what, he asked himself, if not for this, then what?

Locally, people presumed that he had to deal with his property in Wales, knew he had family there at one time, put it down to that. He always was a funny old cove. They dismissed his absence with no further comment.

Inevitably his feelings for Mahalia grew stronger. They were legally 'Mr and Mrs Jenkins', and if people tutted at the age difference they couldn't fault the appearance of a fond couple. Owen and Margaret provided a buffer against the outside world, and acceptance.

They lavished affection on the baby when she arrived. Lily, Eli and Mahalia called her, agreeing the name between them. It was then that they both realised the true depth of their feelings. Eli had tears in his eyes as they bent over the crib. When he looked up, Mahalia understood his sadness – his fear that she might leave now the baby had arrived. She held him close, the gesture natural and spontaneous, reaching up on tip-toe to clasp her hands behind his neck.

"I could never find a better, kinder man than you, Eli. Not in this life, nor the next. Do you think I would ever let you go?"

When rumour came, twenty years after Eli moved away, that he had died and left everything to his wife and child, the entire village was stunned. No one had the least idea that he had married, let alone become a father. The women rolled their eyes at each other scandalised, but the men laughed amongst themselves.

"Who'd have thought it, eh? Old Eli – he was a close one all right!"

THIRTEEN

Howell journeyed to Liverpool with two days in hand before the sailing. ApIvor had given him details of an inn he'd heard about in Old Toxteth. He was surprised a harmless village minister could have known about such a place, given his pledge. Some cleric contact of his from a while back had recommended it, even wrote a piece about it in the local paper, he said.

The reality was no longer 'salubrious' (ApIvor had relished the word). He doubted if the old chap would have directed him anywhere in that particular neighbourhood if he could have seen it with his own eyes. The formerly charming, yet oddly-named, Pine Apple Tavern and Bowling Green had been engulfed by Victorian brick. Gone was the quaint row of Georgian stuccoed buildings, or any hint of lawn described by ApIvor. It had been rebuilt to suit its current surroundings. A more robust, four-square structure shouldered the road, and with it came men who were a harder, unfriendlier breed.

The landlord turned him away, equating his livid face with a brawling lout, not giving him a chance to explain.

"If you value the rest of your teeth, you'll go."

He went. Not for fear of any man's fist. He'd been held to account without explanation, dealt punishment beyond his worst nightmares, suffered the humiliation of defeat. Let these strangers judge him if they must. His inner misery was enough.

Jostled, overwhelmed, out of his depth, eventually he found his way closer to the docks, and into the midst of whole families camped on the pavements. Most were too poor and numerous for even the cheapest accommodation.

No one in his village had ever been to Liverpool, Bristol maybe, let alone London. It must all be like this. Endless walls of new brick. The grimy buildings finished only a year or two before, all bearing construction dates on stone plaques, from the humblest row of terraced cottages to the most ostentatious municipal edifice. The sky above him was dimmed by smoke, the air full of smells that assaulted his nostrils and caught in his throat. How could anyone stand it, and the noise? He fought down his desire to run.

He barely understood what was said. There were alien sounds and rhythms on all sides; the speech harsher, faster than his soft, border-county burr. Despite his obvious youth, his face was discouragement enough to most of the touts and runners angling to relieve a country boy of his money. Those who dared look him in the eye soon backed away from the glimpse of anger smouldering deep within.

In the public bar of another red-brick, three-storey pub he found smoke-filled sanctuary. He couldn't remember the name, there were so many of them: 'The Star' perhaps, somewhere near Warwick Street? It was full of working class men like him. They showed him a peculiar respect, for he stood straight, holding his head up in defiance of his bruises. Labourers, twice his age, made room for him at the bar, and left him alone.

It must have been during that first evening the two men singled him out. No doubt they were a familiar sight amongst the regular crowd in their territory, plying their peculiar trade in the clamour preceding each new sailing. He had been oblivious to any activity around him as he stared into the depths of his glass. If voices were raised, he didn't hear them. His mind was elsewhere, running through woods searching for someone. They had assessed his potential, biding their time.

A growled 'watch it' to his right brought him back to the present. An elbow collided with his and the precious last inch of his half pint of cider spilled across the bar.

"Sorry, son." He acknowledged the apology with a brief nod and turned away. "Son?" A paw belonging to the voice descended on his shoulder. "Another glass for the young man here, landlord. What's that you're drinking, cider? Make it a pint by way of apology."

Howell looked up into the blunt face, with its unmistakeable boxer's nose, and murmured his thanks. The landlord served him with twice his accustomed speed.

"Coming up, Mr Lemp."

The spillage was wiped away without comment and a full pint placed in front of him. A feeling that there might be an unforeseen price tag attached to this incident made him uneasy, but to his relief the man and his companion retired to a table by the far wall and appeared to take no further notice of him.

He savoured the sharp cider, and beckoned to the landlord who, despite the crush in the bar, gave him his immediate attention.

"I need a bed for the night, is there somewhere here?"

"You'll have to share a room, lad." He leant closer to Howell and lowered his voice. "I keep several beds against the sailings, four pence a night, not including breakfast."

It seemed expensive but he was in no position to argue. And tired, so tired he fumbled to count the coins on to the bar. After downing the last of his pint, he followed the landlord up the narrow back staircase to a long room above the bar. A row of four iron bedsteads took up most of the available space. There was a basin, ewer and slop bucket in the corner. He couldn't be bothered with details. At least the linen looked clean. Every muscle ached now. He needed sleep.

"Take off your boots, tie the laces together and hook them round the bars. Keep your papers on you, and your money. You'll be safe enough." He added, seeing Howell's doubtful expression. "There's others already paid up as will take ship early. I run a respectable house here, even if it seems a bit rough. Good night to you."

❧

Wandering towards the queue at the docks, early the next day, he almost collided with the man who'd spilt his drink the previous evening. But he was too depressed about the impending voyage to question the coincidence. His head felt dull, stupid. He could barely lift his feet or follow the signs for embarkation.

The man the landlord had deferred to as 'Mister Lemp' drew him to one side and offered him an astonishing price for his ticket and identity papers. Made it sound like a favour – even normal. He was suspicious at first, before he caught on. Thinking about it afterwards, he realised there must have been hundreds like him shuffling through, in the same compromised position, wearing their sorrows like bosses carved on their faces recording their fall from grace. He'd fitted someone's requirements. They'd read him well.

The lure of easy money, the opportunity to double back and rescue Mahalia was incentive enough. Four times the price of his ticket – a whole twenty pounds. More money than he could earn in a year given his new, desperate circumstances.

This unexpected change of fortune renewed his hope. When he found their secret place empty, the cover pulled from the wall and thrown on the floor, he had feared the worst. Supposing her brothers had beaten the information out of Mahalia? What if they'd hurt her, and forced her to hand over the money? Such thoughts plunged him further into despair. Their honour was at stake. They had held him while Reuben used his fists. But his enemy hadn't been satisfied with that. He pictured his attacker's face. The flash, as a blade sliced his cheek open to the bone – the last thing he remembered before losing consciousness.

This was fate intervening, he was sure of it. With no hesitation, he snatched the chance, slipping away from the docks, and to hell with the consequences. Unaware others marked the transaction for reasons of their own, heedless of danger, unwilling to consider why anyone would pay so much for a country boy's papers and third class passage.

His mind was full of Mahalia. He turned twenty that summer. Another year and he could do as he pleased. All he had to do was find her. He still burned with anger towards his mother, his weak-kneed father, and whichever one of his brothers and sisters had betrayed him. Not Louise, of that much he was certain. Damn his mother, she would take it out on her mercilessly, but Louise was walking out with Jack. He would take care of her. Nor Arthur, he had pledged his allegiance over Louise. He'd never let him down. Nancy. It must have been Nancy, out for mischief perhaps, wanting attention. Yet when he questioned her she appeared not to connect him with the 'Gypsy' she encountered in the churchyard. It remained a mystery. They were so sure they had been careful, right from the beginning.

It had been his job to write up the records, official or otherwise, and prepare the wages. He rarely visited the fields, distributing wage packets from the office while the months progressed, and one crop succeeded another. He knew all the regulars, and most of the itinerants; the seasonable influx of Gypsies that included the Jessels.

As August passed, with no perceptible drop in temperature, he accompanied the hop yard foreman to inspect the start of picking. They walked between rows unannounced. Howell listened as voices muffled by the thick curtain of bines laughed and called in accents as diverse as Birmingham and Bristol. Whole family excursions had come to pick alongside the locals, and the Gypsies.

Tally men and pickers stopped talking, and stood back as they approached. Everyone watched as the foreman ran his arm, backwards and forwards, through the pale green papery hops. Occasionally, he would lambast someone for dirty work. But, as far as Howell could see, the whole exercise ran like clockwork.

The foreman talked to him confidentially as they walked back.

"Words of advice, Mr Pritchard, seeing as how you're new to this, don't interfere with their routines. They know what they're about. I'll keep an eye on things my end. Just let 'em get on with it. It's the locals I've got to watch. They're not so fussy, take it all a bit for granted, so we waste time cleaning out the leaves before drying. See the old lady over there?" He pointed out Rachael, Mahalia's grandmother. "She's in charge of the Gypsies. They rely on her to tell them when it's time to move house." He smiled at Howell's puzzled expression. "That's what they call it when they shift rows. Just check the figures from time to time. Only, one more word to the wise." He nodded in the direction of a huddle of men. One of them, darker, taller, was staring at Howell with open dislike. "Make sure the locals don't get too familiar with them when they come up to the office. There's always a bit of banter, but that one, Caleb Jessel, is a bit touchy, especially where his sister is concerned, though I don't suppose their women will interest you much."

Howell looked away to hide his confusion, he said,

"There's not likely to be trouble between the different groups is there?"

The foreman laughed.

"No, they get on well for the most part. You'll hear them all singing later, I've no doubt. They work better when they do. The Gypsies start and everybody joins in. Remarkable when you consider the difference... ah, well." He stopped himself from saying more. "So, if you've no more questions, I must get on."

Howell walked back to the estate office. Those skilled with letters and numeracy were considered a bit apart. He was expected to eat his lunch at his desk, not sit with his snap on the edge of the fields with the men. It was just as well, for it stopped his eyes straying towards Mahalia though she was ever in his thoughts.

They told each other everything. Their lives were equally closed to outsiders, his in the village of his birth, hers amongst a vigilant matriarchal society. She had been the more fearful of discovery.

"We must be careful. I can't risk Caleb findin' out. 'e has the eyes of a buzzard when gaje are near. 'e's worried I'll be smitten by someone like you. If 'e guessed that you, that we..." she shuddered.

"Why? What would he do?"

" 'e might not risk callin' you out, but he'd give me a hidin'."

He had been dismayed at the picture she painted of her brother.

"Caleb clings to the old ways and woe betide anyone who goes agin him or wants change. If he ever weds it will be to someone keen on the old ways like 'im. Other juvals 'ave run off afore when they met a gajo an' 'ad a chance of a different life. As I'm his only

141

sister, 'e won't let it 'appen to me. He's 'appier now I'm promised to Reuben. I've no say in it."

"Promised?" Howell was incredulous, "Surely not, even in this day and age?"

He had been about to laugh, but stopped, seeing the distress on her face.

"The trouble is my Puro Dai, my grandmother, is superstitious. When my Dai, my mum you would say, and her sister, Reuben's Dai, quarrelled and took it to the grave, she vowed to put things right. I'm supposed to wed my cousin. It's tradition. Chavvis must make good the wrongs of those who went before. She opened her eyes wider, "Besides, his Dai cursed mine with her dying breath."

He had caught her up in a hug, laughing, dispelling her fears.

"Mally, you don't seriously believe in curses, do you?"

She had laughed with him, shaking away the dark mood that threatened to spoil their time together.

"Not when you're 'ere, luvvie, then I forget. Soon we'll be far away, and none of this'll matter. But we must be wary of Reuben, 'e's always about, trading with local farmers, or working as a farrier."

"I think Old Eli mentioned one of your men, though I can't recall the name."

"Maybe, though he keeps out of the gav nowadays. My Puro Dai worries about the drink. He soon gets banned from pubs, and not just because he's Romani."

Mahalia had clung to him then, and he had comforted her, though not in the way he would have wished. She wanted them to run away earlier than planned, but he had held out against it, with more practical things to consider.

"It won't be for much longer, I promise you."

That promise. It still burned him when he remembered. He had lost her through his own fault, his own ambition, for wanting to stay a few extra weeks – earn a little more. He remembered the anxiety in her face each time they met.

"Now Reuben's back from the fairs 'e makes my life a misery. Everywhere I turn 'e's watchin' me. Even brags about me to the others as if 'e 'ad me already." She raised one of his hands to her cheek and held it there. "I 'ad no 'ope 'til I met you. Now I worry he'll try and force me. 'e's the Beng himself when 'e's drunk."

He cupped her face in both his hands.

"We'll be leaving soon. But if he touches you, I swear I'll thrash him."

"No, promise me you won't do no such thing. Promise me you'll keep well away. You don't know 'im. 'e'd kill you!"

He let the matter rest, but the threat of Reuben worried him too. What had, at first, seemed like the thrill of a more dangerous chase became something he'd never experienced before; a matter of survival.

❦

There were better days: moments of lightness when they forgot their immediate troubles. Her life had been a revelation to him.

"How do you contact each other, when you don't write letters and are always on the move?"

She laughed, delighted to have so much secret knowledge that intrigued him.

"At fairs mostly, but there are other folki, loners on the drom who pass on news." She removed a twist of rag from the brambles nearby. "Dikka this marker – left a few weeks ago, I reckon. See the knots and cut strands – the way it winds around the branch with the loose end to the west?" He raised an eyebrow in disbelief. "It's true, let me show you." She selected another faded piece, caught lower down, and twisted it over the barbs. "This is 'ow we mark things. Three twists that way, and two pieces of rag, one above t'other."

"It looks like something wind-caught in the hedge to me."

"It's for us to follow, not strangers. There's other signs, 'patrin' we call them, that everyone uses – even old wanderin' gaje, the tramps on the drom. See them stones set by the church wall? It means 'take care' in this gav."

He had laughed at this, unsure if she was teasing him.

She described the routes they took most years, drawing patterns in the dust beneath the broom thicket. He had sketched them on to paper, and later, married up the symbols with more recognisable lines on a map.

There would be many areas to search before he caught up with them. He would have to be more careful from then on. Having survived one beating, he had no intention of provoking another.

FOURTEEN

Howell's quest took him six months. The closest he risked nearing his village was the far side of the valley down from the Devil's Lip; nothing but the river between him and home.

That September had been exceptionally dry. Throughout the county hop picking finished ahead of schedule. Come mid October, temperatures fell, and the rain began in earnest. Pink dust bloomed blood red at the first drop. Rivulets of bright water seeped down into the road, and flowed past his feet. On either side glistening blankets of Old Man's Beard covered the hedges, their ragged hems tucked in against the coming winter.

In the deserted hop yards wooden poles loomed through the mist, playing tricks with his eyes. Those that remained upright were set in the ground at drunken angles – the rest lay heaped between rows in a tangle of stripped leaves and bines. He felt like an old man with failing sight. Try as he might to focus, objects would fade and elude him.

Higher up the lane, ancient cider apple trees leaned over the hedge. The only sound was a steady drip from lichen covered branches onto his cap. The reek of fermenting windfalls was strong; a tang of scrumpy muddled with rot. It clung to his skin, and tainted his mouth. He spat the offending taste onto the road.

He braced himself for another deluge as laden clouds rolled in from the Welsh mountains. Undaunted, he trudged down the middle of the lane and headed west. Every day the urgency increased. He must find Mahalia soon, or it would be too late.

Instinct told him they would avoid their regular winter quarters, but he made the journey regardless. He circled the area, returning, on the second day, to the same gateway below the Beacons. By then it was mid January.

"They won't be coming this year, lad, if it's the Gypsies you're after."

A gamekeeper, from his appearance – and the gun broken casually across his arm, stood in the lane behind him. He hadn't heard him approach. His exposed ears, raw between cap and muffler, ached with cold. The man eyed him suspiciously.

"You're not one of them though, are you?"

There was a note of authority in his voice.

"No." He was abrupt, and offered no further information, coming back with a question of his own. "What makes you say they won't come? I understood they always wintered here?"

Howell drew himself up to his full height, towering above the little Welshman. He wasn't going to move on until he had an answer. The other jerked his head in the direction of the wooded cleft below the hillside.

"Not always. If they come at all, they arrive after the mistletoe fair, and that's long past."

What a miserable spot to spend the winter, small wonder Mahalia resented coming here.

The gamekeeper echoed his thoughts.

"They're a secretive lot. The old fellow bought the tumbledown barn on that piece of land over there. They own a large plot in the local churchyard too, so I'm told. That's why they return so often. You'd think buying something they'd settle. Never seem to be short of ready cash." He looked across the valley and frowned. "It's hard on their womenfolk, in my opinion, and their kiddies run barefoot whatever the weather, but I suppose it all depends on what you're used to. Still," he tapped his gun, "makes my job easier."

Howell touched his cap by way of thanks, muttered, 'Good day' and turned on his heel, aware of the man's continued curiosity. He didn't look back. His own greenness was fading now, learning to keep his name and business to himself.

Throughout the following weeks he scoured the borders for news. He was beginning to despair. Mahalia had told him they never travelled more than forty miles around the small county and back across the border, what with the weight of the waggons and a scarcity of good horses. At last, in late February, he arrived back in Hereford.

The river Wye, wide and treacherous, brimming with thawed snow from the mountains, had burst its banks on to the Bishop's Meadow. The waters formed lakes of uncertain depth, forcing those who used their feet to reach their destinations by a more circuitous route. The river was a spectacular sight in full flood, dangerous, and compelling, skimming the undersides of bridges. With it came tragedies.

Howell had been halfway through his supper in the public bar of the Barrel when, idly, he picked up a discarded newspaper and started to read. It was folded open. One headline dominated the page.

'WYE CLAIMS MORE VICTIMS.
Once again the deluge of flood water that regularly damages our ancient Cathedral city has brought tragedy in its wake. Three deaths were reported during the months of November and December. Informed sources estimate the toll will rise unless clearer warnings are given about the dangers of sudden elevations in the river level, combined with the fatal temperature of water surging down from the mountains. It is easy to be lulled into a false sense of security when the weather here in our valley is clement for the time of year. Storms forty miles distant can alter this situation in hours, delivering volumes of water to threaten our homes and livelihoods, in addition to loss of life. The victims were one man, Mr Cyril P____, aged 56, from White Cross,

described as inebriated at the time of drowning, and two women; one elderly, a Miss Evelyn C_____, aged 84, of Tupsley, who according to relatives had wandered off unexpectedly. The third, a younger woman, somewhere between twenty and thirty, and several months pregnant, was believed to be an itinerant. This last body remained unidentified having been in the water for several weeks. Although there was speculation about the curse of 'Gone in the Wye', none is thought to have entered the water deliberately. The coroner brought in verdicts of 'accidental death'...'

He went cold. An image of her face filled his mind, remembering how he had laughed at her belief in destiny, reading hands, and tea leaves, calling her 'fey', but gentle in his mockery. Now, it was as if she had spoken, forcing him to look at that particular report, willing him to understand.

Howell left the rest of the article unread, and fled the pub, fighting his rising vomit. He ran down Church Street, across the Cathedral Close, past the school, away from people, on, and on, his boots pounding the pavement in time with his heart.

At the Castle Green high above the river, unable to continue or control his anguish, he heaved up the contents of his stomach until there was nothing left in him but bile. He was alone in the wide sunken park, a grass-covered remnant of an ancient fortress. It was a place of municipal flowers, Sunday-best children, and bands playing in summer. Now, the cold and dark deterred all but his distracted self. He stumbled along the path above the river, and raised his face to the sky, shouting his anger, ranting at ApIvor's deaf and indifferent God.

Later, when he regained control, he made a decision. Whatever the outcome, he must know the truth.

❧

Months of living rough had altered his appearance from clean-living office boy to a man who could pass easily as a casual labourer. He wore a full beard now, almost red against his dirty-blonde hair and roughened skin. It hid the tell-tale scar. The clerk in the town hall enquiry office eyed him suspiciously, assuming a smug expression once he made his request known.

"Your, err, *sister*, you say?"

Howell's face remained blank.

"That's what I said, my sister. Mary Prosser," he added, snatching the first name that came to mind.

"Age, and description?"

"Rising twenty, five feet tall, black hair, hazel eyes…" He paused, before adding, "Light brown skin."

The clerk looked up. His eyes travelled over Howell's appearance. His nostrils flared as if something unpleasant had wafted beneath his nose.

"The woman the city buried, unnamed, was believed to be a Gypsy – hard to say her age." He began to turn the pages in a slow, self important manner.

There was a small name plate at an angle on the counter, but

Howell couldn't be bothered to read it. He wanted to grab the puny, judgemental little rat by the scruff of his neck, and shake his self-righteous, blatant prejudice from him. The clerk ran a stubby ink-stained finger down the copperplate entries.

"Ah, here it is," he said. "She was pregnant, between four or five months. There was no ring on her finger, as is so often the case. The coroner brought in a verdict of accidental death for lack of other evidence." The man's distaste for the subject was undisguised now. He bent his head over the entry studying the details. Howell could smell brilliantine on the slicked hair. "The body had obviously been in the water for some time. I doubt her own mother would have recognised her." Looking up, he saw the appalled expression on the younger man's face, and said, more reasonably, "They say drowning is painless, don't they? With the coldness of the water, it would have been quick."

Howell shook his head, his mind unable to deal with any of it. The clerk, taking this to mean it was not the woman he sought, snapped the ledger shut in a gesture of dismissal. His time was up. He refused to believe it was Mahalia. It couldn't be. There had to be another way to make sure. He would find their camp, even if it proved to be the last thing he ever did.

In early April, after overhearing a local farmer discuss the arrival of Gypsies in his neighbourhood, he caught up with them. They had changed their route deliberately, choosing to return north of Bromyard before crossing the county border into Worcestershire. No wonder he'd missed them. Theirs was one of several encampments near the orchards and gooseberry fields, come for the backbreaking work of pruning and thinning.

He kept his distance, but eventually recognised Caleb with the younger brother. There was no sign of Reuben, or the women he had encountered in his own village – and no trace of Mahalia. He felt sick at heart. What if she had been forced into marrying that bastard? His scar itched at the memory.

A reckless desire to find out more made him bolder. He asked two Gypsies he didn't recognise about Mahalia's grandmother, respectful in his approach. The young couple took pity on him. Maybe they mistook him for one of their own. Their accents were Brummie. The old 'queenie' was ill, said one. In mourning, said the other.

Howell remembered her from his early dealings with the Gypsies on the estate. The younger women would flirt with him when he distributed the wages, vying with each other to make him drop his businesslike guard and smile back. But he would catch Rachael staring at him, and wondered if she suspected; if she read more into her grandaughter's studied indifference than Mahalia intended.

There was no chance she would see him now, but he asked after her again, from a different source, and was given the same response, 'a close family member died' and, despite tradition, Rachael had taken it badly. It was useless to press anyone for the name of the deceased, for it would never be mentioned, but he knew the old lady had pinned her hopes on Mahalia.

The search was over. In his heart he had felt as much when he read the newspaper report. He returned to Liverpool the following morning, using his remaining money to buy a one way ticket to a new life – with a new name. Wiser, hardier, coming full circle to the moment of departure, but his destination different from the one chosen for him the previous year.

Part Two
1921

FIFTEEN

The man known as Harry Jenkins, or sometimes just 'Big Harry', sat with his back to the bar, staring out of the window of Maggie's Place. It was the only pub – if a crude tin-and-timber shack could be called a pub – on the main street of Wintamarra Creek, a one-horse township at the parched end of South Australia. Maggie, washing glasses noisily behind him, glanced over hoping to attract his attention, or at least include him in their conversation.

Her husband Edge carried on his banter with her from under the counter, where he was busy setting up new kegs.

Better humour his nibs, I suppose, or he'll catch my eyes wandering where they shouldn't.

She raised her voice from loud to raucous, joining in the burst of laughter from their Chinese chef Lee, who bobbed his head in and out from the kitchen anxious not to miss anything.

It was time to try a different tactic. She walked over to the table and lowered her voice to 'friendly' again.

"Are you going to sit there all day nursing an empty jar, Harry, or can I get you another?"

He came back to the present, and gave the expected answer.

"Good on yer, Maggie." He passed her the pint glass. It was an opportunity to touch his hand with her fingertips. She was well-practised in that little move. "Better make it a half this time."

She busied herself with his refill, never taking her eyes off him for more than a few seconds.

"You look like you're expecting someone." He took his time before answering, stretched, and locked his hands behind his head.

"No, love, not yet. The truck's not in 'til later this afternoon. I was miles away, you know how it is?"

Maggie knew. She'd watched him often enough. He was one of the regular gang of itinerant shearers, working their way around the district on a strict rotation, or else taking part in competitions. They were rough men, in the main, serious drinkers too, but not Harry. She'd never seen him drunk. There was a reserve about him. It made him a bit of a mystery, and she liked that. Lost count of the offers she'd had over the years, although most of them knew better than to try it on, but from him she got little more than the time of day.

She'd been told he came over from the Old Country, but you'd never guess it to hear him speak. Maggie was surprised when she found out. His accent was a strong as any of them. His skin had weathered to a deep tan, and his face – well his face looked as though he'd been in one dust-up too many. But for all that, she wouldn't have put her money on the other fella.

She set another beer down on his table, and stood beside him, following his gaze out to the bleached and dusty street.

"Bit different from the Old Country out here." She wasn't usually nosey. People told her stuff all right. It came with the territory. But he seemed different today, odd – preoccupied – and instinct told her there might not be many more opportunities like this. He raised his glass, drank half the contents, and looked at her impassively. "So my old Dad always told me," she added, on safer ground here. "He couldn't take the heat, or the scenery. Skin like a milkmaid my mother used to say!"

She laughed at her own well-tried joke. He smiled back, swallowed the last of his beer, rose to his feet, and looked down into her face. She knew her nose was shining along with everything else.

The heat seemed to penetrate the fabric of the wooden building. She could smell warm resin, stronger than the familiar aromas of beer, tobacco smoke, and steak. Above them, the tin roof creaked and protested as the sun beat upon it – even the lizards had given up skittering across. Beads of sweat ran down her temples, and evaporated on her cheeks. A steady flow trickled between her breasts to her waistband. It was too late to change now. She couldn't move or lower her eyes from his.

"Better get on," he said, "wouldn't do to miss my ride, still got a few things to sort out. See you, Maggie."

He edged past her, adjusted his hat to a lower angle against the glare, and went out into the street.

Maggie watched him through the filmy windows, that long lazy stride of his conserving energy. She remained motionless, her cloth forgotten in her hand. A line of foam slid down the inside of his discarded glass.

Bugger, she thought, *I drove him away, me and my big sticky beak.*

She was usually too tough to care about the procession of lonely men who passed through the town. She'd been married so long it was like a bad habit. Started like a prison sentence, she said, and went downhill from there on. Men liked her though, called her 'a good sort', but she'd never met anyone who'd turned her head or tempted her until now.

Maggie glanced at herself in the long mirror over the bar, and her reflection mocked her for a fool. She was still only thirty-four, but in that light even she would put herself the wrong side of forty. The sun did that to you if you weren't careful.

A clatter from beneath the counter brought her back to the present. Turning towards her husband's balding head, as it emerged from beneath the bar, she yelled,

"Strewth, Edge, turn that bloody fan on again before I pass out, or drink the profits!"

Then, as if someone rewound a clockwork mechanism to reset her, she resumed the familiar routine of wiping tables, and put all longing for a man she barely knew out of her mind.

Harry walked back down the main drag towards the shearers' hostel on the edge of the township. He preferred the Spartan quarters, liked living out of his canvas bag, being answerable to no one.

He didn't want to discuss the Old Country with Maggie, now,

or any other time. He'd read that look in her eyes only too well.

Not in a million years, love.

She'd need to be more careful, old Edge wasn't blind or daft. It was time for him to move on to the McKenzie's. This was as far inland as they came for the shearing – a long way from anywhere.

There was good money in it, but it was hard, stinking work. He thrived on relocation, made a few reliable friendships amongst the gangs he worked with over the years and had regular contracts. In this country change was easy. He met so many men like himself, insular, reticent when it came to their backgrounds. If you wanted to talk about your old life that was up to you, but you never asked another man about his origins. Mostly they were glad to call themselves Australian, and leave it at that.

But he felt his soul was being scorched away in that sun-baked landscape. Sometimes he longed to feel the softness of deep sods of earth beneath his feet, instead of the jarring, bone-numbing rocks of the interior.

Maggie, Bless her, well meaning but tactless, had stirred old memories. Images came back to him, with a jolt.

He was a different man now from the youth he had left behind, in spirit, that late spring of 1902. It wasn't his first destination. They'd bought him a passage to Canada in September of the previous year, trusted him to board by himself, but he'd changed his mind as easily as he'd changed his name.

Aboard ship he shunned kindly advances from migrating families sorry for the lad who kept a reserved distance, yet was clearly one of them. Hopeful working class girls eyed him surreptitiously, but met a blank stare of discouragement. He survived the six week trial without incident, kneading his fingers over the forged documents in his pocket until they were worn, greasy; equal to any other presented at the docks.

When he arrived in Sydney his transformation was complete. Harry Jenkins (he thought Old Eli wouldn't mind) stepped onto the quayside, survival uppermost in his mind.

In the land the Aborigines knew stone by stone, he was one more displaced European on the vast continent, one more face without class. Free to move on when the mood took him and lose himself forever if he so wished. His toughness developed young, and stayed with him. He appeared harder than quartz, yet seamed with hurts that were inaccessible. The twelve months since his banishment had wrought a change, and a restlessness. He would see as much of this strange land as he could, and layer each new experience between his soul and the pain.

The last actions of 'Howell Pritchard' came a few months after his arrival. He owed ApIvor the original fare, and his ingrained sense of duty compelled him to repay it. He wrote once and honoured his debt, then severed his link with home forever.

SIXTEEN

A pIvor crossed the railway line, negotiated the half dozen or so steps down to the beach, and stared out towards the twisting thread of silver that marked the receding tide. It was too far away for him to see how the waves fretted and fumed, pulled against their will from the outstretched arms of the bay. Low tide should be about now. Soon the waves would race each other back, hurrying to cover the embarrassment of dirty sand and mud, glossing over the imperfections with smiling, cream-edged ripples. He looked back towards the land, but the hills were wrapped in blue-grey slumber. It was still early and nothing had assumed its rightful colour.

"Breakfast is not until eight, Reverend."

Mrs Ogden-Preece, the landlady, had reminded him, poking her head out from the kitchen when she heard his tread on the stairs. He wondered when she had adopted the hyphen. Perhaps she thought it refined? At this hour her hair was encased in wire curlers. She had looked pointedly at the card of rules pinned to the dining room door.

He held up his hands in a gesture of submission to stem the swell of indignation in her voice.

"Then I shall go for a short constitutional," he replied, "and work up an appetite!"

Judging by the look she gave him eating heartily wasn't something a man of the cloth was supposed to enjoy, along with any other earthly pleasure.

He slept badly, and wished he hadn't bothered to come down a day in hand. He could have driven over that morning if he'd started out early enough, but when he'd told Louise about Eli's funeral, offering to take her in the car, she seemed reluctant. Her husband had hurt himself at work lifting again.

"Better leave it to Jack," she said. So in the end he understood when they decided against it, and had come alone.

The funeral would be at eleven, according to the paper.

'Jenkins, Elijah Bartholomew, aged 71.'

He had ringed the announcement, staring at it in disbelief.

'Passed away peacefully in his sleep.
Beloved husband of Mally, and
father of Lily. He will be sadly missed.
Friends welcome…'

He mulled over all he knew about Eli. He remembered the names of his family, his old school friends – now all gone, and, as far as he knew, everyone in Eli's frame of reference had also been in his. A wife and child was an unexpected, and unfathomable, equation. Who was 'Mally'? He supposed it was a misprint and should read 'Molly'. He had four hours to wait before his curiosity would be satisfied.

He looked around at the neat bay curving away either side of him, like a perfect, symmetrical bite out of the land. In the distance, to his left, a smear of smoke and mist hid everything beyond Swansea. The sky was only marginally clearer than that of his childhood. Nearer still, he could just make out the plume of smoke from the first steam train of the day coming along the front towards him. As a child he had loved that short journey squashed in with all the passengers. Eyes smarting from 'Puffin' Billy', he had fought with Eli for a seat on the upper deck. Never known the carriages anything but full to bursting when he was a boy.

To his right the cliffs rose steeply before splitting into a deep cleft. The road hugged the shore before looping away through the gap towards the lighthouse. He debated whether he would have time to walk there and back before joining the other obedient guests at his lodgings for eight sharp. He looked at his watch, well half-way there, maybe.

ApIvor turned away, disturbing the vanguard of gulls eyeing him for signs of food. They wavered above his head, venting their disappointment, causing him to duck involuntarily. He'd woken in the night, confused, distressed, his breath coming in sharp bursts –

that curious aftermath of a nightmare. For a moment he couldn't remember where he was or what he'd been dreaming about, hearing only the whimper and mewling of an infant. Sitting up, he realised it was a gull roosting above him on the roof. Its cries travelled down the nearby chimney, creating the eerie sensation that it was in the room. Of course, they came in from the sea at night, horrible creatures!

Clouds were clearing before the early September sun rising behind him. It promised to be a lovely day again. He stopped to stare out westwards at the limitless, watery horizon. How thoroughly uplifting it was. He understood why, on a morning like this, young Arthur Pritchard had answered the call of the sea.

He arrived back at the boarding house with five minutes to spare, but when presented with the cooked breakfast (all paid for, in advance) concluded that Mrs Ogden-Preece was more concerned with his punctuality than the preparation.

Throughout his walk he'd been buoyed up by the prospect of one of his favourite meals. Faced with the reality, he hadn't the energy to complain. His fellow guests, he'd hazard a guess, lacked the courage.

"Always look for certificates of competence when dealing with trade," his sister Gertrude had intoned, on numerous occasions, "particularly with food."

Well, it was his fault. He'd been in too much of a rush, as usual. There was not a certificate to be seen, although he would happily award one for truculence. He left most of his meal in the puddle of grease on his plate, gave Mrs Ogden-Preece a look of disapproval which made her retreat(but already starting to bristle), collected his overnight bag, and left.

Away from the after-smell of ruinous bacon and egg, he inhaled the clean air, welcoming the freshness of the onshore breeze. He would drive to the lighthouse, read his morning paper, and watch the surf break over the rocks – a sight he'd loved since boyhood.

〜

The service was at the Anglican church of St Peter and St Paul in Carnegie, a little village just over the Mumbles hill. There were several moments when he thought his beloved motor car might fail with the strain of such a gradient. But his trust in man's progress was rewarded when they arrived together.

He had half hoped the service might be held in the Assembly Hall, something rousing befitting the acoustics, but Eli had been a modest man and steadfast in his Faith, preferring the traditions of his youth to the packed, tightly knit congregations of Chapel.

Seated on the front pew he could see the two bowed heads of mother and daughter. They wore identical black cloche hats and coats, although one was much taller than the other.

Presumably that's the daughter. She must take after Eli.

It was a brief service, in English, not Welsh as he had expected. The coffin was lifted, and carried down the aisle. He lowered his head in respect. Mother and daughter followed. There was one more ceremony to perform at the graveside. He stepped in behind the retinue of mourners as they made their slow progress outside.

The congregation was small, but outside, under the towering

beeches, he saw that the lane was lined with those come to pay their respects. One or two carts were drawn into gateways. The drivers had removed their caps, all save one a little farther off. Well, maybe he was only trying to make his way through. He thought no more about it.

In the cemetery he positioned himself a little way back and to the side of the two women, but it was hard to see their faces under the low brims of their hats. He would know more when he offered them his condolences before leaving.

After the interment he made his way over to the bereaved couple. Mrs Jenkins extended her small gloved hand. He shook it gently. She wore a veil over her face and barely looked at him. There was something familiar about her which he couldn't place. He moved along the line to her daughter and stopped. His hand remained midway to clasping hers. The clear grey eyes of Howell looked back at him. Her face – he glanced sideways towards Eli's widow to confirm his suspicions – yes, of course, 'Mally'. There had been no misprint. This face resembled Mahalia's, but not those eyes, or the wisps of fair curls that escaped her hat.

Miss Jenkins looked at him inquiringly.

"Reverend ApIvor," he said, "I knew your father years ago, when we were boys."

She smiled at him, and left him in no doubt. That smile had broken generations of hearts. She was speaking to him, but he hardly registered a word. His mind overflowed with questions, and this extraordinary picture.

"We'd both be pleased if you would come back to the house."

Custom and protocol dictated his reply. There was nothing for it, he would have to agree. She told him the address and he returned to his car.

The burden of long buried secrets weighed heavily upon him. There had been no recognition from Mahalia. What should he say? What *could* he say? That young woman obviously believed Eli was her father, or did she? It wasn't his place to stir up old feelings, perhaps even animosity, or to hurt these two women already suffering from grief. Eli was a kinder man than most, he'd always thought. Some good had obviously come of it all. As for going to the house, that was out of the question for Eli would surely have told Mahalia of their old differences.

He stretched out his hand to open the car door.

"Why did you come?" A woman's voice cut through the air. He turned round. Mahalia pushed aside her veil revealing red patches of anger on her cheeks. "I know you, mister," she said, echoes of the past causing her to lapse into dialect. "You're from that village. How dare you come here, after all these years, looking to make trouble?"

"No, Mrs Jenk... Mahalia. That was not my intention. I had no idea. No idea at all." She glared at him, but he pressed on, determined to convince her of his ignorance.   "I came to pay my respects to Eli, my old friend. This is as much a surprise for me as it is for you."

Disbelief mingled with her fury, and something else was there too, the beginnings of fear.

"Eli was a good man", her voice caught for a moment, "the only good one from that place, and a decent father to Lily. He's all she knows." She stopped, and corrected herself, "Knew. Do you understand?"

ApIvor, ever prey to his emotions, nodded, tears of sympathy in his eyes,

"Yes, of course." He was not sure how to express the next sentence properly. "It's just that I'm relieved you're alive, after what happened to Howell. I always feared for your life."

Mahalia looked shocked, then uncertain, as if wanting him to tell her more, but pulled herself back to the present, remembering her duty. She turned away and took a few steps towards the rest of the mourners, stopped, and faced him again. She had her emotions under control, Mrs Jenkins once more. Her voice was calmer.

"I would like to know what happened. One day, maybe, I shall have to tell Lily. I should like to assure her that her real father isn't the coward I think him to be." ApIvor nodded his agreement. "But not today," Mahalia said, turning to go, "not yet. Perhaps you could write to me. You have our address now. It will be easier to accept in a letter."

SEVENTEEN

Lily watched the conversation taking place by ApIvor's car. She waited at a discreet distance, puzzled by the short, red-faced, elderly clergyman she'd never met before, or heard mentioned by her parents. Her mother's voice rose and fell, and although she couldn't hear what was being said, she realised her Mam was angry. It was such a rarity. She hardly remembered a cross word in their home the whole time her father was alive. Who was this man, and a minister too, coming here, today of all days, causing an upset?

Indignant at this inappropriate intrusion, she was about to march over and find out when the conversation ended. The little man went round to the bonnet, rested for a moment, as if gathering his strength, and cranked the vehicle into life. A small crowd had gathered about his car, and there were many eager hands ready to assist him. He looked back over their heads towards Lily, but she showed no sign of acknowledgement, wanting him to understand she had seen her mother's distress.

ApIvor inclined his head. The sprightly figure that clasped her hand with such vigour earlier had diminished. He climbed behind the steering wheel and drove away.

This development unsettled her. She wanted to question her mother, but there was no opportunity. It would have to wait.

Lily concentrated on her duty, the usual polite exchanges with friends who had accumulated over the years, but now she was aware of a change. There was an indefinable something in the atmosphere that had not been there before her father's death. The words were all they should be on the surface, but it seemed to her there was a strange undercurrent, a watchfulness. It made her uncomfortable. She felt her father's loss acutely, as if he'd been snatched from them through an act of violence instead of passing away in his sleep.

The room came into sharp focus. She searched the familiar faces for clues to this unpleasant sensation, picking up every nervous tick beneath an eye, each dry cough, measuring the silences between words.

Dada, what is happening? Where are you?

Tears clung to her eyelashes, sympathetic eyes met hers, hands patted her shoulders. No, she was upset, imagining things, that was all.

It was a long day. Her mother seemed to be retreating back into the deep armchair as if seeking protection from the incessant flow of comforting phrases. Their own minister's wife, and close friend, Margaret, beckoned her over.

"This has been too much for your Mam, Lily. She needs to rest."

It was a cue for the wake to disband. Cups clattered against saucers, coats were retrieved from the hall, gradually the murmuring ceased, and it was over. Both reception rooms looked dishevelled, plates piled on every surface. Mahalia got to her feet unsteadily. Lily put her arms around the narrow shoulders.

"Go and lie down, Mam. It won't take me five minutes to clear up, go on now."

Mahalia kissed her on the cheek and held Lily's face between both hands.

"Thank you, Cariad," she said. "I'll be better after a little sleep."

Lily busied herself putting things back in order, half-listening to her mother's movements upstairs, ready to shoo her back to bed if she attempted to come down again. At half past eight, with the maid Bronwyn's help, she finished stacking the last of the best china away in the dining room sideboard, remembering at the last minute to keep all her Mam's things separate. She was eccentric in that way and her Dad had always humoured her. She passed between the rooms straightening cushions and chair backs until order was restored. In the front parlour she went to close the curtains.

There was a man sitting atop a low cart, on the far side of the lane opposite their gate, staring up at the house. She recollected there had been a man wearing a battered bowler, and swathed in a waterproof cape pulled in near the cemetery as they had been driven home. She had dismissed him as just another carter or some tradesman waiting to get by. It was odd. She stood in the lighted window and peered down at him. It didn't take him long to see her. Realising he'd been observed, he flicked the reins and pulled away.

⚜

It was ten by the time she went to bed. Lily slept in one of the two large bedrooms at the front. Her bedroom curtains were wide open. Lily preferred them tied back, relishing the first light. She was a morning person – wide awake the minute her eyes opened.

The carrier, or whoever he was had returned, she could see the movement of the horse in and out of the shadows. Her mind raced with all sorts of possibilities. Perhaps he intended to rob them, but if so, he would have been seen by now. Too many people passed up and down their lane, besides, someone would be sure to have noticed him earlier at the cemetery.

She followed his progress until his image was lost in the gloom, then slipped downstairs and double-checked every lock and bolt. Instinct told her his interest was not friendly, yet she could think of no possible reason for it. She would look out for him tomorrow, but keep it from her mother until the mystery had been solved.

⚜

There was no sign of the man the next morning. She ate alone at the kitchen table. Bronwyn had an errand to run in the next village, a mile away. Thinking her mother might like breakfast in bed, she ran upstairs and tapped on the door to her parents' room, as she still thought of it. There was no reply. Popping her head around the door she realised that her mother must be outside, perhaps in the garden.

She forgot all about the stranger's attention from the night before. There were chores to do, shopping to fetch from the outskirts of Swansea, and she made her way down the winding path towards the kitchen garden and the stables beyond.

Raised voices were coming from an open stable door next to the tack room where she kept her bike. She approached the entrance cautiously and looked in.

The man was there, minus his hat. He stood with his back to her, talking quickly, and angrily, to her mother in a language she didn't understand. Mahalia was hidden from view, but Lily caught her raised voice as she walked in. The strange man swung round towards her, and looked at her face for several seconds, nodding, as if confirming something he'd said.

The air was full of alien smells; a mixture of tobacco, wood smoke and an underlying aroma of horse. He wore an odd assortment of clothes most of which were dirty. He was very scruffy. No, worse than that, she realised, he was a Gypsy. She continued her inspection, unaware of her territorial reaction as her eyes travelled over his appearance. When she glanced back at his face, she saw his look of scorn.

"Never told her, did you?" he said, in Welsh this time, turning back to Mahalia. Her mother shook her head, then looking at her daughter, said,

"Lily, Cariad, I'm sorry..."

Lily couldn't contain herself any longer.

"Told me what, Mam? Who is this man?"

"He's your Uncle Caleb," she said, "my older brother."

"But..." Lily began,

"Oh yes, 'but'," her uncle put in, "but what? He's a Gypsy, is that what you were going to say? No, let me think, not a Gypsy, 'Gyppo' isn't that what you call us?" His tone was bitter. He looked at his sister, and then back at Lily. "We're Romani, you Mam and me, and *once*," he glared at Mahalia again, "she was proud of it."

Lily looked from one to the other, confusion rendering her speechless.

"Go back to the house, girl," her uncle said. Lily rounded on him, so angry at his peremptory tone that she faced him square on, her height matching his.

"How dare you come here and order me around."

But at this her mother held up a hand in protest, stopping her.

"Just do as he says, love."

Lily remained where she was, open-mouthed. This was beyond her experience.

"Never taught her much respect for her elders did you?" he said to Mahalia.

"I give respect where it's due," Lily raised her voice, "my father..."

"Your *father*! Hah, Old Eli wasn't..."

Caleb came back at her, but at this Mahalia jumped to her feet, eyes flashing, stopping him mid-sentence. Lily had never seen her mother so animated or so angry. Her hands flew in gestures as vehement as she shouted a torrent of words in her own language.

Her newly discovered 'uncle' didn't respond in kind. He ignored Lily, and moved towards the door.

"You'd better tell her everything by the time I come back this way."

Lily went out behind him, but he was through the gate and down the road at a brisk walk, without looking back. It was then that she noticed their maid loitering in the kitchen garden, close enough to have heard her mother's raised voice. Bronwyn set down her basket with a thump. She stared at Lily, and when her mistress came out of the stable yard and walked back towards the house gave them both a look bordering on insolence.

Lily chose to ignore her, bolted the yard gate, and ran back into the house. Mahalia had retreated to Eli's old study. Lily followed her in and closed the door. It was then that the shock of her discovery hit her.

Her skin felt clammy as she leant against the panels, unable to take enough air into her lungs. Her legs buckled beneath her and she slid to the floor fighting the urge to cry. Mahalia moved towards her, but she heard her own voice, distant, unrecognisable, saying:

"Leave me alone."

She pushed herself hard against the door, and into an upright position. Common sense began to filter through.

Take a deep breath, deal with the shock, ask Bronwyn to make some tea.

She rang the bell and waited. Mahalia seemed reluctant to look at her. She stared out of the window, with her back to her daughter.

When the bell went unanswered, Lily went to investigate. The kitchen was empty. Bronwyn's coat was missing. On the table was a hastily scrawled note. She read the terse message with dismay.

Don't want to work here no more.

I will send for my trunk.

B. Beynon

Oh God, thought Lily, *she heard us. There will be such a scandal. Well, it's too late now.*

Lily concentrated on the mundane task herself, attempting to regain a sense of normality. She poured out two cups and returned to the study. Mahalia sat in her husband's old fireside chair. Lily set a cup in front of her.

"You'd better tell me the truth, hadn't you? It seems everything I've ever known was a lie. I had a wonderful father; at least, that's who I thought he was. You'd better start with him."

She hadn't meant to crush her mother with her tone, but that was the effect.

Mahalia cried for a long time. Lily watched her feeling curiously detached. She had never looked at her mother from a stranger's point of view before. For that was how she felt: estranged, alienated from this little, dusky-skinned woman who had loved her, indulged her even, all these years. It had never occurred to her to question her mother's origins in a land of small, dark-haired Celts. If anyone stood out it had been her Dada, so tall he often said he felt like Gulliver amongst the Lilliputians.

Now she realised, this was the underlying reason behind the cautious over-protection she had resented, from time to time, while growing up.

She looked at the reflection in the glass fronted bookcase. Her own face seemed unfamiliar. Whose features were staring back at her? Her hand shook as she moved the cup and saucer towards her mother.

"You should drink this before it gets cold," she said, more gently. Mahalia lifted her ravaged face, and struggled to speak.

"As far as I'm concerned Eli was your father. The details on your birth certificate will bear that out. Nothing Caleb can tell you, or that minister, ApIvor, who came to the funeral, will alter that. He was a good father to you, more than any other man ever could have been. I want you to remember that." She took the proffered tea, glancing unhappily in her daughter's direction. "You know, Lily, the word 'Gyppo' has never been uttered in our home until today. Eli wasn't prejudiced the way most folk are, like those from the village where I first met him." She was more in control now. "He liked us. Especially my Puro Dadus – my grandfather. Used to trade horses with my brothers and..." Her mother stopped, a look of distaste passing over her face. "We always camped above his land or on the nearby hop yards. When I fell for you, Eli took me in, helped me, and brought me here for protection. I haven't seen any of my family from that day to this."

Despite her anger, Lily was interested. Her initial indignation was beginning to subside. Her father had often described the farm. It seemed a long way from the seaside town she knew.

"But why didn't you tell me? How could you let me grow up thinking everything was normal by concealing your past? How could you do that? Did you think I'd be ashamed? If it didn't matter to Dada, do you think it would matter to me?"

"We just wanted you to be secure, to have a good life, a permanent home, an education. It seemed best to shield you from the reality." Mahalia sighed, "Life on the road is hard. It's the price of our freedom, that and the prejudice. We've kept you from that at least."

"Not exactly, Mam." Lily showed her Bronwyn's note.

Her mother looked at her sadly.

"I'd better see Margaret, she found her for me. We can manage without help for a while, but I shall have to find someone else soon."

She sighed and looked out of the window again. Lily could barely hear her next words. "I fear we may have worse to put up with than this, since Caleb came here so openly."

❧

Lily postponed her trip to the haberdashers until the next morning. A bike ride was just what she needed. The return journey uphill would require an effort, but for the moment she wanted to feel the rush of speed as she hurtled down to the shore.

By the time she reached the haberdashers, her cheeks were glowing and she felt better than she had for the last few sad weeks. She had managed to put their maid's sudden disappearance out of her mind.

There were several women ahead of her at the counter, so deep in gossip they didn't notice her until she said 'Good morning' to the only one she recognised, Bronwyn's aunt, from the row of terraced cottages nearby. The conversation ceased mid-sentence as they nudged one another, then looked away. Two she didn't recognise left without comment. Bronwyn's stout little aunt, stalwart of the local Chapel, went red, gathered her purchases, scraped up her change, and pushed past Lily with an ill disguised tut before leaving the shop. The word was out, evidently. It was pointless to pursue her and ask after her niece.

The woman behind the counter stared at Lily in an unfriendly fashion, looking her up and down. She hadn't seen her serving in the shop before, but felt incensed. There was no call for that sort of rudeness.

"I've changed my mind," she said, crisply, and moved away from the counter.

"Suits me." The woman came back at her. Adding, as Lily opened the shop door, "Don't want your sort in here."

Believing she had misheard, she looked back.

"I think," she said, in the iciest tone she could muster, "you've mistaken me for someone else."

The shop assistant's face sharpened with animosity.

"No," she replied, "I'm not mistaken. You're the Gyppo's daughter." She came towards Lily and wrenched the door out of her hand. "See that sign?" She pointed to a card in the bottom corner of the window. It read: 'NO GYPSIES OR HAWKERS.' "Perhaps you'll remember in future," Her voice mocked Lily's educated tone, "and take your custom elsewhere!"

With that, she swept the door shut. Lily moved out of the way smartly. The woman locked it behind her, turning over the sign suspended between the net and the glass inset so that it read

'Closed', and watched, with her arms folded under her bosom, until Lily moved away.

A new sensation burned within her, a mixture of shame and indignation, as if she had been slapped, or wrongly punished for a deed she hadn't committed. The rest of her errands would have to wait. The feeling she had experienced during the wake overwhelmed her. She had a new preoccupation now, searching every face she saw for any sign of awareness, a repeat of the sly disdain she had read in Bronwyn's eyes.

EIGHTEEN

Ap Ivor drove straight home, his mind filled with premonitions of further distress from the day's events. Over and over, he admonished himself for not having done more all those years ago. He believed he'd done the right thing at the time, but now he wasn't so sure. Faced with the result of that doomed relationship in the form of a young female version of Howell, he had been overwhelmed with self-doubt. He had given no thought at all to the child.

I must pray, he told himself, *pray for forgiveness.*

As he considered the situation, he realised that Eli had shown a truer Christian spirit than he could ever hope to achieve, and he was plunged deeper into gloom over his own inadequacies.

If only he hadn't antagonised him. No wonder he kept it to himself. Yet what could possibly have happened to make such a man take in a pregnant Gypsy girl? He would never know the answers now. Maybe Mahalia would tell him, though he doubted it. Her anger was raw, and in defence of her daughter, totally justified. He wondered what he should write, and what, if anything, he should tell Louise. It was a blessing she decided to stay away from the funeral, but now he had another dilemma – she might find out. If she asked him about Eli's wife and child he would have to evade the truth (he couldn't bring himself to use the word 'lie') or he would hurt her too.

The letter took him two days to write. He went through many drafts before he could find the right words, trying to eliminate overtones of self-righteousness, defensiveness, wanting only to justify his actions where they were based in fact.

He had trouble addressing her as Mrs Jenkins, even though she had looked every inch a respectable matron in her widow's weeds.

In his mind's eye he remembered her exotic appearance long ago. On that occasion she'd worn her traditional costume, rich with colour, several sets of glinting gold earrings, her arms devoid of the traditional bangles that would have distracted from her fine playing. Unlike the local women who wore their hair up and out of the way even on informal days like the mid-summer fair, her jet black curls had cascaded down her back, held off her face by an embroidered scarf.

They had entertained the crowds, one of the few times when there was no hostility. Their music and singing – every bit as vibrant as their appearance – struck chords of appreciation amongst those who listened. She played the pedal harp, he recalled, and he had watched her spellbound. No, she would always be 'Mahalia', the ancient beautiful name matching her perfectly.

He wrote:

'Dear Mahalia,
You asked me to tell you what happened to Howell, and
I will give you an account of events as I know them.
On the evening he 'allegedly' disappeared, his father, my
old friend, Wilfred Pritchard, came to see me. Howell
hadn't come home at his usual time...

He recalled that painful evening, sighed, and finished writing
the facts, as succinctly as he could.

...It seemed best to sort it out amongst ourselves and
not involve the police thus risking more trouble, either
for you, or for Howell.

   His parents and I agreed a story; that he had gone
to enlist. It was an untruth I have chastised myself for
many times since, but told for the sake of their family. I
paid for his passage to the New World, since he had no
money, to give him a fresh start. He was supposed to leave
for Canada. I was surprised to receive a letter from him,
post-marked Australia, nearly a year after he left. It was
the last and only communication I received from him. I
enclose it with this explanation.

   I do not believe Howell would have deserted you if he
had known you were still in the district. He believed, as we
all did, that you had been taken away by your people.

For my part in any distress you have suffered, I ask you to forgive me. I believe that God took care of you with the blessing of Eli's love. May He continue to watch over and guide both you, and your fine daughter Lily.

If there is any service I can render to help you, anything at all, please feel able to ask.

He ended it there, and sat staring out of his sitting room window, oblivious of time.

How different things were in the present day. He was sure that their transgression would still be frowned upon, but would it have been so serious then if she hadn't been a Gypsy? Other girls had been disgraced before. It was inevitable as long as men and women lived in close proximity. The daughters of Eve would always bring out the weakness in men, from now until eternity.

Could they have made a life together? What about her brothers, and other members of her family? They were as strict and closed a community as his. Would they have let them be? He doubted it. He could still picture Howell's face. Not even Mahalia would have recognised him afterwards. And what of their daughter, that exceptional young woman, Lily, would she have grown up differently? What sort of life could they have given her, always looking over their shoulders, moving around to avoid revenge, and struggling to make a living cursed with that stigma?

He put aside his doubts. Perhaps it was all for the best. Yes, he nodded to himself as he sat, Mahalia had been granted the Blessing of a good, God-fearing man. She had been given a chance to embrace the true way, leaving behind the heathen practices of her kind, with their strange rituals and fortune-telling. God had been watching over them, he was sure of that. As minister, he had acted in good Faith. His conscience was clear. He felt absolved.

❦

There was another letter he wanted to write. An hour later, fortified with tea and Mrs Prosser's special teacake, lashed with butter, he set to with his customary enthusiasm.

He'd been meaning to write to Arthur for several weeks, and embarked upon a lengthy account of recent events. His 'epistle to the Antipodeans', as he liked to call it, and so immersed was he in recalling the details that he smiled and frowned to himself as he wrote. He knew Arthur would be interested in hearing all about Eli, and the events in Wales, though he avoided all mention of Lily's true origins. He described the funeral, what he'd learnt of Eli's new life, and the obvious love his widow and daughter had for his oldest friend. The ending was the same as last time,

> *'I'm sorry, Arthur, I know your invitation is sincerely meant, but at the moment it would be impossible for me to spare the time. My sister needs me. I'm sure you will understand etc...'*

It had become a habit, hiding behind Gertrude as an excuse. The truth was something he had a hard enough time coming to terms with himself. He would never confess it to others.

"You should retire," Doc Bevan had told him just the previous Sunday. On that occasion dizziness and loss of breath had forced him to omit the sermon altogether. "You don't have to continue until you fall from the pulpit, as it were…"

"I know. I know you mean well." He tried to shrug it off, although it had been the worst attack yet. "But what else would I do? It's the ministry that keeps me going!"

Doc Bevan sighed, shook his hand, and left. It was an odd thing for him to have done. He would see him the following Sunday as usual.

ApIvor continued to sit in the gathering dusk, torn between self justification and remorse. As he lit his lamp, he resolved to set things aright with his conscience, if only through committing his thoughts to paper.

He wrote to Howell, pouring out twenty years of doubt, self-recrimination and folly at his own prejudice. It was no more than a cry in the wilderness; for he doubted that so many years later the original post box address would still be in use.

'I use the name 'Jenkins' now,' Howell had written, and he addressed it accordingly, adding 'please forward as necessary'.

The estate manager would call soon before going into the city. He would give him this to post, and there would be no questions asked, no speculation at their local post office. But he would not hope in vain. Too many years had passed. There was nothing else to do but pray.

NINETEEN

Jack came back early from the post office. Louise watched him from an upstairs window as he crossed the stone bridge and turned up their lane. The walk there would do him good, she told him, after being laid up, just as long as he took it slowly.

He stopped to talk to Edith at the end of the row. Her husband and grown-up daughter joined them by the front gate. She wondered what they could be talking about so seriously, for serious it must be as both women started to cry.

Louise hurried downstairs to meet him. She could see from his face that something was wrong. He held her close, saying,

"Ah, love, I'm sorry to tell you, it's the Reverend. He passed away this morning. Mrs Prosser found him in his armchair in the front room. Must have just gone in his sleep, like."

Louise placed her hand gently against his cheek. Disengaging herself from his arms, she filled up the kettle from the pump over the sink. She felt no tears, only a strange sense of release. ApIvor was the last one – the last link with her parents. She had spoken to him only yesterday. He'd been so full of Eli's funeral, but she had noticed then he seemed a little breathless. Promised he'd come round for a cup of tea one afternoon and give her all the details. Now she would never know. She half-wished she and Jack had made more of an effort to go themselves, but with his back being bad it would have made things awkward. She turned to her husband.

"Mary said her Mum was worried about him, but, well you know what he's like, was like," she corrected herself. "He was never one to give in to illness."

Still, to just sit down and close your eyes, what better way to go than that?

Her husband echoed her thoughts.

"At least he didn't suffer, love. The Doctor saw him only last week, you remember, after he had that funny turn during the service? Told him he should have given up preaching long ago, so Mary said. She was filling in for her Mum at the post office."

Louise bustled about making them both a cup of tea. Always tea when you've had a bit of a shock. They sat down together at the kitchen table.

"I shall have to write to Arthur. He was so fond of him, used to write to each other regular. In fact, the Reverend said he was going send him a letter this week telling him all about Eli's funeral."

Jack agreed.

"Time I wrote to Arthur myself. We'll write between us if you like," he said.

Louise pictured her brother's concerned face. He always had

a slightly worried air about him. He'd been closer to the Reverend than any of them and would take it hard. She would sit down after the funeral and write to him, and Jack could add a few words of comfort. He and Arthur had been such good friends at one time.

Wondering what his wife was like, she picked up the sepia picture of Arthur and his bride from pride of place on her sideboard. He had still been in uniform then, though he'd been invalided out shortly afterwards. She looked a nice girl, Geraldine. If only they weren't so far away. Arthur always ended his letters with an open invitation. Maybe she and Jack would be able to afford it when he retired. It was no good asking now though.

The funeral took place the following Friday, and on Saturday afternoon, while Jack went to watch the local football team in the next village, Louise began her letter.

'Dearest Brother and Sister',

she wrote, forming the names in her careful script, adding in her usual best wishes for their health. She thought for a while, unsure how to start, then, imagining her brother's serious face, began in earnest.

'You will be sorry, I'm sure, to learn that our dear friend, the Reverend ApIvor, died last Monday, while asleep in his armchair. Gwyneth Prosser found him when she went in

to clean, said he looked peaceful, which was a good thing
since he'd had several bad turns with his heart lately. You
will miss him I know. He always said how much he enjoyed
hearing from you.

What makes it even sadder is he'd just been over to
Carnegie near the Mumbles for Old Eli's funeral. He
never got round to telling me the details, but I did see
him on Sunday and he said it was well attended. Of
course the real shock was finding out that Eli had been
married for all those years, and had a daughter. A good
girl from what I could gather and bright too. Said they
were both lovely women and Eli would be sadly missed.
I wish I knew more. I got the impression he wanted to
tell me something important, but we'll never know now.
They will be all right though because Eli had a lot of
property in the Swansea area. What a dark horse, eh?
If you wrote it down in a story no one would believe you.

Miss 'ApIvor' came over for the funeral. Of course
that's not the real family name, did you know? She's a
Lady – Lady Gertrude! I never put two and two together
when the Chapel was built. Just knew the money came
from one of those copper barons. It was his family, in
particular his Dad, Sir Ivor Banion-Hartwell, who made
their fortune. Typical of the Reverend to call himself 'Ap
Ivor' and leave it at that. Such a shock meeting his sister.
Gwyneth said she got Mary to contact her, as giving such
an aristocratic old lady bad news would have got her all

moithered. Not like her to miss out on an opportunity for a bit of first-hand gossip, but there you are.

Miss 'ApIvor', as I find it easier to call her, certainly was grand, the exact opposite of her brother. You wouldn't think they were related. I was surprised at how tall she was, and upright (reminds me a bit of Queen Mary), came over in a posh car, though I don't know what kind, a tidy bit of money there still by all accounts. You would never have guessed, would you, from his little place?

Well liked he was though. Ever so many people came from out of the district. The Chapel was packed and they held the wake here in the village hall, couldn't all fit into his little house. Don't know if I mentioned it, but after Godfrey Chalfont died and the estate changed hands, he moved into one of those little terraced houses at the end of the street, so he was only two minutes from Chapel. Made sense when you think about it, but I know he never felt as comfortable there. Missed his view he said.

It was a lovely wake. She did her brother proud that Miss ApIvor. It was all very moving. We are wondering now who will take his place, somebody more modern I shouldn't be surprised, though there will be those who moan whoever we have.

Well, I had better leave space for Jack. No doubt he will tell you all about work.

All for now...'

She left the last half page for her husband.

Jack's approach was altogether shorter, and to the point.

'Sorry to bring you this news, Arthur. The place won't be the same without him. It was a Bentley Miss ApIvor came in, and not the only big car there either, driven by her lady companion! He kept that all a bit close didn't he?

It's a bit tricky at work at the moment. Not growing half the stuff they used to. Remember how it was when your grandfather was head plantsman? I'm sorry to say those days are long gone. I'm lucky to still be working full-time. Everything's being mechanised (although I know you will think that's a good thing from what you tell me about your place). They've been cutting back the numbers, especially since last year. It means I have to do more and more for the same money, and in the same hours (every one the good Lord sends). Hark at me, on to something more cheerful! Watched our team get thrashed in the local derby today, nothing different there (did I just say cheerful)!

We send you all our best...'

Louise read it through and smiled. They had been such a good pair, Arthur and Jack. Her husband had been the perfect foil for her brother's seriousness.

She sealed up the letter, and gazed out of the window, lost in thought. The garden had little colour left, save for the last of the begonias holding out until the frost. They had been her late father's particular favourites, their colours pure and straight from a child's paint pot. She remembered her father's disappointed face, and his smile which grew to be a rare occurrence in later life. That smile... But one face came back to her from the past. She pictured the brother she had loved most, and wept.

TWENTY

Lily tried to push the embarrassing experience at the haberdashers from her mind. She would keep it to herself for now.

She settled at the small writing table in the little back sitting room, and began to read through the letters of condolence, answering them on behalf of her mother, when the letterbox clacked. It echoed through the hall. Something dropped on the mat. It was too late for the post. Puzzled, she picked up the envelope and hurried to the front-room window.

Whoever it was must have run, for there was no one in the lane in either direction. The envelope was brown and plain with no name or address on the outside. The message was brief and graphic. She dropped it in disgust. Upstairs her mother stirred, and Mahalia's voice, somewhere above Lily, carried down from the top landing.

"Who is it, Lily?"

"No one, Mam," she said, chewing her lip as she considered her next move, "just something for me. I have to go out for a while." She moved into the centre of the hall and looked up at her mother. "Promise me you'll stay in bed and rest, and don't let anyone in while I'm gone, will you?"

Mahalia peered down at her anxiously.

"You be careful, Cariad, after yesterday."

Lily forced a bright smile, grabbed her coat and hat, checked the front door was secure, and let herself out through the back.

It was a ten minute walk uphill to Owen's rectory. It had been built on the site of a much grander house. The original building had been raised by fire long ago. The new house was adequate but nowhere near the proportions of the former Victorian vicarage. It was modest, built of white painted stone with a slate roof. The only remaining evidence of grandeur was the view it commanded from the edge of the back garden. There, the land dropped away steeply to a hidden fence. The coast was still a mile distant, but it remained her first glimpse of the sea; a view Lily had loved since childhood.

The bay in front of her was bathed in the pink, blue and violet of an fading autumn afternoon; a sight that ordinarily would have delighted her. Now she was indifferent. The only thing on her mind was that spiteful letter. She knew she could call on her Godfather and his wife any time, and after her humiliation at the haberdashers' and the problem of Bronwyn's disappearance she wanted to talk to Owen before going to Church the following morning. Too many attentive eyes and ears would be following her every move then.

Margaret was in the front garden, cutting Michaelmas daisies from her untidy herbaceous border with a pair of rusty scissors.

"Oh, Lily love, what a surprise!" She started as Lily came towards her out of the fading light.

"I'm sorry to call on you this late in the afternoon, Margaret, but is Owen at home? I need to speak to him urgently."

"Well, love," she said, "he's in, but his Mum's with us for the weekend, so it might be a bit difficult for him to talk."

She was about to say something else when her husband emerged through the doorway. The front door stood open as usual. It was shut during the day only in the most severe weather.

"Oh! Hello, Lily," he said, "thought I heard your voice." The pleasure in his voice was reward enough.

She smiled back.

"Where are you going? Owen, Owen!"

A querulous voice followed him out of the door. Moments later, the owner, Owen's ninety-year-old mother and the bane of Margaret's life – though she would never admit it, pushed her way out into the garden behind him. He turned to his parent, prepared to shepherd her indoors.

"Go back inside, Mum, we're just coming..."

The old woman took no notice and came forward to peer up at Lily.

"Who is it? What does she want?"

Margaret made soothing noises. She put aside her flowers, and took the frail arm, guiding her mother-in-law towards the door.

"It's all right, Mum. It's Lily, you remember, Eli's daughter."

A peculiar gurgling noise came from the wrinkled mouth. The old woman pointed at Lily, agitated.

"Don't let her in this house. She's dirty, a dirty Gyppo, like her mother."

Owen looked at his wife in exasperation.

"Help me take her inside. You know how difficult she is when she gets like this." He looked sympathetically at Lily. "Sorry, love. She doesn't know what she's saying."

His mother jerked her arm free and came back towards her. She thrust her face closer.

"Tricked Eli, she did, that Gyppo, tricked him with a babby. Old fool with a young girl like that." There was no stopping the flow of spite. "Promised he'd leave his money to the Mission before she came along and wheedled it out of him."

Owen and Margaret exchanged glances and went red. In one swift movement they got either side of his mother, lifted her bodily, carried her through the narrow hallway, and deposited her somewhere indoors.

Lily remained where she was in the garden. The day had become decidedly worse. She wouldn't stay now and turned to go home. Margaret came back outside, puffing from her exertions.

"I'm so sorry, Lily," she said, "You mustn't take any notice. She gets confused, and doesn't know what she's saying."

"It doesn't matter. I can speak to Owen another time."

Margaret gave her a quick hug. Lily caught the odour of old, unwashed infirmity that lingered after her tussle with her mother-in-law.

"You mustn't take it to heart, love," she said.

But it was already too late. She had.

It was dusk as she hurried back towards her home.

Mahalia was downstairs sitting by the fire. She studied her daughter's face. "Has something happened, Cariad?"

Lily sank into a chair, unable to hold back her feelings any longer. She retrieved the brown envelope from her bag, and handed it to her mother.

"Well, Mam," she said, looking up through her tears at her mother's anxious face, "In a manner of speaking, it has. And that's not all of it." She recounted her visit to the haberdasher's finishing with, "But I'm not going to let an ignorant shop girl intimidate me. This is 1921, Mam, not the dark ages. People have rights you know."

Mahalia shook her head. Her voice was full of resignation.

"If only it was that easy, Cariad," she said, "but you can't remove people's suspicions. The Romani have lived outside society for hundreds of years. Nothing much changes as far as I can see."

TWENTY ONE

Lily woke much later than usual. When she hurried downstairs her mother was already in the hall and wearing her town clothes.

"I have to go into Swansea. I don't want to leave you here alone, Cariad, so you must come with me."

"But Gwen has arranged to come over today, remember? We were going for a bike ride together."

"I don't want you wandering off anywhere, Lily. It's not safe. I want you with me, is that understood?"

Lily was indignant. She couldn't think why her mother was behaving in this overprotective manner. It was unreasonable to expect her at nineteen, very nearly twenty, to stay in as if she were a schoolgirl. Yes, the circumstances were unpleasant, but a poison pen letter was best ignored.

Mahalia grabbed her arm in a gesture that was wholly uncharacteristic, and propelled her backwards into a chair.

"You will mind me in this. I have my reasons."

"You are not being logical, Mam. I'm going to stay here until Gwen arrives. It would be rude to go out after she's cycled all this way."

Mahalia lost her temper and banged the flat of her hand on the table.

"You will do as I say, girl."

It so completely echoed her newly found uncle's words and tone that she flared in response, banging out of the house to fetch her bike. Even if her mother could get the trap out and harnessed, she would be halfway over the hill to Gwen's by the time she set out. This was ridiculous, she wasn't a child.

☙

Just before the Swansea turning, another cyclist came round the corner. Gwen's sturdy shape and orange crocheted hat were unmistakeable. Dismounting, Lily pulled her bike to the side of the road and waited.

"Gwen, you're early, what a nice surprise!"

Her friend grinned up at her.

"Thought we could cycle round the edge of Fairwood Common. You'll never guess, there are Gypsies camped there, so many adorable ponies. We could ask if they tell fortunes, wouldn't that be fun? Here," she said, without pausing for breath, "have one of these." and held out a paper bag of Victoria plums. "Dad sent these for your Mam. They're the last of them now; the season's finished. Sorry," she added, guiltily, "I did have one or two on the way over. You know me, always hungry." She produced another from her pocket. "Last one. I promise not to eat any more."

"Chump!" Lily said, handing back the remaining few, with a laugh. "Go on, finish them up."

"Mmmh," Gwen spluttered, with her mouth full. "I passed the most amazing Gypsy cart on the way over here, one of those open flat ones. It was beautifully painted with little apples and pears carved in the sides. Gorgeous big piebald too."

Lily looked at her blankly.

Gwen shook her head in disbelief.

"Pied. Black and white. Like a magpie. You're useless, Lily, considering how much your Dad loved horses." She looked behind wistfully. "I thought it might come this way, but the driver turned off at the copse back there." She winked at her friend. "A real rogue at the reins if you know what I mean? Imagine being a Gypsy!" Gwen sighed. "There are others on Clyne Common, Dad said. He's hoping they're looking for work. We could do with help at the moment."

Lily prayed she would change the subject, but Gwen had warmed to her theme.

"Wouldn't it be absolute heaven to live like that, moving around all the time?"

"No, it would be cold, damp, and uncomfortable. No warm kitchen, no bathroom."

"Oh rot! You haven't an ounce of romance in you, Lily, and it wouldn't be cold. The waggons must have little stoves inside. One I saw had a dear little chimney sticking out of the roof." Gwen wrapped her arms around herself, swaying in time to music she imagined in her head. "It would be so thrilling, wouldn't it, dancing in front of a camp fire at night, being serenaded by someone dashing?"

Lily raised her eyes heavenwards.

"No, it wouldn't! You've been reading too much romantic rubbish again."

"Oh, I wish I was mysterious and exotic-looking. Dark and beautiful like your mother." Gwen put in suddenly, crumpling up the now empty paper bag.

Lily had her back to her friend at that moment, in the process of adjusting her pedal ready to ride away. Her foot slipped, and she scraped the inside of her ankle.

"What on earth do you mean by that?" she said, trying to keep her tone light.

"Oh, nothing, it's just that your mother is so lovely. I can see her in one of those flounced dresses dancing the flamenco or whatever they do."

"And what if my mother was a real Gypsy?" she said, watching her closely.

Gwen raised her guileless face and smiled.

"Then she could read my palm and warn me of a tall, dark, handsome stranger coming into my life." She laughed back.

"Seriously, Gwen?"

But her friend was too immersed in her own fantasy to treat her question as other than teasing.

"*Now* who's being a chump?" she said.

Lily decided against taking her line of questioning further. One day, maybe, she would need an honest answer from her best friend. She wasn't sure what the response would be.

"Come back to the house, Gwennie. Mam seemed rather anxious earlier. I should let her know that you've arrived and we can have lunch with her."

Gwen caught her sleeve and shook it.

"Look! Look behind you, Lily. That Gypsy I told you about, he's coming down the lane."

Lily glanced round in dismay. A colourful open cart was heading towards them. Its wheels bounced on the rutted surface.

Gwen waved enthusiastically, in the manner of people everywhere who are drawn to spectacle, waving at train drivers, strangers on ships. It was a naive gesture, and the man curled his lips into a smile that was anything but pleasant. He didn't slow his horse. Gwen groaned.

"Typical!" she said. "He looked at you, not me."

The cart disappeared around the corner, but instead of turning down her lane it continued on. She felt relieved. The man was not her uncle, and showed no sign of recognition.

When they arrived back at the house, Mahalia's trap was missing. She must have taken the main road into the Mumbles, the opposite direction from Gwen's farm.

🖋

They abandoned the idea of a bike ride and passed the morning catching up on news until the hall clock struck midday. Mahalia had not returned. Gwen couldn't stay any longer.

"I'm sorry, Lily, I shall have to go. Give your mother my love though, won't you? Who knows," she called back over her shoulder, as she gathered momentum, "perhaps I'll catch up with that Gypsy rover and run away with him!"

With that, she crouched over her handlebars and pedalled off.

Lily went back indoors. She was beginning to worry.

This must stop, she thought, *now I'm the one being irrational.*

Her Mam would be fine. She should carry on with the letters.

By five o'clock her fingers ached from the effort of writing variations on the theme of 'thank you for your kind wishes'. She hadn't bothered with lunch. Anxiety had driven away any desire for food. There was nothing for it now, she would have to go out on her bike, despite the rain, and try to find her mother.

Owen and Margaret, her first stop, were equally puzzled by Mahalia's disappearance. Lily tried not to sound melodramatic, avoiding the subject of their quarrel. They told her to call back later if her mother didn't return. She continued her circuit of the neighbouring villages, her bicycle lamps wavering in the growing dark.

There was a light on in an upstairs window when she arrived home. Relief flooded through her. Lower down the lane a horse whinnied. Their trusty old cob snickered in reply. She stopped to listen. What a ridiculous notion, she told herself. No one would take a horse out on such a night. Her mind was playing tricks on her, imagining the sound after the day's events.

Lily wheeled her bike into the tack room. As she bent over the saddle to make sure the pedal didn't catch against the wall, something moved behind her. She straightened up, but not quickly enough. An arm imprisoned her neck. The grip was so tight it choked off her cry for help. Her assailant's other hand clamped a cloth over her nose and mouth. He was too strong. There was no escape from the fumes. Inside her head she was shouting for help – falling – slowly at first, until everything went black.

TWENTY TWO

Mahalia had woken before six on that same morning. When she opened the curtains it was dark overhead. As she stared inland, the distant hills were haloed with light. Thin strips of cloud began to form a distinctive pattern. 'Mackerel sky' the locals called it. Clouds like that meant rain later.

Sighing, she turned away from the window, and pulled the bedclothes back to air. Her body had made only a small imprint on the mattress. She felt vulnerable in it alone. Every night, since Eli's death, her dreams had been filled with premonitions of danger. Her pulse hammered against the pillow as she shifted and turned, before sitting up, half-awake, to feel the cold space beside her.

It was foolishness, she told herself, a normal reaction to her loss. Eli had been her shelter. She missed the comfort of his broad back, and smiled as she remembered. She had even grown used to his snoring over the years.

Their lives had been so different. The adjustment required from each of them would have been insurmountable for most people, but they had compromised willingly. Not just for Lily, to protect a child. It had grown to be so much more than that. There could never be another man for her now.

~

Caleb's visit had disturbed her; a stick raking through the clear water of their existence and churning the mud beneath.

"Where's Job?" was her opening question, and knew, as soon as the words left her mouth, what the answer would be.

"Killed at the front, went into the madness with all the others. It seemed like an adventure to him. He always was headstrong, wouldn't heed the warnings. Left not long after you did. I rommed," he said quickly. "Pure Romani she is. Honours the old ways like a proper mort. Met her at the annual fair, at Stow. And we've a chal." He couldn't keep the pride from his voice. "Seventeen this summer."

"Where are they, this wife and son of yours?"

"Back aways," he waved vaguely in the direction of the Gower. "One of her brothers got valleyed out. We came over to help him shift his old vardo. Lost his grais. They'll be close in a day or so. She's a strong-minded mort. I made a good choice."

Words she hadn't heard in nearly twenty years came back to her.

Caleb started, as if a sound disturbed him.

"There's no one here." Mahalia said. "Lily's upstairs, and the maid is out."

"A maid, eh? A proper rawni, ain't yer? I must jal before any of your fine neighbours notice."

But Mahalia had one question she needed answered.

"What happened all those years ago?"

"The afternoon you disappeared, Reuben came back shouting, calling you a whore." His eyes glittered as he looked at her. "He told me you had a gajo from the gav. You were carrying, he said. Told me Eli interfered, and you were hiding up at the farm."

Mahalia listened, recoiling from the indignation in her brother's voice. All these years on still so sure that he was in the right.

"Did you ever consider how I felt? That I hated him?"

Caleb was unapologetic.

"I knew, but you had a duty to please our Puro Dai. Set things straight. You knew how it was. But I never thought he'd risk attacking you, not in front of that old mush."

She was angry now. The memory of that day, so long buried, rushed back to her.

"What did you do, Caleb? Why did you jal, and the hops not finished?"

Her brother stared at her hard before answering. When he replied, his voice was gruff and defensive.

"I meant to give that gajo a hiding for shaming you, but Reuben and Job... "

"Yes," Mahalia cut in, "Reuben and Job what?"

Caleb looked away.

"Reuben was like a madman. He wanted to kill him. Job too; well you know how he worshipped Reuben? They wouldn't

stop kickin'. Reuben took a churi to 'im, sliced open his face.
I knew when they saw that the gavvers'd know it was one of us. I
knocked Reuben out, and Job came to his senses. He helped me get
him back."

Mahalia looked at him with horror.

"You mean he tried to kill Howell?" It seemed so easy to say his
name now. "He couldn't have done though, we would have heard.
Eli would have heard something."

"Our Puro Dai wasn't prepared to stop there until someone
found him. They'd have hanged Reuben soon as look at 'im – all
the fights he started. She ordered us to leave at once, and we were
gone in hours. We'd just started picking, but that didn't seem to
bother her. She wanted us away from that gav. You know she always
favoured Reuben – kept him out of trouble – but trouble followed
him like the crows regardless."

Mahalia's anger was palpable. She could hardly form the words.
When she spoke, her voice was harsh,

"And all this time I believed Howell was the coward. Stay away
from us, Caleb. I don't want my daughter to know any of this.
You've..."

She had been shouting at him as Lily came in. And the damage
was done.

❦

That fateful time, when she had vowed never to marry her cousin,
haunted her. Strange, the way it turned out. They read the leaves
that night. Lymena had been right about Lily and Eli. As for the

rest, Mahalia's life had been so far removed from theirs no one could have misread it. But that was long ago. She had forgotten the other predictions. Now there were more pressing concerns. What of Reuben? He might have heard the rumours, same as Caleb. She remembered how he'd cursed her in front of Eli, realising her condition that day on the farm.

All through the summer he had watched and followed, unnerving her by appearing unexpectedly – like the time in the old churchyard when she had surprised young Nancy. That was the closest she and Howell ever came to discovery. She had needed all her wits about her to distract Reuben and Job, diverting their attention to the little village girl. Easy sport for Reuben, he enjoyed frightening the locals, whipping up prejudice whenever he could. But there was more to it than that. She suspected, deep down, he didn't like women much.

That afternoon, at Eli's, he had threatened revenge. She had seen madness in his eyes that can be sated only by violence. If he learned of her whereabouts - she feared the consequences. A Romani curse is never forgotten.

Her mind was made up now. She would take Lily with her in future. It would not be safe to leave her alone for one minute, not until she had made more arrangements, a caretaker and housekeeper, perhaps, or maybe this was the time to sell the house and move somewhere safer and not so isolated. It was the right time to consult with her solicitors. They seemed honest. She had a good head for figures and had memorised the details of Eli's estate. A Romani head, though she had not thought in those terms for many years

Her quarrel with Lily upset her. Mahalia knew she had been unreasonable. A moment's anger, that's all it was, and soon mended, Lily would understand.

She harnessed the horse quickly, her fingers flying over the buckles. She had learnt to do this very early in her old life. Now, her new found sense of urgency brought it all back. She whipped up their solid bay cob until he was fairly cantering along the lane. He stopped of his own accord at the crossroads and assumed a more sedate pace.

Mahalia looked at the sky. Inland, the countryside crouched under darkening skies, turning its sparse collar of trees against the coming storm. She would leave her trap at the next inn and take the omnibus into Swansea. It was foolish of her to rush out so ill-prepared.

The cob slowed of its own accord and turned into the stable yard at the inn as the rain swept in from the sea. Mahalia had just enough time to retrieve her umbrella from under the seat. Well, she was committed to going now, and would make a day of it perhaps buying a present for Lily, something pretty to make amends.

Her interview with Eli's old firm of solicitors went without incident. No whiff of scandal had penetrated the ornate offices or altered the manner of her reception. She was offered tea and every effort was made to reassure her.

At the drapers in Castle Street she bought a pair of gloves to go with Lily's new bag. In a much calmer frame of mind she retraced her steps, paying one of the lads from the inn's stable yard to accompany her home and deal with all the tiresome business of rubbing the horse down and feeding it. He was glad of the money.

She was tired now, so tired, and dizzy. It would be pleasant to light a fire and spend the evening with Lily, just the two of them.

The house seemed unnaturally quiet. Mahalia stood in the hall and listened. Something was wrong. No light showed anywhere. She hastened around lighting lamps. Without removing her outdoor coat, she called 'Lily' several times, checking each room, heedless of her wet footprints. In the music room her harps remained shrouded out of respect for Eli. Not a day passed, while he lived, without her playing for him. Now, a premonition that she would never play again made her shut the door hastily. She must concentrate on the problem in hand, not dwell on her loss.

A hot bath was what she needed. The world would seem better once she was warm and dry. The range fire had burnt low, and she ran up and down the cellar steps several times with coal before she had banked it up sufficiently. Lily would want a bath too. She lit her bedroom lamp and left the curtains open, illuminating the garden path for her daughter's return.

Downstairs again, later, she peered through the kitchen window. The wind showed no sign of lessening. She opened the back door and listened. A gate or a door must have been left open and was banging against its latch.

She pulled on Eli's old riding cape, which still hung by the cellar door, and hurried through the garden to the stable yard. The lad had gone now, but he had left a single lamp burning by the archway. The cob's head appeared above the half door of a loose box as she entered the yard.

The old tack room where Lily kept her bike, but little else, had a temporary wooden door more like the garden shed. It banged incessantly unless securely fastened. It had been a rare but regular source of irritation to Eli.

It was open now.

That girl, she thought, *never closes it properly.*

The door resisted her. It was slippery with rain, and caught the wind like a sail as she struggled to close it. She glanced through the opening and stopped in alarm. Leaving the door to flatten back against the wall, she went inside to make sure. There was no mistake. Lily's bike lay on its side. Her handbag, new on her birthday, lay open beneath the spokes. The contents were strewn about and the powder compact crushed as if ground under the heel of a heavy boot. She picked up the bag. The purse and keys were missing.

Mahalia clutched the soft leather to her chest. Lily would never have dropped her bag like this. Something must have happened to her. She looked around the room. Nothing else was out of place, just the tangle of wheels on the floor and the spilt powder.

In her mind she relived her cousin's threat. This had to be Reuben's doing. She sensed his presence – his malevolent spirit. He invaded her nightmares. Every demon had his face. She would never be rid of him, not until her life ended, or his.

It was colder now. A chill fogged her breath. Her eyes adjusted to the darkness. Had that boy noticed anything? The door to the carriage house was on the other side of the yard. She hurried over to check. No, there was the trap and the harness hung on wall hooks beside it.

She began to cough. It struck her that she was alone here, without help.

In panic, she hurried up the lane to Owen and Margaret's. Her breathing was painful now, her coughing more frequent.

By the time she arrived at their front porch she had no breath left to speak. When her friends finally responded to the bell, they found her lying insensible on their doorstep.

TWENTY THREE

Lily opened her eyes, but registered nothing. Squeezing them shut, she tried opening them again. Pain ignited – flashing circles of white amidst the darkness. The images subsided. Darkness returned. Like a swimmer dragged under against her will, she fought her way back to the surface, aware that her limbs wouldn't move. Couldn't move...

Shapes formed, close to her. Too near. She was trapped, pinned down in a confined space with little air. Her head was jammed into a corner against wooden panels. Something scratched her cheek. The sharp end of a feather poked through fabric beneath her face. It was mattress ticking. She felt nausea, but a gag, pulled tightly across her mouth, forced her jaws apart. Swallowing hurt. Her throat and mouth were dry. Aware of a different pain now – crushing pain – pressing her back into blackness. She struggled, and in that moment became fully awake.

A man lay on top of her, and she realised, with rising panic, that he had stripped away her clothes. He had his head turned away, but feeling her stir lifted himself up onto his elbows and looked at her. His head brushed against the low ceiling, dislodging dust from frayed material lining the roof. There was no light apart from a paraffin lamp somewhere over to her right, at a lower level.

Sensation returned fitfully. He'd secured her hands by straps which disappeared under the mattress. Her right leg dangled over the edge of the bunk, several feet above the floor; a ridge of wood bit into the back of her thigh. Her left leg was bent, wedged between his body and the wall.

He had...

She couldn't form the word in her mind.

Rape. This was rape – so much a taboo that she couldn't remember ever saying the word aloud. Her life had been ignorant of such crimes. Now this: the darkest recess of nightmare. Perhaps that's what it was: no more than a bad dream. But he moved and pain made it reality.

Lily shook her head and tried to focus. He grabbed her hair, twisting her round so that the light shone in her face.

"Awake are you? Good. It'll be better now. As long as there's some fight left in you."

There was nowhere to go. No hope of escape. She could feel what little strength she had left ebbing away.

"You might enjoy it. I'm sure your little friend would."

He smiled at this. It reminded her of something, but her head throbbed too much – then she remembered. He was the Gypsy she'd seen earlier.

"Go on, struggle." He laughed into her face. She recoiled from a gust of beer, tobacco, decay. "I'm going to enjoy myself with you, now I've taken back what was owed."

He must have read the puzzlement in her eyes. Putting his face down close to her ear, he thrust hard into her.

"He took your mother from me, whoring little bitch that she was. I'm taking his bastard."

He grunted the last word over and over again, timing it to match his movements.

She didn't understand. He couldn't mean her father. It wasn't true. He must have made a mistake. But how could this be a mistake? He'd raped her while she was unconscious – the act of a coward – no, worse, a madman. And what comes next? She stopped her mind spiralling away towards hysteria. Tears streamed down her face, tears of physical weakness, desolation, disgust.

Something inside her gushed warm, as if ruptured. Her period, she remembered. It was due about now, and must have been brought on by this violence. He felt it too and pulled out of her. Her rush of blood covered him and trickled onto the cot. Cursing, he turned away, reached over to retrieve a towel, and slid down to the floor.

Released from his weight, she gulped air into her lungs and with it felt her strength begin to return. It would be wiser to play safe, and not struggle. The damage was done. What else could he do for the present? He wasn't going to kill her, at least, not yet. He wanted to humiliate her further that much was clear. She pushed back waves of terror. It would be easier to shut her eyes and detach her mind from the reality.

Don't let go, her inner voice warned. *If you do, you're lost.*

Lily bit hard on the gag. The roaring in her ears subsided. She concentrated on her surroundings, and her attacker's appearance. He was middle-aged. That might give her an advantage if she could run. She shifted, and pain stopped her. It was more than the usual cramps. Not in a position to run yet.

"Don't move."

He was angry. Her condition appeared to offend him. He pushed aside her leg, and threw the towel over her. Muttering to himself, he drew on his trousers, and opened the door. His boots were outside, on a narrow ledge. Slipping his feet in without lacing them, he clattered down the steps. Footsteps squelched away from the van. It must have rained heavily during those lost hours.

The sky outside was dim and grey, making it hard to tell if it was early or late. In the distance she heard birdsong, the sounds intermittent, but growing in number. Dawn. It gave her hope. In daylight she might have a chance. Emptying her mind of all else, she concentrated on two things: staying in control, and escape.

As the light grew, she strained her head as far as she could to look at her surroundings. She was lying on a high bunk bed, just wide enough for two people, at the rear of the waggon. Everything was lashed down and in little compartments. A scaled down version of a wood burning stove, dirty and unlit, stood against the side towards the front end, nearest the door.

Her clothes lay in a heap on the floor, but from her restricted position she couldn't see her shoes. Both her wrists were sore. The leather straps had rubbed them raw. She stretched her legs out as far as she could, and overrode the stabbing sensation that centred below her navel.

It was cold with the door open. The chill invaded her exposed limbs, and the ache in her abdomen grew worse. She heard his footsteps returning.

The trip outside had altered his mood, and he dressed quickly without looking at her, adjusting his wide leather belt with calloused muscular hands before leaning over to release the straps. A strong man – what hope did she have?

She avoided eye contact, reluctant to show any emotion. Her arms ached from being held in an unnatural position for so long. At first they wouldn't respond, cold dead things that had nothing to do with her body. Willing them to move, she began to feel blood flowing again, restoring circulation. Her fingers tingled.

He seemed detached – indifferent to the damage he'd done. Perhaps he considered her no threat to him now. The floor shook as he moved towards the door. Reaching outside, he retrieved a pail and an enamel ewer.

"Wash in that," he said, indicating the heavy bucket, "and drink from this."

The ewer's rim looked chipped and unhygienic. He placed them on the floor, and began to shut the lower door.

"I'll be close by." he said. "Do as you're told, or I might have other lessons for you. You're my property now."

The door closed, and she heard the exterior bolt slide into place. He pushed the top windows together, his head silhouetted against the light as he peered at her through the gap in the fabric. Footsteps

221

moved away, but she couldn't be sure how far or how long she would have before he returned.

Lily moved slowly, giving herself time to adjust to the different sensations in her body. She looked at the two objects and had the glimmering of an idea. It would be her one chance – maybe the only one. She thought about her gaoler. Her blood had obviously repulsed him.

No, stop, not yet.

She winced with every movement. Her fingers hurt loosening the gag. Numbness became throbbing, increasing to pain as the blood returned. Finally she pulled it down around her neck. Her throat ached from thirst. Putting aside any concerns about the cleanliness of the water, she drank as much as she felt was safe.

The bucket was half full and crouching over it, she relieved herself. She looked at the contents. The water was red enough for her purpose. With both hands, she lifted the bucket, and put it to one side, lest it should spill, then dressed, using her rolled up stockings as a temporary pad. She moved faster now. He must have hidden her shoes, or thrown them away. There was no time to look for them. She dared not risk attracting his attention.

The upper part of the door had two small windows which opened outwards. He hadn't bothered to latch them. The glass was grimy behind folds of curtains tucked into wooden restraints. Her fingers trembled as she pulled the fabric free. It was accomplished with little noise, and nothing broke or tore. There was enough material to stretch over the window area, obstructing his view. With luck he wouldn't notice until the last minute, and she would be ready for him. If she could surprise him as he reached the top step, he might fall. If she could climb over the bottom half of the door, or open it, maybe there would be a chance of escape. There were too many 'ifs' in her plan, but she was resolved. Her throat was so sore... she drank as much as she could, emptied the rest into the bucket, and tested the handle. It wouldn't give way just yet.

Hidden by the curtain, she crouched in front of the lower door, heart racing, straining to hear the first sounds of her captor's return. Within seconds he clambered up the steps, and pulled the upper windows apart with both hands. The contents of the bucket hit him full in the face. Spluttering, he slipped on the platform, and fell backwards down the ladder. Lily released the bolt on the lower door and balanced on the narrow ledge outside. There was so little time to take advantage. As he scrambled to his feet she swung the empty pail at his head. It missed, and her momentum carried her too far forward. She lost her grip on the handle and nearly overbalanced down the steps.

Bellowing with rage when he realised what she'd thrown over him, he swung his fist instinctively instead of trying to recapture her. His hair and face streamed red. A voice spoke in her head at that moment, and she remembered what her father had told her. Ducking beneath the flailing arm, she grabbed his shirt front, pulled him towards her and thrust her knee full force into his groin. He grunted, doubling over. Lily snatched the bucket and swung it at his head.

This time there was no mistake. He grunted again, but struggled back up from his knees. She struck a second blow. The effort carried her round in a dizzying circle. He went down, staggering this time, groping for support as his own blood gushed into his eyes. He kept coming. Lily struck him again… and again. There were several gashes on his brow, but each time he managed to raise himself. She was dismayed by his resilience. Summoning all her remaining strength, she waded in to strike one last blow. His head flopped sideways. He lay still.

Lily was shaking. It was lighter now, but she had no idea where she was or how long she'd been there.

A freshening wind lifted a tarpaulin draped across a nearby cart. The canvas hid bright patterns along each side. It was barely recognisable as the one she saw yesterday with Gwen. There were no others in the clearing, but straight ahead, wheel ruts disappeared around a corner between young woods, a plantation of sorts. Lily wasted no more time searching for her shoes, she would run barefoot. He appeared to be out cold, but she couldn't be sure for how long.

His horses were tethered under the trees. They had backed away as far as their ropes would allow showing the whites of their eyes. Riding didn't occur to her. Lily wanted the security of her own legs. She ran.

Reaching the bend in the track she found herself in another tree-lined tunnel. The path turned downhill. If you're in danger, her father had told her, never go up, go down. Down will lead you to safety eventually, out of a building, or to a river.

She was beginning to feel giddy, but didn't dare slow her pace for fear of recapture. Her feet were cut, but she ignored the pain and ran on, yelping occasionally when a concealed stone bruised her instep. The land sloped steeply increasing her pace. She concentrated on the slippery terrain.

Stitch in her side forced her to stop. She bent over; hands on her thighs, until it eased and her panting subsided. There was no sound of pursuit. She listened intently but the only sounds she could hear above her own laboured breathing were close by, the twigs beneath her feet.

A movement through the gloom below made her start. There were men, two or three in the clearing. She was about to cry out to them when something about the silhouette of one of them made her stumble in terror. It was another Gypsy, perhaps a whole group of them. She tried to stop herself falling but the bank was slippery and as she tumbled headlong towards them she was aware of her own scream in her ears. The bank was steep, her descent rapid, her stop sudden as her head hit a fallen stump.

Pinpricks of light flashed in front of her eyes. And for the second time in twenty four hours her world went black.

TWENTY FOUR

Harry wiped the sweat from his eyes with the end of his singlet, and looked around the shearing shed. The rousies were squatting outside in the shade having a smoke. Their last few fleeces were spread across the tables immediately behind him. Five minutes was the usual break, longer if they boiled up a billy, then back to the unpleasant job of cleaning away debris and faeces before baling. The whole area hummed with flies.

He'd been fortunate to avoid that job when he first arrived in Australia. The two days he'd spent learning about shearing on the estate back in the Old Country were the limit of his knowledge. No more than a harmless experiment at the time. He had tried most of the jobs out of curiosity to gain a better understanding of the men and the difficulties they encountered. Three sheep in all; he kept the number to himself, but at least he knew one end of the animal from the other. His first boss over here thought him green but careful; willing, and cheap. The man's wife thought him young, and in need of a different sort of experience. Between the two of them they'd seen him right.

A stack of wool bales stood at the far end of the shed, ready for transport. Two more days at this pace and shearing would be over before the weekend. He stretched, and settled back to his work again. It was late afternoon, and no matter that he was fit, his muscles were beginning to ache.

He took pride in the precision of his shearing. Not one of his allocated sheep was ever nicked. It was the reason he'd won so many trophies, that and his speed. Every time he relocated he was given the first post nearest the wool tables, the top shearer's position. He was the 'gun', and the gang automatically gave him their grudging respect. He'd earned it the hard way.

Lennie, at the next post down from him, was much rougher. Too many cuts meant animals got infections in the heat, maybe worse damage which could lame or prevent them breeding. The new foreman wanted to get rid of him, but he'd been coming there a long time, longer than Harry, and there was an uneasy solidarity between the men. He would have to remain for the duration or there might be trouble. But he wouldn't be coming back next year - and neither would Harry. He hadn't told them yet, not sure if he intended to make it public. Old habits of secrecy died hard.

He looked out into the holding pen, screwing up his eyes against the brightness. The sun bleached away the colour, making it difficult to focus and count. Another five or so, then he could knock off for the day.

The sheep were squeezed in together, their heads every which way, panting in the heat. He caught hold of the next one up at the top of the chute, and with a deft twist turned it over, gripping the scrabbling legs. It gave up the struggle and its oil-rich wool. He'd lost count of how many sheep he'd sheered over twenty years – could do it in his sleep.

The ewe scurried down the outward chute and bounded around the paddock. It never ceased to raise a smile when he saw that exaggerated leap, as if propelled by jack-in-the-box springs, high above the flock. The newly-shorn animals huddled together self-consciously, bleating their complaints.

At the sheep station they culled a number of animals for their own use. He looked forward to the taste of salt bush mutton at the start of the season. Now he was sick of it, and would give anything for fish, pork, even a sharp cheese as a change. He had a sudden clear picture in his mind of the onions his Dad had grown. Large, white and fleshy, they were best eaten raw with a wedge of Double Gloucester and freshly-baked bread. His mouth watered at the memory.

The men's living quarters and shearing sheds were twenty miles out from Rory's homestead, the other side of mineral rich hills, and the start of vast, salt bush paddocks. Sheep survived well on the grey, low-growing bushes. They'd strip anything more succulent away, but it was this prickly, drought-resistant shrub that gave the meat its distinctive flavour.

The station had been suffering from a shortage of serious rain for three years now, along with every other within a thousand mile radius. They hunkered down and made the best of it, dreading a repetition of the eight year drought that had halved the sheep population by 1903. Most stations were recovering, but it was a slow process and another prolonged drought could put many more out of business.

The McKenzie's station covered a small area compared with some – a mere hundred miles from top to bottom, by sixty across, narrowing in places to a ten mile width. It had the advantage of a homestead near the main north-south route to Adelaide. The white, two-storey stone building, with its skirt of tin-roofed veranda, could just be seen from the distant road, glinting in the sunlight – dust permitting. He felt some sympathy for Rory and his family. They had fifty years worth of heat damage and primitive sanitation to contend with. Jeannie hated it, and told her husband so at every available opportunity regardless of her audience.

His boss, Rory, second generation Scot, had come out earlier that afternoon on his favourite grey gelding, with a light chestnut mare following on a lead rein. He wanted Harry back at the house. The foreman could get on with the final stages of the shearing. He had another use for Harry's many skills. Jeannie had been feeling sick again, another bairn on the way (Rory always spoke a curious mixture of the local accent interspersed with echoes of his father's homeland) and Jeannie's mother was coming up by train from Adelaide tomorrow.

Rory said he needed (and trusted) Harry to take over and help him with the figures and a dozen other jobs. They would go back now it was cooler. The horses could find their way home blindfold.

His mare's name was Sandy, simply because she was sandy in

colour. It amused him that straightforward Australian bluntness, calling a thing what it was with no pretensions. He patted her wet neck, but she chose to ignore him concentrating instead on the flies which aggravated both animals into a state of constant ill-temper. They rode in English saddles, their legs and boots away from anything untoward they might surprise in the undergrowth.

He rolled down his sleeves and drew on a pair of old leather gloves. The horses put them up level with the scratchy remains of wattle bushes overhanging the trail. He presumed they were dead the first time he came to this station. Blackened remains of their gnarled and twisted skeletons dotted the landscape. They had been at the tail end of a drought then too. Several years later he'd almost lost his way because everything looked so different. There had been torrential rain (he was farther north at the time). It resurrected the wattle into grey-green thickets of new growth. He liked the smell of its yellow, dusty, pom-pom blossom. It reminded him of sweeter things: the smell of a woman's skin.

The whole area had been transformed, he remembered, nature rushing to fulfil its seasonable obligations before the last drop of moisture evaporated. But that was several years ago. Now the river beds had dried into natural roads through the parched countryside. Wide red highways gleaming with silicates and fool's gold, their banks lined with eucalyptus trees, always the last to succumb in a drought, and a haven for wild birds. Zebra finches darted from bush to bush; budgerigars performed aerobatics overhead in flocks a hundred strong, flashing green and black feathers, before relocating at a safer distance.

In the village post office of his childhood, the postmaster kept a succession of solitary budgies. They had paced back and forth along a shallow perch. None of them lasted long. Now he understood the reason. They would sit fluffed up against the cold, their heads as far down as possible. That shape, a pouter bosom, reminded him of Mary Prosser.

❦

He had felt sorry for her at first. He, like the other boys of his age, had pressed Mary's growing breasts with the same shared fascination. She was the first to grow them, and they kept growing. But Mary read his interest the wrong way. Everywhere he went, she would appear, staring at him, dumb with desire, until it became an embarrassment, and his mother demanded an explanation.

It might have got out of hand if he hadn't overheard Mary's waspish sisters egging her on, one Sunday, as the last of the congregation drifted home. He had been adjusting a bracket in ApIvor's tiny robing room. There was just enough space for him to stand upright. Concentration made him still and quiet. Near the door, he caught the youngest Prosser girl's intentions.

"You've got to do something, Mary. Make him notice..."

Notice what? Who were they discussing?

"It's his Mum, always putting airs on herself, thinking he's going to do great things... her golden boy. He only works in the estate office after all..."

Him, they were talking about him.

He pressed closer to the door panel.

"Tell our Dad he took advantage. Say he waylaid you coming back from Chapel, down by the river. We'll back you up, mess up your hair and clothes, and swear on the Bible, anything you like..."

Throughout all this he heard no comment from Mary, only loud sniffing, as if she had a permanent obstruction in her nose. She was easily led, as slow to respond as she was in thinking.

Thank God for ApIvor, and his gentle reproof to the silly girl.

He didn't say who had overheard them, but it was enough to keep Mary out of his way for weeks to come - until he began courting that girl from Hereford.

What was her name? No matter...

Sandy snorted, skittered sideways, and nearly unseated him. She sensed his mind had wandered. Pink-chested galahs rose away squawking in a dusty cloud to roost at a distance and comment on their clumsy progress. It brought him back to the present with a jolt. He returned his attention to the trail. If you fell off out here the consequences were serious, but at least he wasn't alone.

Rory rode ahead. There was something odd about the way he was behaving. There was no urgency now. He let the grey meander. Harry watched him. Anyone would think they were on a picnic outing. Several times he made as if to speak, then changed his mind and rode on.

The sky began to turn vermilion. Harry loved sunsets. He would stand outside most evenings after work, beer in hand, watching, as the sun disappeared though every colour in its spectrum. The night sky was even better. Sometimes, camping out, they would lie on their swags and gaze upwards at the whole of the Milky Way – and the hole in the Milky Way as he had discovered. It was a source of endless mystifying wonder, and he could never believe that once his ambition had been to work his way up in an office.

They arrived back at the homestead after dark, and washed up in the outside scullery. Whatever Rory wanted to discuss away from the men, and maybe his wife, had been deferred. The smell of roasting meat came through fly-screens covering the open kitchen windows.

"Beef for a change," Rory smiled at him, "can't say as I'm sorry."

Harry removed his hat and boots, and stepped inside. Jeannie did her best, he had to admit. Everything was spotless. She waged a constant war against the fine red dust, and made damned sure everybody knew about the problem. She smiled at him coyly, and patted her belly.

"Oh yes, he knows, I've told him," her husband put in.

"And don't be nagging him about a wife either, we've got better things to do than listen to your blathering!"

Jeannie looked at her husband with good-humoured contempt. They argued in front of everyone, regardless of status. Their constant sparing had a certain entertainment value, but not on a daily basis.

Jeannie used to eye him wistfully when he first arrived, but they were younger then. She had chafed more at her surroundings. He knew better than to dally with the bosses' wives, but they were usually the ones left too long alone, and with spent husbands. He couldn't put his hand on his heart and swear that he'd never succumbed, but not on this station.

Jeannie loved his quaint manners; the way he held the chair for her as she sat down, even helped clear the dishes.

"What are you doing, you big soft bastard?" Rory had said on that first occasion. "You'll get her into bad habits, and she'll expect me to help her too."

But it had been a good-natured reprimand.

He would have to tell Rory he was going soon, and not likely to be coming back. He hoped he'd understand. Perhaps if he hinted to Jeannie that he wanted to settle... He didn't want to upset them. They were the closest he had to friends amongst the owners.

Jeannie had cooked sirloin of beef with all the trimmings, despite the heat. They were nothing if not traditional. Rory ate two helpings of everything without breaking into a sweat. But there was no dessert, and Harry felt a twinge of disappointment mingled with a rare feeling of nostalgia. Dinners like this reminded him of England, eating to the point of discomfort, but always, always, with a pudding to follow.

He had been concentrating on his food, glad that his unspoken wish for something other than lamb had been answered. When he looked up he saw they were both watching him. Jeannie blushed with pleasure at his compliments, but there was something else in her eyes, he noticed, that seemed more like speculation.

He sat back and surveyed them both.

"What is it?" he said, beginning to feel that the splendid meal had been a softener for something else. They were behaving like two school children, as they fidgeted and smirked, each wanting the other to start. He raised a quizzical eyebrow at Rory, who, knowing his man immediately became more serious.

"We have an announcement. A decision about the future, and want to make you an offer..."

"Yes, something permanent." Jeannie burst in. She had a definite gleam in her eye now. He hoped this would be something he could get out of with a minimum of embarrassment.

"Now don't you go butting in, woman, I haven't finished – and you'll put him off, grinning in that daft fashion – away and clear the table!"

"I will not. Clear it yourself; I want to see his face when you ask him."

"Ask me what, tell me what? Come on! Put me out of my misery."

He was beginning to feel impatient with the pair of them.

"I've bought the Glennock station to the south." Rory said, and his wife subsided as Harry assumed what they both called his 'business-like' face. "No one knows yet. I have my reasons for telling you first. Goes without saying you're the best of all my contractors, no, more than that, you're someone I trust."

Jeannie rose, and cleared the dishes away in silence, letting her husband unravel the idea they'd had about Harry. But she hovered with her back to them, on the pretence of being busy, listening to every word.

"The old fella's found it more difficult over recent years," Rory said, topping up his glass before offering the bottle to Harry. "What with this drought, and short handed, he barely made a profit. After his son died he seemed to lose heart. He wants to retire and go back to Adelaide. It was too good an opportunity to miss now we've another bairn on the way. That new foreman isn't working out. He's too hard on the men from what I hear. So it's a choice between you and Lenny. He's been here longest but you're my first choice." Jeannie looked over at Harry and smiled her encouragement. "There's a better homestead, built less than twenty years ago, and it's bigger. We're going to move over there."

"Hallelujah!" Jeannie laughed, and clapped her hands.

Rory resumed his earnest tone.

"You wouldn't be expected to live in shearers' quarters. You could take over this place. Now that has to be a bonus surely?"

Harry could see Jeannie's face out of the corner of his eye. She was staring at him behind her husband's back. He couldn't be sure, but that old familiar expression had crept back. He wondered about the wisdom of being left alone with her, even now. If Rory suspected her wandering eyes he wouldn't be making him so serious an offer.

Jeannie set down the coffee and sat next to her husband, just out of his eye line. She continued to gaze at Harry speculatively.

He sipped his coffee, placed his cup carefully back on the saucer (when was the last time he'd seen one of those?) and looked at his boss. Rory's face, though the man himself was unaware of it, had creased into a worried frown.

"How long before you need an answer?"

Rory appeared to be holding his breath, now he released it.

"Until the end of the week, no later." Jeannie made an impatient noise, but he cut her off. "I'll be telling the men when I settle up. Most will be glad of the chance for more regular work in the area."

Harry wondered what Lennie would say when he learned of

Rory's offer. Another cause for resentment he was sure. And there, in the background, was Jeannie. Instinct told him 'no' but logically it seemed too good an offer to refuse.

Harry pushed his chair back and stood up.

"Well, I'm going to stretch my legs, look at the stars… and have a smoke."

He smiled at them both, lifted his jacket and retrieved the tobacco tin. There was an invitation implicit in these words to Rory. Both men ignored Jeannie's look of disappointment. She had done her part. There was no place for her between them, and she knew it.

The decision would be reached outside, under the shimmering vault of night sky, while they smoked in silence and gazed above the indigo horizon towards the Southern Cross.

Harry half-opened his eyes. Jeannie's small rough-skinned hand was sliding over his stomach, tracing the line of hairs with exploratory fingers. He reached down and caught her wrist. She giggled, and cradled his growing erection with her other hand. She was sitting next to him on the bed with the sheet pulled back, and began to bend over him. He could feel her breath, warm and moist on his skin.

A man would be a fool to refuse such an opportunity, but self-preservation won through. He became fully awake.

"Enough!" He said, reaching round and catching her other wrist. He pushed her off the bed and himself upright, propelling her, still giggling, towards the door. She squirmed against him, feeling his hardness through her thin dressing gown.

"Oh, come on, Harry, what's the matter with you? Can't say you haven't thought about me, can you? And we'd be safe now…"

He gave an exasperated sigh, but she leaned closer. Moonlight illuminated her upturned face, exaggerating the hollows, giving her a predatory, feline look. Rory's snores resonated through the wall.

"Go back to your husband," he said, keeping his voice low, but unable to disguise his annoyance.

"Another time then…"

She didn't give up; nor would she. He had noticed the determined look in her eye before now. What was the matter with her, she had a good man, why take risks that could hurt them all? How could she climb back into bed beside her husband with another man's musk on her fingers?

Little Jamie, in the small bedroom next to his parents, stirred in his sleep and murmured 'Mummy'. The door was open, and he could see the child's outline on the bed from where they stood. Jamie moved again, and Jeannie went quiet in Harry's grasp. Disentangling herself with an abrupt movement, she pushed past him to settle her child. He retreated into his room and shut the door. Rory's snoring had stopped. Harry leant against the panels and listened, then slid the old fashioned thumb-lock into place. That should prevent any further nightly intrusion, but her intentions unsettled him.

He moved over to the window, his bare feet making no sound on the cool linoleum. Resting one hand on the wall he looked out over the barren moonlit landscape towards the road. He was still engorged, painful now with the lack of relief, and closed his eyes against the alien hills trying to picture a woman, any woman he had known, to have the desired effect. But the image he recalled only intensified his frustration.

❦

They had found the only safe place they could to make love undisturbed, a room in the deserted oast house below the village. There was a pile of unused hop-sacks baled in the corner. He cut the twine and shook the dust out making them both cough.

It was the first time he had seen her naked, and he had been mesmerised by her. She was so delicate and dark against his pale virgin skin. Despite the crowded conditions in which he had been raised, total nudity, even amongst his brothers, was frowned upon. Ungodly, his mother said, imposing rigid rules regarding modesty, citing the expulsion of Adam and Eve from Paradise.

For Mahalia too – she had been the more hesitant; hers was the stronger taboo. But that first time was a release. He lifted her up and she had wrapped slender muscular legs around him, laughing with pleasure, her hair tumbling onto his face.

But it was too far from either of their homes. They had few opportunities to repeat it; stealing kisses and furtive couplings whenever they could, under the trees in the old churchyard or amidst the broom thickets on the Devil's Lip.

She told him about the broom that May, breaking off two branches laden with yellow and red splashed blossom. It was considered lucky, she told him, to wed when it was in flower. They held out the branches for one another, in the absence of anyone's blessing, leaping over them without touching. They twisted the narrow, leathery leaves into temporary rings, promising each other gold as soon as they could free themselves and be together.

"We are Gypsy husband and wife now," Mahalia said. Their small ceremony justified their passion – intensified their need.

It had been a month like no other; one of those exceptional Mays when every plant blooms at once. The countryside danced on gentle breezes, clothed in enough creamy finery for a wedding beneath skies of unblemished blue. Mahalia found a snake skin shed on a stone near the top of the 'Lip'.

"It's kushti..." she said, "for luck." Lifting the delicate casting with reverent fingers, she placed it in his hand. He had kept the papery talisman in his breast pocket until it disintegrated, leaving nothing but silvery scales.

Mally – in his mind's eye she was as clear as if she stood before him. Mally – he could almost taste the salt of her skin. Their omens for good fortune had turned to dust. He pictured the brown swirling water that had taken her from him, and all desire leached away.

❦

He had ached for her, at first; crying her name in his sleep, or believing he had; waking suddenly, his throat tight; running as far as he could from everything that reminded him of England. He blotted out the pain with temporary comfort in the arms of women who wanted nothing more from him than sex. Women without ties, or plans for long-term involvement, whose names he'd forgotten, and faces had blurred into one another.

The memory disturbed him, and not just physically. His eyes ached from the moon's eerie searchlight. It pinpointed his position on the bed, for the box room was devoid of curtains.

Turning his face to the wall he shut his eyes, but no matter what image he sought as an antidote, sleep eluded him. Now, it seemed, he had another dilemma. Here, under Rory's roof, festered discontentment in the shape of his wife. Was he aware of it? There had been hints and rumours among the men before now. Jeannie threatened the wisdom of this new commitment.

By five o'clock he was dressed, sitting on the edge of the mattress listening for Rory's tread on the narrow stairs. He followed him down to the kitchen. There was no sign of Jeannie. A wall clock chimed the half-hour. Another few minutes and little Jamie would bounce down the stairs. Rory was not at his best so early and had mentioned his son's enthusiasm for each new day. This morning he'd be glad of the distraction a small boy could provide, but the child's disturbed rest must be making him sleep late.

"Listen, mate," he began. Rory stopped what he was doing. "I need a bit of time to think things over. I really appreciate your offer... don't get me wrong. It's just that it's such a big change, and will mean giving up my next contract."

The anxiety on Rory's face gave way to relief, he managed a smile.

"I'll put the coffee on. Worried you were having second thoughts – after you'd slept on it..."

Harry looked away uneasily, as guilty over last night's encounter as if he had taken advantage of Jeannie's offer.

"No, don't bother on my account. I'll get my tucker back at the sheds. Thanks again for the meal, set me up for the rest of the week."

But Rory's mood had lightened.

"Aye, me too." He waved in the general direction of the paddock. "Keep that mare until shearing's over, and ride her back then."

It was another concession for this final week. The horses worked hard on the station. They were lean, thin-skinned and used to the heat. Sandy was a sweeter ride than most in the wranglers' string. It made droving more enjoyable. His large pack could return on the mule cart at the weekend.

Harry crossed the yard to the pump, and sluiced away his fuzziness. Rory ambled out behind him, yawning, and helped him saddle up. Slapping the mare's dusty rump, he waved him off.

It was still early, time enough to ride back at an easy pace, but as he walked her out onto the main trail, she seemed eager to be off.

He held her to a slow canter, feeling the animal's power reined in beneath him. Away from the homestead, she surged forward, ears pricked, snorting her enthusiasm for the early morning coolness.

Pure instinct – why couldn't he react like that? Another, less welcome, thought occurred to him, unsettling in its truth. His life had changed too often, too radically through mistakes, making rash judgements, rushing headlong into strange territory, acting, so he believed, on instinct. This proposal of Rory's might be another such catastrophe.

He let the mare have her head. Maybe she sensed his mood. It was time to run.

Lennie barely acknowledged his presence when he returned to his post. For one so garrulous, he seemed reluctant to talk this morning. Harry sensed the other man's eyes on him, but when he looked up expecting comment, Lennie dropped his gaze and concentrated on his task. Everything about his demeanour seemed hostile – if that wasn't too strong a word for it – from the sour expression on his face to the hunched shoulders. No doubt someone had upset him. It was bound to come out during the day. It didn't take much – an imagined slight – or preferential treatment given to someone else on the gang. The man had a peculiar idea of his own worth, furious, at the start of this contract, when Rory installed the new, and in Lennie's view, inexperienced foreman.

He remembered that original outburst, followed by a sudden surprising change of tack, expressing indignation on *Harry's* behalf, 'If any one deserved that post it should have been his mate Harry', was how he put it. Lennie had worried at it, like an ill-tempered terrier, until he had reassured him that the last thing he wanted was a permanent post, tied to one station.

The expression on Lennie's face together with that odd remark, with hindsight, made Harry uneasy. He tried to remember his exact words. They had been returning to the shearers' quarters from the wool shed. Lennie had looked disbelieving, and smirked,

"Oh, I get it, mate. I've seen the looks she gives you..."

Harry had cut him off before he could say more, or find an excuse for gossip. Lennie was always the first to speculate about bosses' wives or daughters, and there were others willing to join in.

It was dangerous territory, as he knew to his cost. He had passed it off as insignificant – now he was not so sure – if Lennie was jealous of him, as Rory implied last night...

"I told him I couldn't confirm or deny any rumours. He didn't like it, fished a bit, almost as if he'd got wind of my plans, though I don't understand how. He's always so cocksure of himself. Sorry, mate, but you need to watch your back..." Rory had started to say more, but checked himself, perplexed that Harry should have formed, what on the surface seemed such an unlikely friendship. "The odd thing is Jeannie seems to like him. There's no accounting for women sometimes. Maybe he's different with them, but you'd never think it to hear him talk. He's got a wife down in Adelaide, did you know that? Probably some poor downtrodden little Sheila with a posse of barefoot children round her apron!"

They had both laughed, curious about Lennie's domestic set-up. But as for the man being jealous of him? No... He dismissed the idea as before. Throughout the years he was the one person Lennie singled out for conversation, the only one he treated with respect. He wouldn't bother if he considered Harry his rival. Nonetheless he would keep these particular plans to himself.

He stopped for a smoke and handed his tin across to Lennie.

"Looking forward to going home, mate? These last few days must drag for you."

Lennie stood up, stretched, and took the tobacco tin all in one movement. His eyes flickered over Harry's face.

"Yeah, there are times when I think I could do with something permanent, you know, move the family nearer to work..."

It was a leading remark given the recent conversation back at the homestead, but Harry wouldn't be drawn. He removed a strand of tobacco from his lip, stared away into the distance, and tried a different tack.

"How many kids have you got now? Three did you say?"

Lenny looked smug, despite his mood, and launched into his second favourite topic, his progeny.

In his view, patronising Harry with his tone, a real man was measured by his ability to sire children. Harry let that pass. Coming from such a large family, pregnancy was something that had occurred with the seasons. He liked children well enough, had a way with them, but had put up a barrier to his own loss; the unborn child that died with Mahalia.

"You're a lucky bastard."

"Too right."

The tension evaporated. There had been times in the past when he'd taken bigger risks. Jeannie would soon have her hands full with a new infant. Rory would allow him a free hand, he said, employing whom he wished. If it all went sour he could walk away.

TWENTY FOUR

A hand held her wrist lightly. It was warm, the skin smooth and brown, unlike the rough, stained hands of her attacker. She was being carried over the shoulder of a young man. Lily could feel his right arm gripping the back of her legs. His left hand, the one level with her face, balanced his burden. Upside down, looking past the even stride of her new keeper's legs, she registered the limping gait of another, older man in front of them. He pushed back the brambles that threatened their progress.

She must have fainted. No, her head was throbbing, knocked herself out perhaps when she fell? These men were not captors then, but rescuers. She decided to remain unresponsive until she was released, although being carried in this position was decidedly uncomfortable.

There were other voices around them now. She couldn't look about her from this unnatural angle. Her hair had escaped from the tight roll at the nape of her neck, the only way she could control it.

She wished she'd been brave enough to cut it like Gwen's. Now it hung about her head in a damp tangle of disobedience.

A woman's face appeared close to hers. She was bending over, lifting the wayward curtain until she could see into Lily's eyes, peering at her with grave concern.

A conversation was taking place, accompanied by much arm waving.

She was lowered, carefully, to the ground and into an upright position. Everyone was talking at once. She couldn't understand a word of it, but seeing the assembled waggons and tents around her, knew they were Gypsies. It sounded like the language of her mother and uncle.

She winced as her feet took the pressure of her weight. The young man who'd been carrying her registered her pain with anxious brown eyes, and scooped her up again. He placed her gently on the nearest waggon's steps. They formed a semi-circle in front of her, a uniform expression of concern on their faces.

The woman appeared to be older than her mother. Her dark hair was streaked with grey and arranged in looped braids held back under a floral scarf. She wore several sets of gold earrings which caught the light as she moved. Around her shoulders, and secured by a large lapis lazuli brooch, was a woven, intricately patterned shawl of many colours. Her long skirt reached to her boots, the hem decorated with an uneven band of mud. Everything was caked in mud for they were in another clearing, criss-crossed with deep ruts from the wheels.

Looking back at the woman's face, she saw that the eyes which met hers were kind, and Lily knew from the compassion in them that she understood more of her plight than the men. She spoke to Lily, her tone a question, but when Lily looked blank and shook her head, the younger man broke in, translating in faltering English.

"This is my mother, Rosa. Rosa Magdalena," he added, as his mother looked at him sharply for not using her full name. She nodded at Lily. Rosa Magdalena was clearly in charge here. She held up her finger in a gesture that meant 'wait a minute', climbed into the waggon and brought out a blanket which she folded around the girl's trembling shoulders.

Lily clutched it to her gratefully but still felt nervous of them, unwilling to speak.

Rosa gestured to her son and he continued,

"I'm Jem," he said, "and these", he indicated the man with the limp, and another older man who stood beside him, "are my Uncles, Silas, and Abram."

The men nodded to her as their names were mentioned.

Lily attempted to say 'thank you', but could only croak. Her throat was bruised, and she was thirsty. Rosa handed her a china cup full of water and she gulped it down noisily, struggling not to cry. Rosa held up her hand to silence Jem from further questions, waved him over, and spoke to him in low, urgent phrases. He looked towards Lily, translating for her.

"My mother says it's important that she treats your feet to stop any infection. They're badly cut and full of dirt."

He paused, waiting for her response. Lily nodded, uncertainly.

"I'll carry you into the vardo. The waggon," he explained.

"No." Lily struggled to her feet and limped across to the woman. "No, I'll manage." She stumbled, but as he leapt forward to help, flinched away. Lily hobbled up the steps. Rosa followed, pulling the door to behind them, but at this Lily panicked and tried to push it open again. Rosa caught her hand gently, and held it. She tried to pull away, but the older woman didn't let go and patted it, looking into her face murmuring soothing noises, as if to a child. Jem came over to the door.

"She says you mustn't be afraid. No one here means you any harm." He paused, adding, "But someone has hurt you, and I'd like to get my hands on whoever it was."

Lily heard the anger in his voice. His eyes blazed, reminding her of Caleb. She formed her next question carefully.

"Are you the only ones camped here?" She spoke to him in Welsh this time. It might be easier. He seemed relieved, speaking more fluently in the familiar language.

"Yes. We're heading back to our main site tomorrow. My Dad's there. It's just outside the Mumbles."

"The Mumbles?"

Lily sat upright, looking from Jem to his mother. She had to trust them. Perhaps there was hope after all? Was she this close to home? If they could get her back to her Mam? If she could make them understand that her mother was Romani too, but would they believe her?

"How far is it? I come from near there, I must get back. Oh God! My Mother..."

"How did you get here?"

249

It was the question one of them had been bound to ask.

She was wary now, unsure of how to phrase her explanation.

"I was kidnapped."

Rosa's kind face tried to follow the gist. She looked at her son for a translation, but Jem shook his head, horrified.

"Go on," he said. She faltered, wishing she'd used another word. How dramatic that sounded, almost too extraordinary to be believed.

"Someone drugged me, and brought me to a waggon. Like this one," she stopped again, not sure how to continue.

Jem frowned as he translated this statement for his mother. Now Lily had started her explanation she needed to finish – to tell someone what he'd done to her. No, not all of it, she wouldn't, couldn't say all of it.

"I was tied up." She held out her wrists as evidence. No, don't say any more, she decided. The word itself was best avoided. It was too ugly. She was soiled. It would remain her secret.

"Yesterday, I think it was. I'm not sure how long I was unconscious."

With that, the image of his face caused her to stop. She took a deep breath, pushing away the memory, his weight crushing her. Rosa put out her hand and stroked Lily's tangled curls.

"I escaped," she said, managing to continue, "I must have run for at least a mile, I think, through the wood to the bank where I fell."

No more. Please don't make me say any more. She closed her eyes, and leant back against the wooden panels.

Jem exchanged a few words with his mother, and turned to go.

"You must keep warm." he said. "There'll be food shortly," and walked over to join his uncles.

The interior of Rosa's waggon was different from her captor's. It was full of polished brass, coloured glass, china; each flat surface covered with lace and crochet work; every inch of the varnished interior decorated with flowers and fruit. On the walls, either side of the small iron stove, two oil lamps with amber glass shades were mounted on brass brackets. Rosa swung one of them round so that it illuminated them more clearly. Even the ceiling was lined with floral material.

It's an arbour, Lily realised, a refuge from the gloomy skies outside, and despite her ordeal, she felt safe.

Rosa's face was full of concern at the extent of her injuries.

Lily's left foot was bathed and bandaged with a poultice on the sole to draw out impurities. Her right foot likewise, though by now her legs were sagging from the effort of holding them out. When she'd finished, Rosa pushed open the door and pointed in the direction of the camp fire. She made eating motions with an imaginary spoon. It must have been twenty four hours since Lily had eaten, but fear had driven all thought of food from her mind. Yes, she must eat, she told herself if only to have the strength to run away again.

While Rosa bustled around preparing the meal, Lily sat cocooned in the blanket and stared at the flames.

She had lost any real sense of time. Yesterday, she had been abducted, or was it the day before? If she had been gone more than two days the police must surely be looking for her? And her mother? Her mother would be frantic.

She was colder now and started to shake again. Rosa poured strong sweetened tea thickened with condensed milk into the pretty crown derby cup and Lily nursed it gratefully. She concentrated on sipping the tea, everything around her at odds with the delicate bone china in her hands. It was similar to the set her mother treasured at home.

A figure loomed out of the dusk and stood at the edge of the firelight staring down at her. To her dismay she saw that it was her newly discovered uncle Caleb. They looked at each other for several seconds in both horror and amazement. Their expressions, had they but known it, mirrored each other's exactly.

Lily attempted to get up. Jem moved to help her. At this a row broke out. Caleb shouted at Jem, Rosa came forward and shouted at Caleb, and within moments all three were yelling at each other. Caleb pushed the younger man away, then half raised his fist at Rosa who subsided. Now she had a different expression. Fear and suspicion had replaced her former friendliness. Jem, however, looked down at her with fascination and a hint of warm appraisal. In her confusion she looked away.

What would they do to her now they all knew the link between them? This troublesome stranger in their midst; this outsider who was family, by blood, yet not family. Never could be, nor, if she was strictly honest with herself, would she ever want to be if it meant living like this. There had been no acknowledgement that she was a niece. No effusive Welsh welcome for a long lost relative. Only suspicion and reserve, and something akin to her own initial reaction, disapproval. It puzzled her. She needed a little physical comfort, an arm or a hand holding her against so many perils. But she would not reveal her weakness. The last thing she would do was cry.

A chill seeped through the ground, numbing her bruised feet, pervading her limbs.

Jem took his father aside and spoke rapidly to him in Romani. She saw Caleb's shoulders droop, and he turned his weathered, shocked face towards her. He made no comment. After a minute's silence, during which he stared at her unmoving, he strode across to Rosa, and in a low voice issued some instructions. His wife drew her shawl tighter around her and disappeared up the steps of their waggon. Without another word, Caleb, Jem and the two older men disappeared into the darkness.

Lily could barely swallow. What next? Would they find that madman? He was one of their own. Surely they would help him, believe him? Fear threatened to overwhelm her once more but she steeled herself. She must run if possible, but where? And how?

After an hour or so, Jem reappeared at the edge of the clearing, brusque and in a hurry. She had not heard him approach.

"He won't hurt you again."

Lily got unsteadily to her feet.

"Why, what did you do to him?"

"There was nothing to do. He was already dead. Killed by a blow to the head."

Nausea rose within her. She couldn't control it. Turning away from him, she retched onto the grass. When she had recovered and could face him again, he continued.

"We put him in the vardo and set light to it. There were enough bottles about the place to make local people think he'd been drinking. With any luck, they'll believe he burnt himself to death accidentally. It won't be of much interest to them. He'll be one less Gyppo in their eyes."

His tone was matter-of-fact. He looked across at his mother, and Lily read something else in his expression, something he didn't intend. He knew the identity of her assailant.

Caleb returned minutes later, walking heavily. He avoided her eyes, and taking his wife's arm moved her out of Lily's sight. When they both returned, the mood had changed. Rosa scurried up the steps of her waggon. The others began clearing the encampment with a speed born of long practice. Lily sat down again. Her feet were throbbing painfully.

Jem crouched beside her. He began to explain.

"We're moving on. Dad says we have to jal as quick as may be. My Dai, my mum," he added, "has already started to pack. That vardo's heavy loaded up. Sometimes we all have to push..." he said, catching her wistful expression as she looked towards the waggon. "We're making for the border, but it'll be slow, no more than a few miles each day, with stops to rest the grais. You'll need these." He placed a bundle down beside her. He had retrieved her coat and shoes. "I'll take you back to your mother, but you'll have to ride."

She shook her head.

"No. I'm no good with horses, a bit frightened, I suppose."

"There's no need to be. I'll lead you on our old mare until we're out of this gully, she'll carry us both. I won't let you fall. You'll be safe enough. Can't walk with those cuts on your feet, and we are eight miles, at least, from your farm."

She looked across at the lighted waggon. Comforting shafts of golden light spilled out into the dusk. It was cosy in there. She would have preferred to travel inside it. The shadowy form of Rosa moved across the windows. She heard drawers being opened and the clatter of china and glass.

Lily eased her feet into her muddy lace-ups and attempted to stand again. She felt more secure in her shoes, but the pain made her wince.

It was beginning to rain, starting with a few desultory drops. There was an occasional hiss and crackle as the water hit the flames. The fire sputtered, and smoked. Jem kicked it out. Within minutes, the wind increased from sighing accompaniment to a keen autumnal rough house. It unravelled ropes as soon as they were tied, and snatched at their clothes. It was as if the very elements had caught their sense of urgency.

Jem pulled a cap down over his eyes, and wrapped an old coaching coat around his slim frame. He led a shaggy brown horse across the clearing. Without waiting for further protests he picked Lily up and placed her atop its broad warm back. The horse shuffled beneath her. In panic, she clutched its mane. The old mare blew indignantly through wide nostrils.

Jem smiled.

"Careful, that's the same as me pinching you. This old grai is safe enough and I won't let you fall."

He held onto her coat as they move forward. Lily was alarmed at being so high up. She couldn't explain her reluctance to anything horse related, certainly her Dada had tried his best to encourage her, but to no avail. She thought even the newfangled combustion engines were safer. Who could tell what a horse would do next? She had heard reports of accidents in the town when something as simple as a discarded newspaper fluttering in a horse's path caused chaos.

Jem repeated his promise, more gently, once they were away from his father's hearing.

"I won't let you fall. When we reach level ground you can ride behind me."

She wobbled and clutched the horse regardless of his reassurances, but eventually they reached the open heath without incident.

Jem swung himself up behind her. He said.

"On second thoughts, this way's safer."

She relaxed a little. This reminded her of being a small child again when her father had seated her in front of him. Now was her chance to question him. This cousin of hers seemed more amenable than her uncle and aunt. She said the words 'cousin', 'uncle', 'aunt' over to herself inside her head. As an only child, the words were a novelty. Now, despite their obvious social differences – and here her inner voice chided her for even thinking in such terms – she longed for siblings, a cousin, family, envying Gwen her house full of brothers.

"Jem, why is Caleb so angry with my mother?"

Jem sighed.

"It would take more time that we have to explain our ways to you, Lily. But my Dadus had only one sister, and she brought shame on him by running off with a gajo, an outsider. There's no forgiving that. But despite our tradition, when he learnt she was dead, he was shocked and sad. There was a report of a young woman, you see, one of us, drowned in the Wye. Our Boro Puro Dai, our great grandmother didn't recover from the loss. She burnt all your mother's things and threw her crockery, even her harp's metal parts into the river, and banished Reuben. She died not long after. See, she blamed him for driving your mother to such a desperate act. He dishonoured our family in other ways, with his drinking. My Dadus took the whole business hard. Finding her alive has brought it all back. And now, with Reuben taking you, he's angry that it'll bring trouble on us again."

They arrived at Owen's drive. Jem pulled the mare up inside the gateway. He slid from her back and holding out his arms took Lily's weight, lowering her gently to the ground. Standing upright on the gravel was too painful, and she crumpled against him.

"Hold on to the gate," he said, looping the reins through the bars. With little effort, he picked Lily up and carried her across to the front porch.

"You'll be all right now, Lily." He turned to go, but she caught hold of his sleeve.

"No, wait, Jem, please. Owen will want to thank you."

He shook his head.

"There's no call for that. I have to get back. I'm needed. We must put some miles between us and what happened."

"I understand. But," she hesitated, "will I see ever you again, Jem?"

He grinned at her, hearing the wistful note in her voice.

"I'll see you from time to time, Lily, though you may not see me."

She leant over and quickly kissed him on the cheek. His skin smelt of wood smoke. She would remember him this way; his handsome, smooth face, not yet a full grown man. She saw him redden in the porch light. He slipped away then into the shadows, and she waited until the old mare's hoof beats faded into the distance before rousing Owen and Margaret.

At last she could put it off no longer and braced herself for the ordeal to come; the questions, and, worst of all, the realisation of her mother's fears.

TWENTY SIX

Blake threw down the newspaper cutting in disgust, and glanced towards Lemp. He shook his head, more in disbelief at his own folly than at the inevitable resurfacing of his nemesis, and only son, Jeremiah.

"Can you believe this? The very thing I dreaded..."

He snorted. Lemp continued to stare at a point midway between himself and his employer, "...and I think we can safely assume that Knoller is dead after all this time. There's been no trace of him either here, or sightings from our contacts overseas. He was too fond of the drink not to have surfaced in one bar or another. What am I to do? All secrecy has gone. I told them I had taken care of business, put things right, rectified my one mistake." He stood up, leant his considerable weight on his knuckles, and stared across at Lemp's downcast face. "Thank God his mother is no longer alive to see this."

Lemp's eyebrows moved a fraction. He shifted in his chair. Blake began to stride about the room. His mirrored image loomed and faded between wood and glass, filling the room with disquiet.

"I was happier believing him dead, but now, there he is, large as life. The one thing I tried to avoid while he lived at home – his face in a newspaper." Blake snatched up the offending picture. "And here it is now with a reward for information. I should have dealt him when I had the chance, ended it there. All these years without a breath of scandal..."

He stared at his longest-serving and most trusted henchman.

Lemp dwarfed the chair in which he sat. The expensive Worstead suit failed to disguise musculature honed by twenty years of unofficial pugilism. His head had sunk so low his chin almost rested on his chest. The rigid shirt collar disappeared beneath a roll of flesh, but seemed to cause little discomfort to the bull neck. He winched his head up, unfolded his arms, and sat upright. Only when his face was level did he flick back his eyelids and look directly at his boss. Their expressions were of one accord. Whatever it cost, they must track down Jeremiah before anyone else, or risk exposure. They would need to move fast. Blake continued his rant.

"At least this felony occurred in the Antipodes, All we can pray for now is that our sources there are reliable." Lemp waited, out of habit, until given short, unequivocal orders. The pacing recommenced. He paid close attention. "That lad, the one whose identity we bought, all those years ago, did you finish him, I can't remember?"

Lemp shook his head. He thought back to the money he'd split with his former colleague – the one occasion he hadn't carried out orders to the letter.

Blake had taken him into his confidence once he had decided to spirit Jeremiah away.

"Find me a suitable lad," he said, "someone prepared to sell me what I need. No questions asked and fifty pounds for his trouble."

Lemp had shown no emotion. In reality the impending departure of so unpleasant an object as Blake's son would be a blessing. He drew the line at calling him a lad, or even a young man. In his view, the little basket should have been strangled at birth. Any one else's son would have been tossed in a loony bin, or had his throat cut, long ago.

"Oh, and one more thing, Lemp, see that our benefactor gets all of the money. I want no come-back, no messiness. It must be someone as is willing, do you understand me?"

In those far off days Blake had been more eager to buy off, or pay for what he required. Times were harder now. Lemp remembered the name of the ship as if it was yesterday...

When the local paper announced that the Lynmouth had berthed, he went straight out towards the docks with Knoller. Not too direct, nor too close, ignoring the hopeless, picking their way through in search of a young man down on his luck. It didn't take them long. On the second day out they found a likely candidate.

They had trawled up Northumberland, cut through Caryl, and turned down Warwick to the corner of Grafton Street. They were known, but those who recognised them looked away. They sidled up to him at the bar, and inspected him discreetly. Two huddled men, minding their own business. He'd do. Same height, same age, more or less, and he'd already had a beating – saved them the trouble. His clothing was poor, and he had little in the way of possessions. A country boy, from the occasional word he'd spoken to the landlord, ideal. They'd exchanged glances, clinked their glasses, and agreed. He'd settle for as little as twenty by the look of him. They would share the profit between them. It was easy money.

They moved away from the bar and watched him for the rest of the evening. Lemp stayed on, but never let him out of his sight until the exchange was over.

Knoller lost the toss. He had accepted his duty without comment, charged with delivering young Jeremiah Blake to his destination. He hid his nervousness well – there was too much at stake. Lemp guessed he had more funds hidden about his person than the allowance Blake had given him for the round trip. He also held the tickets. His was destined to be one-way – surely that must have occurred to him? Lemp would have staked money on it, then as now.

When Knoller disappeared he'd taken it as an omen, and kept to his own code ever since – absolute obedience to Blake. He'd survived this long. Maybe if Knoller hadn't been so greedy he wouldn't be dead, for dead he most certainly was after all this time. He felt it deep in his gut (used to give his old Mum a turn when he came out with things like that).

"Lemp!"

He snapped back to the present, his reply delivered in short bursts, as if unfamiliar with regular speech, and now defensive in tone.

"You said a good price – someone down on their luck – no comeback – just to give him a beating – make identification difficult if there were questions. Spread the word Jeremiah was attacked and convalescing. It all worked out, didn't it? Why is that so important now?"

Blake jabbed his finger at the picture once more, his exasperation growing.

"Because *that* name and *this* picture don't go together. Because anyone who knows me knows this is *my* son. Twenty years on, and there he is, looking not one day older, every curl in place thanks to the improvement in photography, and the eagerness of law enforcement agencies to use it." Blake's voice rose in volume and pitch. "It's in a national newspaper. You must realise by now, if anyone traces this back to the lad's family *they* may well question it too. And there's always the possibility that they will want to know what became of him. Worse still, they may prompt the police to investigate whose name belongs with *this* face, and why he's masquerading as Howell Lewis Pritchard. You should have found a John Smith or a Jim Brown, something more commonplace... Bah! Knoller said they had only their age and height in common." He waved his arms around in a gesture of disbelief. "Any normal person, given Jeremiah's history, and all the problems we had getting him away, would have changed his appearance, kept low – but not him!"

Blake sighed, stood to one side of French windows that would have graced an embassy, and peered out. The back of the house boasted a long terrace which overlooked gardens the size of a municipal park. Despite his faith in the armed guards he could see patrolling below, he was careful not to reveal his silhouette against the light. Once these grounds had been far beyond the outer limits of Liverpool, now, sprawling suburbs threatened to encroach upon his stronghold. No one could guarantee his fences were safe.

"I don't want any more trouble, Lemp, or police attention. It will be difficult enough sorting out our side of things." He sat back at his desk and opened the top drawer. "I want you to settle this business. You know what to do..." He slid a wad of bank notes across the desk, and Lemp, with a swiftness that belied his appearance, spirited them away into his pocket. "...Wire me through the usual sources if you require more funds. I'll expect you back in early December."

Taking this as a cue to leave, Lemp rose to his feet. The chair creaked in relief. His boss made no sign, but he waited, sensing there was more. Blake leafed through the papers in front of him.

"These are the notes Knoller made; a copy of the lad's details, home address, and so on. I'll send that little Welshman, Merrick. He can ferret around without causing too much comment. I don't want any loose ends. If the family's still living, and in touch with him, I want to know, but if, as Knoller suspected, he left home in disgrace – and presumably for good – so much the better."

"And when my part of the job's done?"

"Take an indirect route back, through the Americas. There must be no links back to me, no repercussions. It ends there."

Merrick had done his homework. He consulted military records under the guise of tracing a long-lost cousin, checked copies of Parish registers for the district, went back through old newspapers, and pondered over a map of the village before setting one foot in it.

He travelled by motorbike, something he'd enjoyed since the Great War, and afforded him a more expedient means of departure, should the need arise.

Blake valued Lemp from long association – the only one he trusted implicitly – his 'number one'. The others accepted this position. They knew exactly where they stood with him; he was one of them. Merrick was different. Around him you kept your mouth shut, and gave no one cause to question your loyalty.

In appearance the man was genial, if unremarkable. He might even be considered non-threatening, in a physical sense, but it was a mistake to underestimate him. He missed nothing, and his memory made him dangerous. Over the years, his reputation had grown out of proportion with the real workings of a quick, logical mind. Some said his ability to make leaps between connecting events bordered on intuition. He was happy to fuel the myth.

The village pub served cold cuts, cheese, and pickles at lunchtime. Apart from the landlord, and a couple of elderly patrons who seemed indifferent to his presence, the public bar remained empty.

It was a disappointing start. He spread a road map on the ringed table, drank his shandy, exaggerated his Welsh accent, and played a sightseer for parts elsewhere – just pulled off his route. He was good at deflecting interest if it suited him.

He had noticed the post office on his way in, and chugged back down the road when he was sure it would be open. The woman behind the counter, although in late middle-age, was well-preserved and buxom. Like many small men he was drawn to the type. His eyes twinkled at her from the other side of the grill, and he watched her blossom in response. Surely if anyone knew the local gossip it would be this Mrs Prosser?

☙

Forty minutes later, plied with cups of tea, and included in their conversations by the succession of women making their daily pilgrimage for news, in addition to their groceries, he had filled in the gaps.

They told him about the Chapel, where a plaque had been erected to the three Pritchard boys who had died in 1916 (Joe and Will), and 1917, Eddie, a close friend of his late son (so he hinted). Eddie's girlfriend had taken it bad, the all-knowing Mrs Prosser told him. She'd married someone else later, and moved away. He'd been a good boy, Eddie, like Arthur, the one who'd emigrated. Merrick's ears pricked up at this, allayed a moment later by the news that this particular brother had been discharged from the Royal Navy, lived in New Zealand, and had stayed a close friend of their Minister. One of the informants on his side of the counter took up the theme.

"Oh, but d'you remember...?"

A door opened behind Mrs Prosser, making her jump. The others stopped as if throttled. From where he was standing, Merrick could see the outline of a large solid woman in her late thirties.

"Oh! Mary love, there you are!"

Mrs Prosser tried not to sound as flustered as she looked.

"Dad's back now. He said to tell you."

Her glance took in the assembled women without enthusiasm. She seemed not to notice him as he leant back against the corner of the counter. Her face had a sad, almost sullen expression in repose, and Merrick wondered who she had set her cap at, years ago, only to be so disappointed. She went back through the door, and shut it behind her.

There was a long pause. His would-be informants fidgeted with their bags, and looked everywhere but at each other. Mary's entrance had thrown them off their stride. They would tell him more if encouraged, but he must not let them lose their enthusiasm for the topic. He decided to up the stakes.

"Is there any family left here? I have a few keepsakes I feel should be passed on, that's all. Not much, but it seems unfair to hold on to them."

"Well, there's Louise, of course." The women relaxed visibly, glad to break the silence. They hummed a comforting chorus, agreeing with the postmistress as she resumed the conversation. "But she's had so much to put up with..." Louise, he remembered, from the Parish register, so close in age to the brother he sought. "Nice girl, Louise, not like that fast piece, Nancy!"

This was better; they were gaining momentum now, nothing like bit of spite for bringing out the half-truths of a situation. They were shaking their heads as if conducted. One of them, with a down-turned mouth, nudged him with her elbow,

"Ran off with one of them jump jockeys."

There was a chorus of contradictions.

"No, he was a gambler."

"I heard he was a spiv."

"And I'm *telling* you he was a jockey! Saw his picture in the paper not long back, won at Cheltenham races on a horse with a daft name, Pingo or Pongo something."

His conspirator, having re-established her position, continued. "Anyhow, she moved Gloucester way. Or was it Cheltenham, no matter. Not far enough, if you ask me. Right little madam she turned out to be." She enlisted Mrs Prosser's approbation. "D'you remember, Gwyneth, when she turned up late at her Mam's funeral? Not an ounce of decency. Still called herself Pritchard then, but she sat down like a married woman..."

The humming became a drone of disapproval.

Time to go.

He had what he wanted, and would learn more from this flighty sister. She should be easy enough to trace. Any further show of interest on his part might arouse suspicion.

"Well ladies, you've been so kind, so very kind..."

He beamed at the postmistress, anxious not to stem their flow, and eased himself out of their company. This was the right moment to leave; they had warmed to their topic now. By the time they got round to analysing him, he would be long gone.

TWENTY SEVEN

The McKenzie's yard was in chaos. A pall of dust churned up by the mule cart, and the to-and-fro of a dozen men, coated everything in orange grit. Despite the bandana protecting his nose and mouth, Harry could taste it.

They were all bone tired; more than ready for a beer with a good steak and gravy dinner at Maggie's Place, before they moved on to their next contracts. He was still undecided about Rory's offer; his indecision almost a decision in itself. But he would have to make up his mind in the next couple of hours. His boss needed an answer.

Time enough.

There were a dozen jobs requiring his attention before the waggon left for Wintamarra Creek.

Lennie was in unusually good form. He'd been regaling the men with his latest snake story. Rory had sent him out to check on the water troughs where he'd found, and shot, a King Brown. The others, Australian born and bred for the most part, listened enraptured. They all had snake stories, but Lennie had worked as a snake wrangler for a while, in the Northern territory. It earned him a curious respect.

There had been a couple of dead wallabies near one of the shadier troughs. He found the culprit close by. The 'brown' had been unable to move quickly as jaws distended it ingested a lizard.

"Jesus! You should have seen at the size of that bugger! Must have been cornered under the trough and struck out from there. I couldn't see any other reason for it. They're territorial bastards!"

Lenny crowed about the remains, but to Harry it was ten feet of lethal, venomous unpleasantness. He had a healthy fear of such creatures, but stayed resolutely unimpressed by the account of its subtle colouring, sizeable fangs or anything else. In his view the only good snake was a dead one.

Rory was fascinated by all the local species, 'browns' in particular. He'd taken to stringing the skeletal heads of his kills outside the big barn. It impressed the gang, but Harry found the sight of those gaping jaws unsettling. Rory's four year old son shared his father's obsession, much to Jeannie's concern. There were too many hazards for the young and vulnerable in her opinion.

With all the confusion in the yard, little Jamie had been confined to the veranda. He spotted Harry and waved, his high voice carrying above the circus of mules, horses, men, and dogs. He waved back, grinned, and returned to sorting the shearing tools.

Jeannie's advances had thrown him. The McKenzie's whole set up was in jeopardy. That vague feeling of disquiet resurfaced.

It was too small a sensation to call fear. He was being watched. Lenny emerged from the shadow of the barn wall and sauntered over.

"Been looking for you, Harry. Boss said to take that mare's tack down to the end barn. Didn't say why."

He turned away without waiting for Harry's response. It was an odd request, but he had no time to question the logic. Rory was usually happy to let them throw the saddles over the rails in the yard so he could check them in.

He collected the blanket, carried the saddle on his arm and hooked the bridle over his shoulder. The barn was empty. It had a small tack room – more of a general dumping ground for old harness – at one end. As he went through the door, a blow caught the back of his head.

Coming round, minutes later, he found himself on the floor minus his hat and tack. The saddle blanket was trapped beneath him. As he staggered to his feet, he saw that he was not alone. In the far corner was a sack, and unwinding itself from the folds, the burnished slippery coils of a King Brown.

He pressed back against the farthest wall praying that it would not notice him immediately. He was defenceless: no gun, no knife, and with no inclination to try any of the tactics he's heard described for such encounters.

The snake, sensing another creature close by, raised its head off the floor and flexed round in a circle, searching for a means of escape. It gathered speed and without warning struck at the blanket he held in front of him. As it recoiled, he shook the dusty cloth violently, hoping to distract it, but the second strike caught the edge only inches from his leg. The lunging and circling grew faster.

The reptile's head flattened, its body seemed to grow in length, filling up the space. He steeled himself against another strike. This time it found his gloved hand, catching one of its fangs in the tough leather. The inside was wet with venom. He felt the smooth needle slide next to his finger.

Missed. It had missed him. Using this slight advantage, he threw the glove, with the snake still attached, back into the far corner of the room. He didn't know who was the more terrified. The lethal knot bowled over and over in the dust, finally banging into the wall and disentangling itself. What now? He couldn't protect his hand against another strike. But the snake found a thin strip of sunlight and, in one fluid movement, slid through the gap beneath the corrugated iron and disappeared.

His relief overwhelmed him. He picked up the blanket and stuffed it into the gap. His hands were shaking, and when he tried to call out found his throat was still constricted in fear. The door was barred on the outside. He began hammering on it with his fists.

Others were shouting out in the distance, and above their voices he heard the piercing cry of a small boy. Christ! Jamie wouldn't stand a chance.

There was a thud – followed by a cheer – then the whole yard erupted. No one could hear him. He tried again. At last running footsteps approached the door.

"Hold on, mate."

Young Lucas, sixteen or so, and one of the rousies, opened the door.

"Strewth, Harry, how d'you get trapped in here? You missed all the drama. One of the black fellas killed a King Brown – nailed it to the barn with his spear. Helluva throw. Gives me the willies thinking about it..."

"Thanks..." Harry pushed past him, and ran outside.

Where the hell was Jamie?

Up ahead, Jeannie, with her small son clinging to her skirt – obviously unscathed, was shouting at her husband. Lenny launched straight in as soon as he saw Harry, though he placed himself on the far side of his boss.

"You pallack! You useless bloody Pom'! Why didn't you kill that snake? You were in the barn. You know Jamie follows you everywhere. He'd be dead by now if it wasn't for Bill."

The men fell silent, watching to see who came out on top. He'd like to smash that slimy creep to pulp for setting him up, but sensed goading him to a fight was the next stage. He'd witnessed several brawls stirred up by Lenny. He wouldn't give him the satisfaction.

Jeannie glared at Harry, vigorously nodding her agreement. She continued to upbraid her husband in front of his men.

"And to think he was your first choice for this place..."

She flounced up the veranda steps with a theatrical snort of disgust and went indoors. Lenny picked up Jamie and followed her. It was a gesture so intimate and familiar that no one could miss the implication, and told him more than countless rumours throughout the years. Harry stared up at the big man and realised that he knew

– must have known all along the reason Lenny kept coming back. Had Jeannie played a part, or was this all Lennie's doing? All those years they'd worked together, he would never have thought him capable of this. But it would put him even further in the wrong if he spoke of his recent encounter... or claimed that he had been assaulted, and shut in deliberately. They would call him a liar, and a whingeing Pom to boot.

No. It was best left. The damage was done – the decision made for him.

Rory lumbered up the steps after his wife and her lover. His shoulders drooped in humiliation.

❦

Harry didn't waste any more time. He retrieved his pack from the cart, checked his rifle was loaded, and strode off in the direction of Wintamarra Creek.

At the end of the homestead, where the trees gave way to bush, he found Bill, their occasional tracker, sitting in the shade. He got up when he saw Harry and glanced nervously towards the house. His brother crouching behind him began muttering in his own language.

He translated.

"Nigdi say Irwardbad, that King Brown snake, he meant for you. You lucky fella." The muttering continued. "Says you off Maggie's Place we come alonga you. Not that way."

He pointed to the long straight dirt road leading to the main north south route, and looked back at the white two storey house.

The windows facing them reflected the sunlight, effectively concealing anyone who might be watching. Bill pointed his spear at the bush.

"Safe this way."

Harry followed them along their time worn trail. They walked in single file. Occasionally Nigdi would say something to his brother and they would stop, but neither man spoke to Harry for the entire journey. Usually, carrying a pack, and in this heat, it would have taken him at least two hours. They made it in one along a diagonal route. He wouldn't have risked the track alone.

℘

In the dry creek outside the small township, a group of Aborigines had lit a fire. Bill and Nigdi left him and walked over to join them.

Nigdi was right. He was lucky. That walk had steadied his nerves. He could think about the encounter more rationally. One in three died from a bite, so he'd been told. The venom attacked the muscles. Whether Lenny had meant it to kill him or merely get him out of the way didn't matter now. He had his wages and his bonus – Rory had given it to him in advance, no doubt as an inducement. Just as well, although he wasn't bothered by the prospect of finding new work. Years of living this nomadic existence had taught him to survive on next to nothing. He spent little enough, the occasional beer and his smokes, not much else. Had a good bit put away too, but that was no one else's business.

For once, Maggie was not behind the bar. He was disappointed. Her irreverent banter would have taken his mind off things. Edge looked past him into the street. Realising Harry was alone, he said.

"You're early, mate. I was worried we'd have a rush on our hands and Lee not ready yet."

"I'm hoping to catch the down train, if it's running on time. The others will be another hour or two..."

And I'll be long gone.

"All's well, according to the telegraph station. 'No foreseeable delays'." Edge laughed at the standard response. It meant anything could happen. "You'll want a steak then?" He poured Harry a pint without being asked and set it on the bar. "Oh, I've just remembered... lucky you came in first, or it would have gone clean out of my head, and I'd have had to send it on to the McKenzie's. You've a bunch of letters. One of them looks as though it's followed you around Australia!"

Edge handed him a bundle of post, mostly catalogues for shearing equipment and the like, but tucked in the centre was a letter.

Seeing ApIvor's educated script gave him such a jolt he almost dropped it on the floor. He ignored the eager inquiring face in front of him, and gulped down his beer.

"Thanks, mate. Another one of these and I'll be right!"

Edge poured a second pint, said something incomprehensible to Lee through the serving hatch, and rummaged under the bar for cutlery.

"Steak, mash and gravy coming up, Harry."

He sat at his usual table and did justice to the simple meal, conscious all the while of the letter in his pocket.

There was another hour to wait before the train came through. He didn't want to be in the bar when the rest of the gang arrived. One more beer and a coffee later he walked down to the stopping point. It was too simple a place to be called a station – just a raised wooden platform, no more than fifty feet long, with one seat.

The light was beginning to fade, but still strong enough to read by. He could resist no longer and opened the envelope.

"My dear boy," ApIvor began, "I hope that after so many years you will have found it in your heart to forgive me..."

The letter resonated with long forgotten words and phrases, conjuring the melodic voice off the page and into his head. He read and re-read the letter, disbelief his over riding emotion. Mahalia lived – and he had a daughter. And Eli, Old Eli had married Mahalia, *his* Mahalia. He couldn't square that at all. Eli had married *his* wild Gypsy love, and raised their child. *His* child. How could that be? And the unkindest stroke of all... he and Mally had been separated by no more than a field all those years ago, hidden by two kindly old men who had disagreed over the subject of Gypsies and kept their secrets to themselves. Yet those circumstances had saved Mally's life and given his daughter more than he could ever have achieved.

For several minutes he was torn between the urge to shout with joy or punch his fist into something. But his feeling of elation quickly passed, and he subsided into melancholy..

The train was on time. He clambered aboard without a backward glance, and settled near a window to study the letter again. This was fate. That elusive fate Mahalia had believed in. He would go back, if only to look at his daughter from afar.

He stared, unseeing, out of the window, his mind half a world away. Was this a reprieve, one final chance to set his life right? He felt hope again, an emotion he had abandoned long ago.

He would return to England. His burnt-out eyes longed for a protective covering of grey clouds, to feel rain on his face once again, a cooling balm for more than just his eyelids. By the time he reached Adelaide he had cast off his adopted life. Harry Jenkins was going home.

TWENTY EIGHT

Lily hammered on Owen's front door. It was several minutes before she heard footsteps in their hall and the door opened. She was surprised to see Owen's worried face. Usually Margaret answered, if only to spare her husband some of the trivialities of parish life.

Owen gave a cry of relief and caught her up in a hug.

"Thank God, oh, thank the dear Lord you are safe. I've been all over the place looking for you. Your mother's in the hospital on account of that cough of hers. Margaret's with her, you're not to worry, mind. Your Mum's very poorly, and she's not making a lot of sense. Claimed you'd been taken by someone. Later, she thought you'd gone off in a huff, but I said that wasn't like you..."

"Owen, please." Lily struggled free of his arms.

"Sorry, love. It's just I'm so glad you're safe. I..."

He stopped short and looked at her carefully. She saw his growing dismay at her dishevelled state.

"Dear God, Lily, what happened?"

"Please, Owen. I need a bath, and a hot drink. I didn't want to go back home in this state."

Her pallor must have alarmed him.

"What you need is a glass of brandy. You go on up and help yourself to anything of Margaret's that you need. We'll have a proper talk when you're sorted. I'll make you something to eat."

She managed to smile at him as he hurried about, putting first a very large glass of brandy in her hand, a pile of fluffy towels in the bathroom, Margaret's best dressing gown on the hook inside the door.

"Welsh rarebit on toast all right for you? It's about all I can do."

He ran downstairs to complete his mission, calling over his shoulder. "Margaret will be back soon, she'll look after you properly."

Lily shut and locked the bathroom door. She must avoid Margaret's over solicitous care. Neither she nor her mother must ever know the details. The shame of it would kill her.

Once inside the large old fashioned bathroom, she filled the bath almost to the brim and lowered herself through obliterating clouds of steam into the hot water. There was an unused bar of carbolic on a metal rack across the end of the bath, and a round cake of lily of the valley which must be Margaret's. She chose the stronger smelling red soap and rubbed so much into the flannel it changed colour.

She scrubbed the dark pink sludge into her skin. Over and over, she soaped, rubbing herself almost raw in places. She would never be clean again. Never be rid of the smell of him, that stickiness mixed with her blood. Did men and women really join together in such a way for pleasure? Was that what procreation meant? The thought of it made her gag. No man would touch her with such intimacy – ever. She fought back her nausea. Never, not as long as she drew breath.

Wrapped in Margaret's wine-coloured velvet dressing gown, with the glow of brandy beginning to take effect, she went down to the kitchen where Owen was buttering a mound of toast.

"Ah, there you are. Here, get this inside you then we can have a real talk."

He drew up a chair and joined her with a mug of tea.

Everything looked so cosy and familiar. She raised her knife and fork, then dropped them with a clatter. She must tell someone. Owen, with his clergyman's oath of confidentiality. This kind man, her Godfather... Tears were streaming down her face now. Owen reached across and held her hand.

"Tell me." was all he said. And Lily dissembled. The story came in broken phrases, until the hardest part. She looked at Owen calmly, and said in a low voice.

"What I tell you now, Owen, neither my mother nor Margaret must ever know. Promise me."

He squeezed her hand gently.

"I promise."

The word 'rape' made tears start up in Owen's eyes. He stood up and began to pace the room, running his fingers through his shock of iron grey hair. Without warning he punched the side of his hand against the kitchen table. Everything in the room rattled.

"He must be found and punished. I will send for the police straight away. They won't need to know all of it. It will be enough that he kidnapped you and you have been assaulted. For your sake we'll avoid using that word if we can."

"No."

He turned to her in astonishment.

"What do you mean, Lily? A monster like that must be punished."

"He has been, but it is worse than you can imagine, Owen. Much worse. He's dead."

"How come? Did those Gypsies tell you that? How do you know they didn't protect him? He's one of their own. Perhaps they said that to help him."

"I did it." She cut him short. "I killed him, I had to escape and... I did it. There was no one else involved."

Owen collapsed into the chair opposite her and laid both his palms on the table. He didn't speak for several minutes.

"No one must know, Owen. My mother's family rescued me. They burnt his body in his waggon. They dealt with it in their fashion. If the police are involved they will be blamed. It wasn't their fault."

"And if the police are involved," Owen's voice was thick with emotion, "the real truth may come out. It's a hanging offence."

"What will you do?"

"Me? Nothing. What can be done? As you say, the matter has been dealt with. This must remain a secret between us. You've suffered enough in your short life. You must convince your mother that you went off in a temper. Better that folk think badly of you for something minor than the truth gets out."

She studied Owen's downcast face and realised that his would be the greater dilemma. One day he must answer to a Higher Authority for his silence.

TWENTY NINE

Lily sat in the musty splendour of Lady Gertrude Banion-Hartwell's drawing room, trying to find a comfortable position on the stiff upholstery, and waited for her hostess to return. She rather liked the audience of dust-embalmed relics, the museum cold tones, everything muted, and not its original colour. It would have been garish when everything was new, at the height of Victoria's reign, all those patterns and influences shrieking for attention. She tried to picture the room full of young Banion-Hartwells and failed. Her former school governor must have been a stately child.

As if conjured by the thought, the lady herself came back into the room, followed by Bates, though whether the latter was a Miss or a Mrs, Lily didn't dare inquire.

"Put it there, Bates, will you? And order our tea now. I'm sure Miss Jenkins would appreciate cook's scones, and Dundee cake, if there is any."

Bates, whose age was hard to determine, carried a large leather suitcase over to the hearth and placed it by Lily's chair. If it was heavy there was not the slightest indication from her gait or posture. She neither smiled, nor bobbed, nor demurred to, or acknowledged her mistress in any way. She merely obeyed. If anything, she was even more terrifying than her employer.

Her hostess waited until Bates left the room before turning to her guest.

"I asked you here today, Lily, because I believe there are certain items amongst my late brother's effects that should rightfully pass to you. I have already given your poor mother the letter Geraint wrote the day he died. I hope the content gave her comfort."

No, it didn't. She read it, cried for two days and refused to show me the contents.

Her mother had locked the document in her jewellery box, her 'little treasure chest', as she called it, the miniature key impossible to spirit away from the gold chain she wore around her neck, and seldom removed.

But instead of voicing these thoughts, Lily smoothed out the crease in her frock and looked up.

"It has all been such a shock, learning about my parents in this way," She said. "Although, as I'm sure you appreciate, to me there can be no other father than my Dada, Eli Jenkins."

Stop it. You sound like a naïve little girl after all that's happened.

Looking up, she saw Lady Gertrude nod approvingly. It was the modest reply she had expected.

"Yes, you were fortunate. It was such an act of Christian charity when Eli took your mother in. Unprecedented one might say. He

285

was more of a father than most, given the life he provided, and your education. The odd thing is I didn't connect him with *that* Eli Jenkins, the one I knew as a child. I never heard his first name mentioned during my time as Governor of your old school. But of course I rarely met parents face to face. He was just another Jenkins. There are so many hereabouts. Yet he and my brother were close as children. I am a little surprised he didn't renew our acquaintance when he moved back here..."

Yes, why was that?

Why had the old minister attended her father's funeral yet never visited their home? Small wonder it had shocked her mother. She returned her attention to her hostess, who had not paused for breath.

"...But I gather, through my brother's long involvement with the village, that Eli showed an interest in several of the Pritchard children. Your natural father was the eldest, I believe. Had such good prospects too, at one time..."

Lily chose not to be rattled by the patronising tone. If she was ever to learn about her real father, it would surely be from the late Reverend ApIvor's records (finding it difficult to associate the short, breathless minister with the formidable titled lady in front of her). She concentrated on keeping calm, not giving way to the excitement she felt at these discoveries, and her own Machiavellian approach.

"...My brother spent a good deal of his time and resources in that village. He was particularly interested in capturing images of rural life, festivals, that sort of thing. It was an interest he shared with Eli. I'm rather surprised you haven't any records at home."

Lily looked suitably blank. Yes, where had all those photographs gone? Maybe her Dada gave them away when he and her Mam married? Receiving no rejoinder from her young guest, Lady Gertrude continued. "In that suitcase you'll find all his photographs going back to the wedding of, well, I suppose the people who were your grandparents." Lily bent forward eagerly and began to pull the suitcase towards her. "No, don't open that in here. It's extremely dusty." Lily smothered a smile. "You'll find that Geraint wrote all the details on the back of each one. He was meticulous."

She sat up again, conscious of her deportment, noting that the old lady's straight back didn't rest against the chair. Such discipline, yet she must be eighty if she was a day.

"I'm most grateful to you, Lady Gertrude..." she began, but was interrupted by the maid bringing their tea into the room. To her dismay, she saw that it was Bronwyn Beynon. She wondered how such a girl had managed to secure a post in this household, with no reference from her mother.

Bronwyn set out the small tables, and stood back waiting for further orders. She stared at Lily openly, her mouth sullen with disdain. Lady Gertrude caught the look, and frowned.

"That will do, Beynon."

She bobbed, and left, eager, no doubt, to rake over the scandal with the kitchen staff. Lily watched her disappearing figure.

You won't last long here either, Bron', if you can't control that face of yours.

Lady Gertrude lifted the elaborate silver teapot, filled translucent porcelain cups with amber, smoky tea, and handed one to Lily.

"It has all been most unfortunate. You, of all the brilliant young women from my old school. Now tell me your plans" She didn't wait for Lily's answer. "I should advise your mother to sell up and move away. Preferably somewhere you're not known. Of course, attending any college now is quite out of the question given your mother's origins."

Lily's polite expression vanished. Was this the real reason she had been summoned? To advise her informally that all her future hopes were crushed by an accident of birth, because of the ingrained prejudice of others? Her hostess evidently hadn't noticed her reaction. The imperious voice continued.

"Now you have this additional, if unforeseen, handicap it is in the interests of all concerned that you should not apply at all rather than risk the inevitable rejection, or worse, generate any scandal. However, there are many other avenues open to you, given your late father's assets and position. A gal like you shouldn't have to work. There are causes you could espouse in other districts. As you know I have dedicated my life to fighting for the unfortunates in society. Women's minds, in particular, must be opened to the possibility of governing their own destinies. It takes decades. Believe me, I know. One day soon, all women will have the right to vote, not just those of us who are older with property."

As she listened to the old lady revisit her pet themes – the subject of many a speech day. Lily's thoughts turned to matters nearer home.

Yes, one day maybe, but too late for my mother. We would be offered more opportunities if we were fallen women.

Lady Gertrude had stopped talking and was sipping her tea. When she set down the cup her air of dismissal was only too clear. She had done her duty. Lily was of no further interest. It was time to leave.

❧

Lily had driven their trap to the mansion, but had, out of deference, parked round the back by the tradesman's entrance.

The suitcase, when she attempted to lift it, was surprisingly heavy. It was hers now, this unexpected gift, this chest full of clues. She would discover the truth, she was owed that much. Too many secrets had been kept from her.

THIRTY

Louise stayed longer at the post office than she intended. Jack had a half-day, and she wanted to get on with her chores in order to spend time with him, but Mary Prosser and her Mum had been holding court. It was difficult to get away from them once they started. She found it hard to believe what they had told her. Such a scandal by all accounts!

Listening to them, she thought how sad it was that the ripples had spread as far as their quiet village.

She didn't know what to think about Old Eli, but recognised the name of his widow – careful not to react in front of the Prossers. Even after all this time she knew better than to let something slip. But there couldn't be two Gypsy girls of the same age called 'Mahalia', and Eli was always so tolerant of them. It had to be the same girl, but if that was the case, what had happened between her and Howell? Maybe that was the cause him of him going off so suddenly. But Mahalia had been her brother's only real passion.

He'd never been in love like that before – the way you fall for the first time – when you let nothing stand in your way. No, none of it made any sense. She wouldn't be able to concentrate on anything until Jack came home.

As she approached her cottage, the front door opened. Louise stopped at the gate, disconcerted by the appearance of a woman emerging from her house. It was Nancy, her closest sister at one time, but now, well she hadn't seen her for many years since their mother died. It was typical of her to let herself in.

"Louise!"

Nancy came down the path, and hugged her before she could gather her wits or respond.

"Knew you wouldn't mind if I let myself in. Came all this way and was desperate for the loo."

Louise kissed her sister's cheek. It smelt of face powder. Nancy produced a handkerchief and dabbed at the place, buffing away the mark of her sister's affection. The make up left orange traces on the flimsy cotton.

"No, love, of course not." Louise said, "It's nice to see you, just caught me unawares. You'll stay for a bit of dinner with us, won't you? Jack'll be home soon. He's generally back by half past twelve on a Thursday."

Nancy stopped in front of the mirror which hung above the china cabinet. Dissatisfied with the image, she perched on the arm of the sofa, took out her powder compact and studied her face minutely, applying a fresh layer of lipstick to the already crimson lips.

Louise watched her, dismayed. Living in Cheltenham hadn't

diminished her vanity, or improved her manners. Long ago, in her role as older sister, she might have been tempted to say so.

Nancy concentrated on the painted mouth, pressed her lips together and removed a smudge from the outside edge with her little finger.

"Dinner? Oh, I forgot, that's what you call luncheon. We eat in the evenings, so don't bother on my account. Besides, I'm banting again, can't afford to let myself go. What do you think of this suit, then?"

She stood up to show off her clothes. Obviously it was the latest fashion, though it did nothing for her bust, that slack shapeless look, or the low waistline. Still Louise had to admit that her sister, although only just over five feet tall, did look slim and stylish.

"Very nice. How's Jim?" She said, changing the subject.

"Oh, I thought you knew..." Nancy frowned. "No, of course it was Ruby I told, not you. Jim and I have split up. Oh, don't look like that," she said, as her sister's face fell. "We were much too young. I'm getting a divorce. It'll be final soon, and I'm thinking of trying again." She burst out laughing. "You should see your expression, Lulu!" She reverted to her childhood name for her sister at the first sign of disapproval. "You look just like our Mum."

Louise frowned.

Please don't let that be true.

"I'm sorry to hear it, Nancy, that's all. It must have been dreadful for you to have taken such a step."

"What? Oh, yes, well it was a bit difficult for a while. Jim was nasty to begin with. But he's got someone new himself now..." She stood up and moved over to where Louise was standing. Catching her arm, she pulled her sister to the window. "I've something to show you. See that car down there?"

Louise looked towards the corner where the road widened. There was a pull-in Jack used sometimes when he had one of the estate's vans. Now, an open-topped tourer took up most of the space. There was no one in it. *Surely Nan' didn't drive all the way over in that?*

"You mean that big car, with no roof?"

"Yes, silly. Frank, my intended, bought it for me. What d'you think, eh? That'll have wiped the eye of a few of them round here, won't it?"

"It looks..." Louise began,

"Expensive? Yes, it was, but Frank can afford it. He comes from Liverpool, talks funny, not a bit like us. I had trouble understanding him at first. A gent though, not like Jimmy." Louise stood quietly in her own front room, at a loss for something to say. Nancy gave her arm a little shake. "Oh, Lou', you mustn't worry about me, you are a dear. I'll be fine. And I'd love a cup of tea..."

Louise went to the kitchen to comply with her sister's request, having lost her appetite. Nancy continued to talk, but, being just out of range, Louise couldn't hear her properly. There were a great many 'I's punctuating what she said was all she registered. When she returned with the laden tea-tray Nancy was still talking.

"...I came over for a couple of reasons. There's something you should know. Just before Jim and I split up, this chap came to see us, a little Welshman called Merrick – I think he said he was a

293

detective – must be a couple of months ago now. You'll never guess what he asked us?" She hurried on, eyes gleaming. That 'knowing' look in her eyes, as her elder brother had called it, despairing of Nancy's honesty, even as a child. "He was asking about Howell!" She paused, scanning her sister's face for a reaction.

Louise tried not to shiver. It was as if someone had stepped on her grave. "Yes, Howell! Imagine?" Nancy rolled her eyes and continued, "As if we'd know anything about him after all this time. Jim didn't like the look of him, didn't trust him; said he wasn't like any policeman he'd ever met. You know how he always believed he had a nose for them. Told him all our brothers had died in the War, except Arthur of course, got cross with me when I mentioned where he lived. What harm could it do? I said, they're hardly likely to traipse over to New Zealand to see him, now are they?"

Louise was stunned by this piece of news, following on from her earlier discoveries.

Whatever next? Everything comes in threes.

Nancy didn't give her the chance to interrupt.

"I've just remembered something else; you had a visitor while you were out. You'll never guess who that was either! You remember Old Eli? Well this girl said she was his daughter. I didn't listen properly to what she was saying" She looked at Louise with malicious delight. "And there she stands on your doorstep, brazen piece too."

Surely not? No girl lucky enough to have Eli as a father could possibly be brazen. Though (Louise glanced at her sister) *there's one a bit closer to home the description would fit.*

But Nancy hadn't finished yet. Louise wavered, caught between sadness and disgust at her sister's attitude.

She's relishing every nasty detail. That's the pity of it.

"Did you know that Old Eli married a Gyppo? Ruby told me, got it from that friend in Swansea whose hubby goes to one of those big Chapels."

"Yes, Nancy, I had heard. What of it?"

Nancy's face fell. She set down her cup, picked up her bag and looked at her sister with something close to contempt.

Tread carefully, miss. Louise frowned. *You can't have forgotten that my Jack's old grandmother was half a 'Gyppo' as you put it.*

"Oh, well, I thought you ought to know that's all. I didn't let her in. You can't be too careful. Sorry to be off so soon, remember me to Jack."

Oh yes, off you go, overstepped the mark and now you're running away.

She'd been doing that all her life.

Nancy opened the door and walked quickly to the gate. When she turned to say, 'Goodbye', the malice was back in her eyes.

"She'd done all right out of it, that Jenkins girl, by the look of her. He must have left that Gyppo woman a fair bit of money. All that property he had. These old boys when they fall late in life they fall hard, don't they?"

"He was a kind man, Old Eli. Don't you go saying otherwise, our Nancy."

Louise could feel herself getting all 'warmed up' on the subject, as her Jack would say.

"Oh, I know." Nancy said, "That's not what I meant, but he was an old fool to be taken in by one of them!"

She ignored her sister's pursed lips of disapproval, and looked down the road with pleasure at her latest acquisition. Louise moved towards the door.

"I mustn't keep you. You've a long drive back."

Nancy ignored the tone, and rummaged in her bag. She handed her a small printed card.

"There you are, Lou'. If you ever need anything, I'm on the telephone now. You ought to get one, you and Jack, being so far from all of us."

They kissed each other in a perfunctory manner. Louise was glad to see her go. She watched the diminutive fashion plate clip down the road in her thin-soled shoes. It was sad. There was something almost comical about her desire to be noticed still, not so far removed from the little girl let loose in the dressing-up box of yesteryear.

It's a shame. If she wasn't my sister I doubt I'd ever speak to such a self-obsessed creature. What ever happened to the bright child she once was? Old Eli would have been disappointed to see it. He had a real soft spot for Nancy when she was little. Yes, and for Howell too. He and Nancy had been the clear favourites.

She looked up and down the village street, wondering why Jack was late. It was after half past twelve. What a pity he didn't have the van today, she could have sent him off to find that Miss Jenkins before she went home, and invite her back. She wanted to see for herself what sort of job Old Eli had made of raising a daughter.

THIRTY ONE

Lily stayed up until two o'clock in the morning, following her
visit to Lady Gertrude (or 'Miss ApIvor' as she thought of her
irreverently), sifting through the photographs. Apart from a dozen
or so formal studies of visiting dignitaries at fêtes and music festivals,
the Pritchards featured in every one.

Faint similarities to her features gazed back at her passively. A
small child chewed on a thumb the way she once had; familiar blonde
baby curls fell over a high forehead; and two sets of distinctive pale
eyes looked out across the years from the stiff sepia prints. She studied
the picture of Louise and Jack Millward on their wedding day. ApIvor
had printed the date, with their name and address, on the back.

Margaret insisted she spend time on her own.

A letter had come for her mother concerning the farm back in
Herefordshire. She opened all the important post for her mother
and decided that, since one of the solicitors was going over to discuss
their lease with the tenants, she would accompany him and take the

opportunity to look around at the village where her parents met. Besides, she would be travelling by car, something she relished. One day she would buy one of her own, despite her mother's innate fear of such machines.

❦

They arrived in the village late morning. Lily decided that if she couldn't locate the woman called Louise, her aunt, she would find the places her Dada had described to her. Try to picture him in a different environment. It had piqued her curiosity now. She wouldn't be satisfied until she knew more. The solicitor had thoughtfully provided her with a small hand drawn map.

The driver pulled in by a row of cottages. A stylish new Morris was parked incongruously in the narrow rural lane. No doubt the villagers would be agog at two enormous motor vehicles arriving on their quiet streets in one day.

Lily agreed to find her father's old farm when she finished her walk, but as she waved goodbye her air of confidence vanished.

There were a couple of good photographs of the Pritchards in her bag, just in case they were needed. She checked her appearance in her handbag mirror. Her face was clean, her hat on straight, shoes and gloves tidy. She wouldn't be letting her Dada down.

It was so quiet: no traffic, no children, no dogs barking or distant farm noises. There was no sound at all except for her footsteps on the loose gravel at the edge of the road. The cottages were uniformly neat with matching green doors and gates. They must belong to the local estate.

Number four, where her 'Aunt Louise' lived, had a brick front path edged with half-moon terracotta tiles. Fuchsias and begonias in pots clustered either side of the front door. There was no bell, only a well-polished brass knocker in the shape of a horseshoe.

This Mrs Millward might not welcome her intrusion. She took a deep breath and knocked twice. The sound echoed hollow through the cottage, and down the empty road. There were no windows open. Louise must be out. She turned to go.

The door opened. One set of pale grey eyes narrowed, and looked her up and down. This was not Louise, but the one labelled 'Nancy', last seen staring at her from beneath a large white hair ribbon in her Sunday-school best.

"Yes?"

There was no welcoming look from the woman. She knew this wasn't the right sister, but in order to preserve appearances she went along with her own charade.

"Mrs Millward?"

"She's not here. What do you want?"

Faced with such hostility, Lily could feel her confidence ebbing away.

"Err, I was hoping to speak to her..."

"What about? I'm her sister. Who are you?"

Lily strove to keep her face polite, ignoring the intended rudeness.

"Oh, I see. My name's Lily Jenkins. My father used to live in the village at one time..."

"Oh yes! I know who you are now. Heard all about it from my

sister." The woman she knew to be Nancy sneered, "Old Eli must have been off his head marrying a Gyppo. You should be ashamed of yourself coming here where people remember him."

Lily was aware that her mouth was open, and shut it. She had not been expecting sarcasm, or open dislike. What could have triggered this sort of spite? She turned to go. There was little point in asking this woman to pass on a message, or even mention that she had called. The door slammed behind her before she reached the gate.

Lily walked past the gleaming metal motorcar. She didn't doubt it belonged to the creature called Nancy. What price had she paid for that? She looked hard and over-painted. Her hair was a surprising shade of red. Lily didn't think such a woman was in a position to call her names.

She walked through the village, and turned right up the steep hill towards the location of her Dada's old farm. At the top, on her left, was the gate to the old cemetery. The derelict church looked so beautiful in its tattered surroundings, silhouetted against the autumn sky. According to her map, the farm should be just over the rise.

A man was coming towards her, carrying a canvas workman's holdall. His hair was grey and curly, but he was still recognisably 'Jack' from the wedding picture. He touched his cap out of politeness.

"Are you all right, Miss? Are you lost?"

"No, but thank you for asking. I'm just stopped to admire the old church."

He looked at her closely.

"Do I know you, Miss? Your face seems familiar."

Lily didn't know how to respond to this. She felt indignant. If this man was going to be rude to her, she would just forget the whole business.

"I'm Lily Jenkins." she said, with as much confidence as she could muster. "My father used to farm here years ago."

But instead of insults he beamed at her, then looked upset.

"Oh, Miss Jenkins, my wife and I were so very sorry to hear about your Dad. We wanted to come to the funeral, but I was laid up with my back. Louise should have gone with the Reverend, but she didn't like to leave me. We both have such fond memories of Eli." Lily smiled at him, and held out her hand. He made an apologetic face and indicated his own dirty palm, but she reached out and shook it anyway. "You must come and meet my Louise," he said, "she should be home by now. I know she'd like to see you."

"That's kind of you, but I did call in. She was out, according to your sister-in-law, Nancy."

She supplied the name even though they had not been formally introduced. He seemed to understand her meaning, although she had tried to be tactful.

"Ah! Well, suppose we pop back, then if her visitor has gone perhaps you'd like to come in?"

That was an odd way to refer to his sister-in-law. It seemed there was a lack of enthusiasm on his part too.

It was exhilarating walking downhill, despite the gradient. Jack chatted to her as they walked, pointing out this landmark and that until they were outside his cottage. The car was no longer there. With luck Nancy had gone.

Lily waited while Jack went to find his wife. Louise was a different sort of person from her sister. Before Lily could offer her hand, or a polite explanation, she had been grasped warmly and kissed. Her aunt was crying, she realised, and swallowed hard, lest her own tears should give her away.

Jack took his wife's arm, steering her back inside their cottage.

"Come on, love," he said, "you'll frighten her away!"

He beckoned to Lily, and she followed them into the front parlour.

"Tea, that's what we need, my wife's standby, only this time I'll get it. You sit and talk."

He went out into the kitchen.

Louise stared at her, in between mopping her tears, and said an odd thing.

"You look just like your father, the very image of him."

Lily felt disconcerted. She didn't look remotely like Eli. Surely if this woman knew him at all she must realise that? Did she mean her brother? Did she know the truth?

Louise dried her eyes. She seemed to be summoning up her courage to say something. Lily reached across the table and touched her hand. She would take the first step.

"I know Eli wasn't my natural father." She said the words as quietly and carefully as she could. "Eli's name is on my birth certificate. As far as I am concerned he was my Dada, and a wonderful one at that."

"Yes, he was a kind, generous man. We all loved him. He was especially fond of your... my brother."

Louise let out a sigh. Her words came in a rush.

"Your mother, Mahalia, and my brother, Howell, were planning to elope, but one evening he disappeared. No one has heard from him since. All I knew from my Dad was that he had gone to enlist, but it didn't seem possible at the time... and I'm not sure I believe it even now."

Lily relaxed a little. It was going to be fine. They would tell her the truth. She could fill some of the gaps in her life.

"I've only found out something of my history recently, Mrs Millward."

"Louise, you must call me Louise," she said, "and my husband is Jack." She looked up at him lovingly as he came back through with the tea. "How is your mother?"

"She's not well. I think losing my Dada has been such a shock to her. They were devoted. You may find this hard to believe, Louise, but I didn't know that my mother was a Romani until recently."

Jack looked at Louise. There was agreement in their eyes. He turned to Lily,

"I remember your Mum, Lily, if she's the same Mahalia that used to come here. Jessel, her name was, I believe."

Louise took the cup of tea from her husband,

"She knows about Howell being her real Dad, love. But she's only just found that out too." Louise smiled sympathetically. "This has been a lot for you all coming at once, hasn't it?"

Lily was unsure of how much more she should say.

"I suppose the first thing I wanted to do, when I found out, was to find my natural father. There's so much that is still unexplained. I hoped you would know what happened to him?"

"I only wish I had more to tell you, dear," Louise said. "You see, he and I were so close. Then for him to just disappear, we're not even sure..." Jack put his arm around his wife. "...if he's still alive. We lost three of our brothers during the Great War. If he did join up it's likely he was lost too."

It was a possibility that hadn't occurred to her. If that was the case, what was the point in chasing ghosts?

They sat in silence for several minutes, occasionally sipping their tea from politeness, and the need for something to do. That was enough for now. Lily stood up.

"You've both been very kind. I'm sorry if anything I've said today has upset you."

They rose together, and smiled at her.

"It's been a joy to know that you exist, Lily. Eli made a fine job of raising you, and your Mum did too. I hope she recovers soon. You're welcome any time, both of you."

They hugged her. It seemed the natural thing to do, and stood outside their cottage, watching as she walked away.

Jack sighed.

"Well, I never expected that, did you, love?"

He looked at his wife anxiously, but she seemed to have recovered.

"I'm all right, really I am. Just a bit shocked. And that lovely girl having to find out all this, after believing Eli was her Dad." Her smile faded as she remembered her sister's visit, "Nancy was telling me about it. I'm afraid her tongue is sharper than it used to be, I can't bear to hear it."

She told her husband about the gossip circulating at the post office.

He didn't like it, any of it, yet kept coming back to the most puzzling part of all.

"And Mahalia Jessel married Old Eli Jenkins. How can that be possible?"

He frowned and looked over at Louise. Both shook their heads as if unable to accept it as a fact. To them Eli had always been an old man.

"Eli." Louise echoed his mood. "He was so solitary, and to have married late, that was enough of a surprise."

"What difference can it make to anyone," Jack said, "if that poor upset little girl is Howell's love-child. She didn't want anything from us, only the truth it seemed, and none of us are qualified to give her much of that."

"I think I should write to Arthur," Louise said. And Jack agreed. It would give her comfort.

❦

Louise sat at her little table. This would be more news to add to the already sad catalogue she had sent in previous weeks. What would Arthur make of it all? Such turbulent water had flowed through their village since their elder brother had fallen in love with Mahalia Jessel.

THIRTY TWO

O utside her eyelids, it was bright. Mahalia held them shut. She
was in a bed somewhere. She blinked away the needles of
light impairing her vision, until her pupils contracted, and the world
re-formed into recognisable shapes. A nurse stood at a nearby table,
with her back to her, busy with the clink and shuffle of equipment.
Edges blurred into shadow. Tall screens of soft-coloured fabric
separated her from what she supposed was the rest of the ward. It
was as if her bed alone was illuminated. The white linen seemed to
glow and crackle, like the uniform of her attendant.

"Where am I? This is a different place."

Her question brought the nurse to her side; the woman's face a
professional mask.

"You were moved here yesterday, remember? To the sanatorium."
Mahalia tried to sit up, but the nurse sighed with exasperation, and
loomed over her. "No, Mrs Jenkins," she said, "please lie back and
try to keep still."

"But the sanatorium," Mahalia said, anguish in her voice now, "that's for consumption."

"Tuberculosis." The nurse corrected her. "Yes, the doctors ran some tests." Mahalia looked about her, too frightened to think clearly. "Now, now, there's nothing to worry about." The nurse's expression softened fractionally. "You're in the best place. The doctors will be back later. They'll have the answers for you."

These standard reassurances were no comfort to Mahalia.

"Where's my daughter?" she asked, "Where's Lily?"

"Mrs Lewis has gone to find her. She took the keys to your house. She'll bring her straight back. You mustn't fret. They'll be here soon."

Mahalia had to be content with this, and gave herself up to the routine, knowing her daughter would be angry with her if she obeyed her natural inclination, and tried to leave. She had promised Lily, promised. Lily had told her she must get well. She mustn't leave her on her own.

Poor Lily. Poor little girl.

Tears slid down her cheeks as she admonished herself once more. This was all her fault.

It was dark now, she realised, trying to make sense of lost hours. The high window behind her bed was devoid of curtains, but she could see nothing beyond the black rectangle. Inside, light reflected off tiled walls and far above on the vaulted ceiling. The strange brightness was caused by lamps suspended from metal rails, the naked undersides of bulbs. It made spots dance before her eyes. She shut them again.

She was dazzled, walking through the sunshine of an early April morning. Their caravan of vardos creaked up the hill through the centre of the village, the men watchful of the brakes, dividing their attention between the loaded waggons, and the horses. She had been among the women threading their way on foot, wary of villagers who had gathered by their front gates to watch.

Outside the chapel, a young man stood bare-headed beside the short, red-faced cleric. She'd seen ApIvor before. He'd watched her play, tears in his eyes as he applauded their band's performance at the mid-summer fair. The minister's glance caught the attention of her grandmother, and the two old people had nodded their acknowledgement of one another.

She had been walking ahead, ignoring Lymena as she flirted with someone. When she turned, Howell was there. They stared at each other, oblivious of their surroundings, until Lymena warned him off.

That minute was enough. There was a feeling of hope again, a lifting of the dread she had lived with all year. She would see him again, she knew it.

Mahalia shifted uncomfortably on the high hospital bed. She tried to focus on Howell's face in her mind, but it eluded her. Physical sensations resurfaced: she remembered him carrying her easily, how they had fitted together despite the difference in their height, the warmth of his hands, his laugh, but not his face.

The day in the churchyard came back in a rush. She was so sure they had been seen by the little girl, Howell's sister, as she found out later, and Reuben's face leering at her – the sickening fear of near-discovery.

Reuben and her younger brother Job had walked her back to the encampment between them, grinning at each other over the top of her head as if they had a plan in mind, something to do with her. When she returned to the vardo they parted company, and Job hurried away. Reuben followed her up the steps. He tried to push her inside and shut the door, but Caleb saw him and intervened. Her elder brother could be interfering, but on that occasion she had been grateful.

It was Reuben's face she couldn't escape. She turned on the bed again, but the image overwhelmed her. Now back in the barn, she moaned in her delirium, burying her head in the pillow as she recoiled from his fist.

The nurse eased her back into a more comfortable position. Mahalia tried to speak, but the imagined figure bending over her had no gentle voice, or soothing hands. She struggled against it. Something pricked her arm. Letting go, she sank into the whiteness again.

She had been planning to abandon her old life, but not in the way it happened. Eli had spirited her away just in time, he told her. That old tinker Riley appeared in the village earlier than usual that autumn, working his way around the district with his handcart full of grinding wheels. He missed nothing as he talked up business amongst the local women, treating them to his black-and-gold smile, and smelling to high heaven. Eli guessed why he'd come.

Sold him milk and eggs, even brewed him tea. Told him he could camp on his top field. Let him see he was alone.

Didn't do the nosey old fellow any good. She was miles away, sitting by the front window of Owen and Margaret's first home, safe with Eli's dearest friends until he could join her. She had rested her hands on her growing belly, feeling the baby kick, watching the sea. Maybe that was why Lily had loved it so when she was little.

Her baby; her daughter; their Lily. The one reason she had never looked back, never changed her mind or given her affection to another man. Eli, with his bachelor habits, had come more than half-way to meet her, even indulging her traditions in the matter of hygiene, custom, and folk-lore.

They had both tried hard for Lily's sake, but on one thing she had taken the initiative – though neither of them could have foreseen the repercussions. She made a deliberate choice to leave the Gypsy life behind. If Lily was to have any chance, if they were to protect their secret, Mahalia knew she must sever all ties to her Romani past. She must remove herself from all possibility of coming face to face with her tormentor.

At the beginning, she had done it willingly, from gratitude, but eventually out of love and admiration. No other woman could have been so cherished.

❦

Where was Lily? She tried to speak her name but was conscious that no sound came out. Lily spoke to her. She could feel her daughter's strong young hand clasping hers.

Mahalia slept, but when she awoke, although she tried, her eyes refused to open properly. If there were people in the room with her, they were too far away to understand what they were saying.

She missed her husband. As if in answer to her unspoken wish, she recognised his footsteps coming closer to the bed. She sighed, and let go of Lily's hand. She would be all right now, and so would Lily, her Dada was there. No, she began to struggle again, something was wrong with that, but she was too tired to remember. Eli's face bent over hers. He was smiling.

Eli was there. Eli. He'd rescued her just as he did before. He held out his hand. She'd been unable to move earlier. Why was that? No matter, there was no pain preventing her now. She placed her small soft palm over his old gnarled fingers, safe at last. He had come back for her.

THIRTY THREE

Lily hadn't noticed him, at first. It was only as they turned to leave the church that she saw his tall figure in the shadowy corner behind the door. He looked at her directly, and in her confusion she turned away.

Margaret's arm was round her shoulders. She still had the irrational feeling that she would wake up, that all of this was part of an imaginary scene, a precursor for a future event. It couldn't be happening now. She ought to be weeping, but felt weak, unable to swallow. Nothing around her had any substance. Her feet moved over the flag stones, Margaret's arm gripped her tightly, and now there was someone else there too. Someone she ought to know, who seemed familiar, but she couldn't concentrate, couldn't even speak.

It wasn't over yet. They were outside again, in the mid-December drizzle, walking the short distance to the cemetery for the interment.

Lily's curious trance continued as she sat in the funeral director's imposing car for the short journey. It was mid-afternoon and gloomy, everything dulled by fog.

People had tried to talk to her during the days preceding this event, but she had no memory of any conversations, couldn't be sure if she'd managed to speak today. She sat in silence, her eyes drawn to the lighted windows of neighbouring houses.

Owen and Margaret had taken over. The wake was a simple affair, family and close friends only. It was odd being in the house without her mother. No one tried to pull her in one direction or another now, all too shocked by the suddenness of Mahalia's death. In her stillness and silence they let her be.

The walls and floor shifted. She set down her cup, with a clatter, spilling the tea. Margaret caught her as she swayed and held her close.

"Oh, little love," she said, "this is all too much."

❧

The following twenty four hours passed in a blur. She felt too weak to make any comment. It was taken out of her hands. Margaret hovered, and disappeared. Voices broke through the thick gauze around her, but were too indistinct to recognise. Occasionally, when she half-opened her eyes, she could see Gwen, sitting on her bedside chair, clutching grapes and toffees as if on a hospital visit. Gwen had sobbed all through the funeral, there with her parents, solid in their support.

Lily's earlier ordeal had brought about a change in her friend.

She couldn't stop apologising, aghast at what had happened, no longer romantic, chiding herself over and over for going home early, and her frivolous remarks.

Gwen had reproached her when Lily called at the farm. She had been rather stiff, looking at her friend doubtfully when told that Mahalia's origins were news to her too, but she softened when her Dad surprised them by coming in and giving Lily a hug. He had known her Mum was Romani all along, he told her. Saw her play years ago – regular beauty she was.

That explained all the fruit throughout the years.

Like her Dada, in the days when he had farmed, Gwen's father relied on the Gypsies, liked them too. Her friend's romantic notions about their way of life may have taken root from his daydreams. But her father had more practical help to offer. Didn't like to speak out of turn, he said, but if he could advise her in any way she only had to say the word.

But it was too much of a struggle to think. Now her future was blank. All her plans for college had been crushed. What was the point? She was conscious of just being, nothing more, standing there washed, dressed and fed, but motiveless, inert, devoid of feeling.

On the third day after the funeral she had a desire for fresh air, wanting to fill her lungs with sea breeze and dispel the numbness. She and her Dada had always loved the wildness of the sea in winter.

At that time of the year the beaches were empty. She had taken the omnibus to Langland bay. Gwen accompanied her, linking her arm through Lily's and trying to keep pace with her friend's longer stride. They walked around the cliff and back.

A solitary man stood on the sea wall, huddled against the cold in a long coat. A woollen scarf covered most of his face, his hat pulled well down to his ears. He'd been staring out to sea until they crossed his vision, then she became aware that he watched their progress.

Lily didn't break her stride or turn back to look at him. They were two young girls out for a walk: he was a man. Men look at girls, simple equation. When he didn't move, or follow them onto the returning omnibus, she felt relieved.

At four o'clock he knocked on the door. Lily peered at him through the nets at the study window. She could see him more clearly, his face in profile, the tanned skin: she knew who he was. Inside she was churned up with excitement and fear. Once she opened the door and spoke to him there could be no going back. But this was what she had been searching for. This was what she had to face in order to get on with her life.

In the days following her mother's death she had learnt so much. There was ApIvor's letter. She imagined the effect its contents must have had on her mother, yet Mahalia's last words returned to her,

"Remember your Dada, Lily. You had the best father. I have no regrets."

The man at the door sensed her watching and turned towards the opaque net. She saw him sigh, his disappointment evident.

Before Lily could rationalise her actions, she rushed to the door and opened it.

"I know who you are." she said, "Please come in."

Her first impression was how tall he was, and muscled, filling up the space in the hall with his thick woollen overcoat, obliterating the welcome mat with his boots. But there was no mistaking her parentage. His grey eyes matched her own. She ushered him into the front parlour and politely asked for his coat.

"Please," she said, as if entertaining a minister, "sit down, may I offer you a cup of tea?"

His mouth twitched, holding back a smile, but it was there in his eyes. She realised how daft she sounded. Her natural father had just walked into her life. She should be exhibiting some wild emotion: crying, raging, laughing, instead she felt nervous and overawed.

He took off his hat, removed his coat, and held out his hand.

"My name's Harry, Harry Jenkins. I left the name of Howell Pritchard behind a long time ago."

She put her hand in his, but he didn't shake it, only held it gently and looked at her.

"I didn't know that you existed until two months ago, didn't know your mother had survived, or that she'd married Eli."

Lily withdrew her hand, but kindly. She gestured to the sofa and Harry sat down.

"I arrived too late." he said quietly. "It seemed fate intervened again, and I wasn't destined to be with her. She had a different life from the one we planned together." He took in every detail of her appearance. "I imagined you would look like her, but you're fair, like my family. You have her mouth, but not her eyes."

"I know a little of what happened from a letter written by the

Reverend ApIvor and sent on to my mother after his funeral. His sister felt we should have the facts."

Lily took the envelope from the bureau drawer, placed it in his hands, and went out to make the tea.

When she re-entered the room with the tray he was standing at the window, looking at the garden. He handed back the letter.

"I see from the date that he wrote to me on the same day. That's why I'm here. I had to come, Lily. You see I thought Mahalia died all those years ago. Even if you hadn't been prepared to talk to me, it would be enough for me to know you exist." He smiled down at her. "You have a comfortable life here. Eli must have been a wonderful father; I know he was always a good friend to me. He liked children, and was so kind to all of us through the years. It came as such a shock to me to learn that he married Mahalia. Will you tell me what happened, Lily, if you know their history?"

It was costing him such an effort. She saw the pain in his eyes when he mentioned her mother's name. She had been his first real love, Louise had told her, and you never forget.

They talked for several hours, first one, then the other, filling in the blanks in each other's lives. He stopped abruptly, and rose to his feet.

"I must go, you look all in. It wasn't fair of me to spring this on you so soon..."

She looked into the hall mirror as he left, and saw what he must have seen, her own pale, exhausted face. She touched his arm.

"Come back tomorrow, won't you? There are people I'd like you to meet."

That was a week ago. The man she would always call Harry, stood, and stretched, accidentally knocking the lampshade as he did so.

"Sorry, love, not used to such grand houses any more, well, perhaps I should say being inside a house. More used to living rough, in the outback," he added, catching her look.

His eyes twinkled, ready to tease her at the first opportunity.

"Seriously," he said, "you should see the spreads out there. Acres of land. If you knew what most immigrants left behind, Lily, you'd understand. He put his head on one side, determined to lighten her mood. "Besides," his grin broadened, "with your Gypsy blood you should yearn for more space, the open air, you'd be right at home."

Lily smiled back. He was hard to resist. Despite her loyalty to her father's memory, she liked this man. From all that she had learnt recently, Eli had liked him too, treating him as a son when he was younger. She didn't think her Dada had been too bad a judge of character.

"Will you go back to the village?"

"No, I'm not going to stir up a lot of old memories."

"Not even to see Louise?"

"I'm not sure I'm ready for that. Too many bad things happened in that village. There are still some outside the family who might recognise me. I value my freedom too much to jeopardise everything."

"So you'll return to Australia eventually?"

"I only came all this way to see you. But now I'm here, I see no good reason to hurry."

Lily looked alarmed.

"You won't take any risks, will you? What I mean is, I wouldn't want the authorities to-"

"No, love, don't fret about that. I'm legally Harry Jenkins as far as everyone's concerned." He sat back down again. Lily perched on the arm of the sofa opposite to listen. "I'm planning to buy a parcel of land when I get back, and try a new venture. I once worked for an estate that produced hops so I'm going to price equipment and stock while I'm here..." He reached across, and caught up her hand. "...You know, Lily, I can never hope to be the sort of father that Eli was to you, and I don't want you to think that I'm trying to muscle in and replace him. But you are my daughter and I would like the chance to get to know you better. You've given me hope, something to shoot for. Come with me, just to take a look. If you hate it I'll put you on the next boat back."

Lily didn't withdraw her hand, and waited for him to finish. She stared at the floor, feeling conflicted. She wanted to know this man better, but still remain loyal to the memory of her parents.

On the other side of the world she could hold her head up, confident that no one would pass judgement or spread malicious rumours. There were no visible scars. She could get on with her life. There was nothing to stop her going. She could always come back with her own funds to rely on, but she was afraid. She couldn't define the reason. Maybe it was simply a basic fear of the unknown, or, and this was more disconcerting, that she might enjoy it so much, she wouldn't want to return.

Impulsively she squeezed his hand, and bounced to her feet.

Harry stood, believing that their conversation was over. He looked disappointed. Lily further surprised him by putting her arms around him in a brief, enthusiastic hug.

"Let me sleep on it. I need to get away, but it's a big decision."

The next fortnight passed in a haze of goodwill and excitement for Lily. She had made up her mind to go with Harry. If her friends had anxieties, they kept them hidden. Owen was in charge of her affairs and although she sensed his misgivings, he approved a change of scene for her. Even if it proved temporary.

At the end of the month, when he had finished all his business transactions, Harry would join her and they would sail together on the evening departure from Bristol. He would arrive at ten sharp that morning, he said, and buy both tickets, keeping them with him in case of delay.

She felt a prickle of fear at those words. They would have one last farewell meeting with those she loved. Gwen had volunteered to see them off.

On Thursday, Lily woke too early. For the first time in that dark autumn and winter she felt hope. The prospect of a different environment kept her mood buoyant, despite the thick sea fret that had crept in overnight.

At nine-thirty she went from window to window overlooking the lane, straining to see each approaching vehicle, willing it to stop.

Gwen and her parents arrived at half-past ten. There was still no sign of Harry, but Gwen's Dad said he was sure to have been delayed on the road, what with the weather...

But when eleven passed, and the half hour, they were plunged into gloom. Lily felt angry. He had let her down. Cracks appeared in Harry's story. His relationship with her mother ended badly. Would he leave in the same way? Just take off with no message. Perhaps he had doubts of his own, and had taken the easy way out? Perhaps?

At one o'clock Owen set off for Harry's hotel, half-expecting to encounter a reason, like an accident, or a blocked road, that would account for the delay. They would never make the sailing now.

Lily went to her room and threw herself on the bed. She had been a fool to believe in a fairytale ending. There was no hope. Owen would learn the truth. There would be time enough to pass judgement when he returned.

THIRTY FOUR

Nancy sat at her ornate dressing table and contemplated her reflection. Ever since she saw the announcement in the newspaper, she had been brimming with spite. That girl! That spoilt bloody girl, getting the lot now. Well she'd go to the funeral. No one could prevent her doing that. Funerals were open to all comers – but as for paying her respects.

A mean look slid across her face as she picked up her glass perfume dispenser and squeezed the miniature tasselled bellows. Her new perfume, 'Parisian Nocturne' would knock them for a six, but the nozzle spluttered. It was already empty. She pouted her lips, and added another layer of glistening carmine. Nancy Pritchard, as was, would give them something to talk about. Make sure everyone saw her too, and if there was a chance she could speak her mind about that Gypsy upstart, she would. After all, what could they do? She would only be voicing what others dared not say.

She had kept her real feelings well hidden from Frank when she mentioned her wish to attend the service. He had patted her hand.

"Tell you what, Nancy, why don't you take the Rolls? I'll get Reg to drive you in case it's too much for you, my little petal."

Inside she was crowing. Mildred, at the dress shop, had been overheard to say only bookies like Frank could afford a Rolls, 'them that wasn't toffs', as she had so crudely asserted. Let them envy her, let them talk. She was the one on the inside, not them.

She checked her lipstick, careful not to smudge the outline, and pulled on her new hat. It was a low-brimmed cloche with a sable rosette and matching pom-poms fixed to one side. They bounced whenever she moved her head. Her coat had a wide sable collar and cuffs. Everything about her shouted 'rich', nothing spoke of class. Frank gave her a look of benevolent approval. He liked her to wear his money, and she was happy to oblige.

Outside it was misty, with a promise of thicker fog as they drove west towards the border. Reg kept his eyes on the road, making no attempt at conversation. Nancy made a point of ignoring him. She also ignored the scenery. Her inner vision of the day's promise unfolded before her eyes.

It made her shudder to think of it – Old Eli and a Gyppo girl. Let that trollop of a daughter object to her presence. She was ready for all of them.

❦

The little village of Carnegie was shrouded in fog so dense it obscured every detail. She rubbed the inside of the car window thinking it dirty, but the surroundings were no clearer.

Damn! A light concealing mist would be helpful, not this pea souper. Nancy was reluctant to park too close to the church entrance for fear of drawing attention. But in these conditions, if they parked too far away she would miss everything.

Reg pulled in and waited with gloved hands on the steering wheel until she gave him instructions. They were an hour early. He opened the glass partition.

"Do you want me to cut the engine?"

His tone was peremptory, just this side of dislike.

"Did I ask you to cut the engine?"

Bloody chauffeur, who does he think he is?

"I only meant that it'll be a long wait until the funeral's over." he said, with exaggerated patience. "I need to find more fuel if I'm to keep the engine running and the interior warm enough for you. It might be difficult to find a garage down here."

His attempt at being conciliatory was not lost on her.

Yes, that's right. You keep a civil tongue, my man.

She tossed her head so that each of the sable pom-poms jiggled provocatively.

"Drive down into the Mumbles, and let me out at the first hotel advertising coffee."

He nodded, and moved the car forward at a crawl until they drew level with the Anchor Hotel. It was small, but respectable. A sign, illuminated in the gloom, read 'Morning coffee'.

Nancy rapped on the glass, too impatient to bother with the speaking tube.

"This'll do, fetch me in half an hour."

Reg stopped the car, and Nancy waited pointedly until he opened the rear passenger door. He seemed to be taking longer than usual. She climbed out, with an audible 'Tut', and walked towards the hotel steps.

He wasted no time in driving off. Nancy turned back to glare at the disappearing car – and froze.

A man walked out of the mist and past the hotel steps in front of her. A man whose long stride and silhouette she would know anywhere. Disbelief stopped her mid step, but she had just enough presence of mind to follow him before he disappeared into the wall of fog. The Rolls Royce was still visible; small pinpricks of lights moving slowly for fear of collision.

It's Howell. I swear to God it's him, but it can't be. What's he doing here?

Her heart was drumming loudly in her chest. She slowed her pace as he hesitated and looked up and down the road. Nancy clutched the brim of her hat to conceal her face. He went up the steps of a small boarding house, and in that split second she made a decision.

She half ran back to the Anchor hotel, positioned herself in the window of the coffee lounge, and waited for Reg to return. Her former plan was discarded. She had but one goal now, to find out why her brother was here. All the hurt she had buried long ago at his disappearance surged through her on a wave of bile. She pushed her half-finished coffee to one side slopping it into the saucer, ignoring the dark brown stain spreading onto the snowy cloth.

What had that funny little Welshman, Merrick, said? Ah yes, he had sympathised, with her, she remembered. About the only person who had, all these years down the line. There was always one black sheep in a family, he said, but in this instance it was more serious. He had hinted there might even be a reward for information. She naturally assumed he meant the police, but first she had a little investigating of her own to do.

She wondered how much help she could expect from Reg. He was not much use except to drive the vehicle, and she didn't trust him. Something about the way she caught him looking at her grated.

She wondered if she had the nerve to talk to her brother, but the old anger wouldn't subside enough for that. It would be more prudent to watch, and wait. There was an outside chance he was going to the funeral.

Reg returned fifteen minutes before the service.

Nancy was eager to get as near the lychgate as possible for the best view.

"Park about twenty feet away, Reg, I haven't decided whether or not to go in yet. It might be too upsetting."

Reg followed her instructions, letting the engine idle. Nancy pulled her compact from her bag, and applied touches to her make up, angling her mirror to watch for the cortège.

She opened the car door without waiting for Reg to oblige.

"I will go in after all. I feel a little better now. You needn't hang about for me. Go and get yourself something to eat, but be here by one. That will give me time to talk to the family."

With a show of solemnity she walked up the path, waited until Reg pulled away, then doubled back and hid amongst the grave stones.

She had a clear view of the mourners. She didn't have to wait long, recognising the slim figure of Eli's daughter in the company of a large plump woman. Funny, she didn't look much like Old Eli. She was fair. This thought hovered at the back of her mind, as she watched the company go in.

The last of the mourners' transport arrived, and her brother emerged from the one of the cabs. As he stood in the church porch, under the light, the truth of Lily Jenkins's origins struck her with the impact of a physical blow. She clutched the nearest headstone for support.

Images whirled through her mind: the Gypsy girl in the graveyard, her brother's reaction when she mentioned 'his girl', all that secrecy, Eli's mystery note to Howell the day he disappeared, Eli marrying a Gyppo and coming to live here, and that girl, with her fair curly hair and those grey eyes – their family's eyes.

How could she have been so slow and stupid? The mother *was* that Gyppo, the one who grabbed her in the churchyard, and the father, the father had been her own brother. He'd obviously been sent away in disgrace. Bloody right too, brought shame on the lot of them. But that Gyppo, she must have got round Eli, he was always soft on them. Must have wheedled her way into making him believe it was his child, conniving bitch.

Her anger spilled over. And here was Howell come to pay his respects. It made her want to spit. Well she'd fix that. If they were all going to kiss and make up, she'd make bloody sure they didn't.

She was impatient to go home now, and regretted her decision to send Reg away just when he could have been useful. It was too far to walk down to the town and back. Should have stuck to her guns with Frank, and brought her own car, but she was well aware that Reg had been sent to keep an eye on her. Time to make a few plans while she waited. God, it was so cold. That bloody Reg had better not keep her waiting.

First of all, she would use her own car; pretend she was off to see Louise again, then visit the detective agency her friend Madge had used in Cheltenham. If she could find out Howell's plans, she would know when to have him arrested. She wondered about the size of the reward. It would give her a bit of independence from Frank.

She decided it would be prudent to move away from the church and meet Reg as he came up the lane. When she rounded the corner, she was surprised to see the rear lights of the Rolls. He had obviously decided to park up and wait. She wondered if he had stayed in the car for the duration, or whether he had been watching her.

Before she reached the vehicle, Reg got out. He looked displeased, but said nothing. Nancy decided to bluff it out.

"I'm glad you're back early. Couldn't bear to wait until the end, all too upsetting. Home, I think, away from this gloomy atmosphere. And don't stop on the way."

Reg drove off in silence. Nancy retreated into her inner world once more. No doubt he would complain to Frank about her odd behaviour, but she could forestall all that. She had a mission now; a chance for revenge. After all these years she wanted to enjoy its sweet taste.

The Montgomery Detective Agency appeared neither seedy nor particularly prosperous. Nancy was not sure what she had expected. The exterior was bland, discreet. Its small outer office contained the minimum of furniture, no pot plants or flowers, just one side table with several of the day's newspapers set in a neat overlapping row.

Hardly had she closed the door, when a man emerged from the back room. He was not much older than her, mousy-haired, dapper, his eyes intelligent behind wire-rimmed spectacles. Everything about him matched the low-key environment, and for a moment Nancy regretted her decision to come here. She would have to be careful how she phrased things. If he suspected her of tracking the movements of a wanted man, she might miss out on the reward.

She introduced herself as 'Miss Millward', but before she could elaborate he came forward with an ingratiating smile, and solved the problem for her.

"Is this a domestic matter, Miss? Someone you would like us to trace?"

He had mistaken her reticence for shyness.

Projecting herself into the role of injured fiancée, Nancy began her tale. By the time she finished Mr Montgomery was engrossed. Yes, he assured her, he would have all the information for her by the end of the week.

"You understand why I must ring you?"

Nancy repeated her question, anxious about her own domestic arrangements.

"Yes, of course, Miss Millward. We pride ourselves on our

discretion; you may be assured of that. And it is you, as the client, who sets the contact arrangements to suit yourself."

Her plan was perfect. She returned to Frank's apartment in a brighter mood.

❦

The week passed slowly, with Nancy starting at the sound of the telephone, despite Mr Montgomery's repeated assurances, and chewing her thumbnail with a distracted air. She accompanied Frank to various race meetings, but could not have named any winners if pressed. At the end of the week she made a return trip to the agency, and found the information exceeded her expectations.

The news of her brother's departure surprised her. He had bought two tickets – one for himself, and one in the name of a Miss Lily Jenkins, due to sail the following Thursday. Time enough to stop that, but first a long overdue visit to the police.

It took a while to convince the tired detective assigned to speak to her, that she wasn't a vindictive ex girlfriend, but wished to amend certain iniquities caused by the person who had shamed their family. 'Civic-minded' were the words she'd used. He was unimpressed.

He denied all knowledge of anyone called Merrick, but became thoughtful at her description. Could she come back, he said, once he had made his own inquiries? In the meantime he needed her full name and address. When she hesitated, for that brief second, his gaze sharpened.

Oh Hell! What does it matter? Frank won't care. He's a respectable bookmaker, not a low-life.

On her return visit the detective had more questions, and information of his own. Her brother may have sold his papers illegally – they could question him about that – although it was a long time ago. They'd been used by a known criminal, Jeremiah Blake. He had said the name slowly, watching her reaction. This man had subsequently died, he continued, out of the country. There were ends that needed tying up, so no doubt her brother could help them with that.

But his last words were the most upsetting.

"There was no reward. It seems certain the man who visited you was nothing to do with us – most likely an associate of the man, Blake."

"But you'll act on my information?"

The detective's expression remained professionally non-committal.

"We will probably question him, yes."

"Oh, I wonder. Must I be called on to identify him? There are others, my closest sister Louise would be better able. She is only a year younger than him. I would prefer to stay out of it."

If there was nothing for her financially, she didn't want to know.

"I shall have to confer with my superiors about that, Miss. I'll be in touch."

Nancy left feeling extraordinarily pleased with herself.

Back home once more, she let herself in by the side door to the apartment block, and ran all the way up the sweep of stairs to the top floor. On the hall chair sat her old doll, which she took everywhere for sentimental reasons. Her battered portmanteau was on the floor, with her one good suitcase next to it. They were obviously packed. What was going on? Were they moving? Frank never said.

Reg emerged from Frank's study. His expression showed open contempt. He sauntered across the room, too near to her for comfort.

"Seems you'll be leaving us, and not before time. Don't bother," he said, as she looked towards the door, "Frank won't see you. You're to go." He lowered his voice. It was all the more threatening. "Think you're such a clever little madam, don't you? Left a trail even a fool like him could follow." He jerked his head towards the study door. "One thing he doesn't forgive is chasing after other men."

"What?" Angry now, she pushed past him. He took his hands out of his pockets, prepared to manhandle her out of the apartment. Nancy was an old hand at deflecting this sort of intimidation. She screamed loudly up into his face, and yelled,

"Get you hands off me! Frank! Frank!" The door opened behind them. Frank stood in the entrance. She marched over to him. "Perhaps, instead of listening to your hired help, you'll at least let me explain my side of things. If you think I've been chasing after another man then say so to my face, don't turn your guard dog loose on me!"

She swept into his office. With a dismissive nod towards Reg, he shut the door. He kept his back to her, and looked out of the window.

"If you'd asked me, Frank, you would know that I've been helping the police with their inquiries about my brother. He disgraced our family and left for Australia years ago. I saw him at the funeral, and I've been investigating his return for reasons of my own."

Frank looked back at her, over his shoulder. His tone was disbelieving.

"A brother?"

"Yes, my eldest brother, Howell Pritchard. You can check everything for yourself if you don't believe me."

He moved over to his desk, sat down heavily, but seemed reluctant to look at her face. His broad hands played with the gold signet ring on his right little finger. Good. He was sitting down. Once she told him the full story he would be putty in her hands again, might even dismiss that basket Reg for his meddling. Adopting her sincerest tone, she began.

"When I was still with Jim, this chap came round, said my brother had done something illegal. Told me there was a reward for information. So naturally enough, when I saw him back here, after all this time, bold as brass, I thought, well, someone should tell the police." Frank nodded. This was better. He obviously remembered the incident. She and Jimmy had been part of his set. Nancy began to elaborate, confident now that all would be set straight. "Apparently he sold his papers to a gangster. All sounded a bit too far-fetched for me. You know how these so-called detectives are always so full of their own self importance? This one said the man was a fugitive, had an odd name, Jeremiah Blake, something to do with a crime lord in Liverpool and..."

She got no further. Frank made a strangled noise in his throat, and clutched the edge of the desk. He stared at her in horror.

"What did you say? What have you done, you silly bitch?"

"What do you mean? Don't look at me like that, Frank."

Nancy went cold. Frank never swore at her, hated it, wouldn't have any of his men use profanities. Now he glowered at her as if he wanted to hit her, or worse.

"I always knew you were greedy, but I never dreamt you could be this stupid. It seems I was mistaken."

He clutched the glass paperweight she had given him, and banged it hard upon the desk. Reg came back into the room.

"Problem, Frank?"

"Pack her things in the tourer. It's in her name, not much I can do about that. And all her clothes, except the furs and jewels." She was terrified by the change in him. He was having difficulty breathing, and stared past her with frightened eyes. "Give him your keys." When she didn't move his voice rose, barely in control. "Your keys, woman!"

Reg came forward. Nancy backed away and fumbled in her bag.

"All right, wait, here..."

She tossed the keys on to the leather-topped desk. He snatched them up, and left the room.

Frank's hands stopped trembling. Nancy wanted to ask more questions, but self-preservation, ever her strongest suite, won through. He shuddered, and seemed to regain his composure. When he spoke again his voice was resigned, but there was obviously little point in trying to argue with him.

"If you could see beyond your reflection, you might have realised your danger. So let me spell it out for you. Both sides know about you now, and if you value that face of yours, you'll keep as far away from me as possible. Let this be the moment you learn to keep your mouth shut." When she didn't move, he reeled round, shouting at her. "Go on, get out!" He looked towards the door in alarm, and lowered his voice. "If you're wise you'll stay away from the police and forget all about the name of Jeremiah Blake, for both our sakes."

Reg came back. Nancy tensed, expecting more trouble, but he dropped the keys into her hand. When she moved to the door neither man made any sign. From the doorway she had the oddest impression that the tableau before her was skewed. It occurred to her that Reg was in charge.

He kicked the door shut behind her.

Nancy fled.

Outside, she paused, undecided upon her choice of destination. This time there were no obliging friends impressed as long as she was on Frank's arm, worse still, no open wallet from her indulgent lover. She needed money, but she couldn't sell the car; it was her freedom. There was one place she could go, and a source of income that was hers by right.

She climbed behind the wheel and headed back to her old village. Even if Louise was home at this time of day, she could get round that particular obstacle – if she was alone. Better yet she'd wait until her sister went to help at the Chapel then leave a note, an excuse so they'd know it wasn't a robbery. It was all a matter of planning, knowing the other person's habits.

The whole operation took her ten minutes from entering the village to driving back onto the main Hereford to Ross road. Simple, what did her sister want with the bronzes anyway? It would all have gone to Howell if he hadn't fallen out of favour. And after Howell, she was the next favourite. They'd be worth a bit now, and easy to sell. She would be set for a while, until someone else came along.

As the road became less familiar, and the landscape opened up on top of the Cotswolds, she went faster.

It was exhilarating, she decided, being free of her obligation to Frank. She would go to the Smoke, change her name, and her hair colour. There would be money in her pocket once again, and money meant freedom. The initial feeling of panic passed. No one would find her if she set her mind to it. They all underestimated her, everyone she'd ever known – save Howell, and she'd savoured that particular payback.

In a mood of defiance she put her foot to the floor, exalting in the power as the vehicle surged forward. Funny, it wasn't handing as well today. Something was rattling. What a nuisance, she didn't want to waste precious money getting it serviced.

Approaching the first steep downhill gradient, an appalling thought occurred to her. She took her foot off the accelerator and let the tourer coast. Now she had it, knew what had been niggling her. That expression on Reg's face as he slammed the door. It had been triumphant.

THIRTY FIVE

It had been Harry's intention to leave his holdall at the boarding house, but when he came down early the next morning there was no hot breakfast, and no landlady. He had not encountered the husband before, although he had been aware of his presence from occasional raised voices, and a whiff of pipe smoke from their back parlour. His landlord's face was set and unsmiling.

"There's been inquiries made about you, twice now. Not the police or I'd have had you out of here double quick. But twice is too many. We run a respectable house here, and I intend to keep it that way. You're to go, right now. My wife's too upset to cook this morning."

He stared at Harry with growing belligerence.

This was unexpected, and would upset his plans for the day. He frowned, and risked a question.

"I'm confused, since I don't know anyone hereabouts. Who was it, you said two?"

"All I know is there were two, on separate occasions. One of them put the wind up my wife proper. You say you don't know who these people are, but they clearly know about you. Now, that's as much as I'm prepared to say. You've got five minutes." And he left the room abruptly.

Harry was stunned. He must act fast. There was no time to contact anyone or go back to the house. He had appointments. All his arrangements *must* be clear and settled by ten the following morning for his departure with Lily.

By the time the train arrived at Bristol, he was convinced he was being followed.

At first, seeing the same man pass through the carriage several times didn't seem so very out of the ordinary. He decided to double back once on the station, and, sure enough, his 'shadow' did the same. This man didn't resemble any member of the constabulary that he'd ever encountered. He was tall, close to his own height, flashily dressed, and when he looked at Harry directly his expression was sardonic.

It struck Harry that his pursuer, whoever he was, wanted him to know he was being followed, but if not the police, then who was he, and more importantly, why? No one else knew he was back in England. No one who could associate him with the name of 'Pritchard'...unless... No, it was too far fetched to imagine there was some older connection; that all these years later anyone would remember, let alone care.

Over lunchtime he thought he'd lost him. He relaxed and concentrated on the tasks in hand. As he caught the return train, having decided to throw himself on Lily's hospitality for his last night, even if it meant the sofa, he saw him again. This time he was wearing a large mackintosh over the loud suit, and was accompanied by another, older man. Perhaps he had imagined it; the whole incident was no more than coincidence. Yet there was something familiar about his companion. The recollection of his physique, that broad slab of a face partially concealed beneath a greying beard triggered a warning. He had met the intimidating 'Lemp' before.

"Remember," Lemp had repeated, slowly for good measure. "You are no longer Howell Pritchard, and never will be again if you know what's good for you."

Harry stood, stretched, and concentrated on the men sitting at the far end of the carriage, overtly reading their early evening newspapers. His fears were confirmed, and with them a certainty that he must do nothing to endanger Lily.

The train slowed as it approached the outskirts of Swansea. His fellow passengers roused themselves, buttoning up their coats, adjusting hats, retrieving packages from the parcel shelf. He took advantage of the clamour to stand nearest the door, ready to leap onto the platform and make good his escape.

Out of the corner of his eye, he saw Lemp nudge the other man, yet remain in his seat. He was peering through the window, and obviously didn't like what he saw. Harry looked again. There was a policeman on the concourse and a pair waiting by the barrier.

Two women behind him, handicapped by their thick winter clothing, struggled to disembark with their bags and parcels.

"Allow me." Harry smiled at the older woman and helped her on to the platform. "Is someone meeting you? Can I carry these to a taxi?"

He wound his scarf closer and pulled his hat brim over his eyes. Neither woman questioned his actions. It was cold, foggy, the station filled with steam and smoke. Everyone was similarly muffled. He shepherded both women towards the barrier laden with all their baggage, inclining towards them as if he belonged. They were tired, grateful. A perfect shield against authority.

He walked away from the station in the opposite direction from the main town. He saw no sign of his pursuers immediately, and took a roundabout route towards the docks, moving quietly from the protection of one dark entry to another.

A car, unusual by its appearance in such a rundown area, cruised past the end of the alley. He recognised the passenger's profile. When the noise of the engine had faded into the distance, he forced the door of an empty building. Its lock was rusty and gave easily. The entrance stank of urine. A place for tramps; down and outs, misplaced persons like himself. He would hide here for the present, another twenty four hours if necessary. The risk for Lily was too great. If anyone traced his ticket, they would be disappointed. He had no intention of making that particular sailing now. Lily. This subterfuge was all for his daughter, though she would not understand.

By Thursday evening, he felt sure the threat had moved away. Dusk offered a temporary respite, keeping him hidden from prying eyes while he agonised over his deepening turmoil concerning Lily.

It was easy to lose himself amidst the constant stream of activity around the ships and goods' yards. No one paid his tanned, scarred face any attention. There were so many foreign faces on these busy quays.

What was he doing? Now there were unknown would-be assailants; police interest; scandal and recrimination to add to the mix.

Leaving his bag in the back room of a small public house, for a price, he walked the few miles out to Lily's home, hiding in fields each time a carter passed.

A single light burned on the top front landing. The rest of the house was closed and silent. He stole around to the back yard and found the key Lily had described for emergencies.

Once inside, he breathed more easily. Those irate protective friends he might encounter were minor considerations compared with forces outside.

He tried Lily's door, but before it was fully open she murmured, "Who is it? Margaret, is that you?"

Lily struck a match, and he heard her gasp. Before she could chastise him or call out, he crossed to the windows, shut the curtains, and using his own matches, lit her lamp. He realised she must be half asleep, unsure of what she was seeing. He spoke to her in a fierce whisper, anxious not to wake the rest of the house.

"Lily, listen to me. Don't be frightened. I know you believe I let you down, but circumstances have altered. You need to hear me out, as I haven't much time. Do you understand?"

Shock and surprise, combined with the urgency in his voice, had their effect. He watched her come fully awake regaining control. She didn't speak, just stared at him wide-eyed.

He sat on the edge of her bed and reached for her hand.

"When I was sent away from home all those years ago, I did something reckless, even stupid. I sold my identity papers to a stranger on the dockside for a handful of bank notes. I have no excuse other than that I was young and desperate. Now it seems that I am being followed, either by the police, or by those who've had time to reflect on their mistake in not taking what they needed then, by force."

She gripped his hand tightly, but didn't interrupt.

"I have only two choices, and neither option is a happy one. If I admit to being Howell Pritchard then I will probably be arrested, as, although I was under age at the time, it was still a crime to trade my identity for money. If I stay in my present disguise, those who have recognised me will consider me 'unfinished business' and continue to track me down. They followed me to Bristol and back. God knows how they found me. I have no alternative but to return home as best I can. There are passages aplenty from Swansea to ports all over the world. It may take a while by a roundabout route. Once back in Australia, I don't think I will have any further problems, but I need time to be sure. Above all, Lily..." He sensed she was about to protest, and cut her off. "Above all, I must keep you safe."

She was crying now, repeating 'take me with you'. He longed

to comfort her as he might a toddler, rocking her back and forth, but it would weaken his resolve. He must tell her his plan, and go before she could protest.

"Not now, Lily, but soon. Long ago, Old Eli made a pact with your mother to keep you both safe. We must do the same. If he could manage such a secret, despite greater odds, then so can we. Promise me, Lily. Promise you will say nothing until I can send for you, and we have the chance of a new life. If the rest of the world vilifies me, calls me names for deserting you twice, a weak man incapable of love or commitment, do not enlighten them. Tell Owen, as I sense you can trust him with your life, but only if needs must. Lily?"

He stood up, preparing to leave, but she leapt from the bed and hugged him. Her arms formed a tight band around his chest. He relented enough to caress her hair, and held her until her grip relaxed.

"We have each other now, Lily, father and daughter. I swear I will not desert you. This is only a temporary setback. Everything I do, from now on, will be with you in mind. You're a bright girl. Don't give either of us away."

She didn't attempt to argue, instead she clung to him. He gently disengaged himself, pushing her away until he could see her face.

"Tell me you understand, Lily."

She nodded, and began to smile, slowly at first, until it transformed into a radiant reminder of her mother. He touched her cheek, and left as quickly and silently as he came.

As he began the long trudge back to collect his belongings, he sensed she was still smiling. It kept him going. She had understood.

Epilogue
1964

She had never wanted to return to England, but Harry made her promise – the journey now a matter of days not six weeks by sea.

As the plane approached Heathrow, Lily craned forward in her window seat, watching the ground come steadily closer. Five decades of change had transformed the landscape. The trauma of her long-distant departure from the country below had faded, but not the long-term damage.

Once the finite arrangements of her parents' wills had been clarified; property sold or rented, furniture stored, for the present, and all matters financial supervised by Owen, she was able to consider Harry's proposal in earnest. It was not without opposition. Eventually Owen conceded her right to make up her own mind, and two years later than originally planned Lily set out to join her natural father with the prospect of a new life.

It was a bitter-sweet reunion, but she had come to love him.

Years later, Louise visited alone. Jack had insisted, being reluctant to travel himself 'on account of his back.' Her joy at seeing Lily again was evident; the reunion with Harry, as anticipated, on the surface all they had hoped for. But beneath the tears Lily glimpsed something else in her aunt's eyes – a mote of anger for the hurt. She sensed that at a deeper level the disappearance of her brother would remain unforgiven. She doubted the hardened insular man known as Harry registered his fault.

He outlived all his brothers and sisters, succumbing finally to the ravages of the sun in his eighty second year. She felt a curious release amidst the loss. His last words had come as a surprise, rattled her even now as she tried to picture her natural parents together.

"I married her, Lily, Gypsy fashion. We were Gypsy husband and wife, that's what she said, when the broom was in flower."

His mind had wandered, sliding in and out of lucidity, preferring the morphine-induced dreams that released him from pain into that lost reality.

"Take me back," he begged, repeatedly, "back to the 'Lip', where it happened." She had agreed, more to stem his wandering and fretfulness than anything else. It distressed her. When she sat with him, he would clutch her hand. There was strength left in his grip, but his skin was sun-withered and blotchy, raw in places. The nurses discouraged him, gently disengaging his fingers from Lily's. He seemed not to notice.

"So many mistakes, Lily. Every choice I made was wrong. And when I tried to make amends, I only made it worse."

She had ignored directives and held his hand right until the end, unable to make a coherent tale from the ramblings, conscious only of his sense of loss.

Her Mam and Dada lay at rest together in the small cemetery overlooking the sea, had done for over forty years. Owen and Margaret, their friends and close neighbours in life, had joined them later, their grave a dozen yards away.

Despite her long relationship with her natural father, Eli had raised her and remained first in her affections and memory. Yet curiosity, and the desire to take one last look at her birthplace, enticed her back.

Her encounter with Reuben had marred her life, altered her outlook so completely that she had avoided men, never marrying or even enjoying a courtship. Mingled with her latent anger was shame, for despite all logic, she could never escape the memory of her abduction. It revisited her dreams in times of fever and illness.

She had filled her life in different ways; a career in teaching, drawing warmth enough from friends and family in her adopted country.

During the long flight home, she compared the similarities between Harry's life and her own. All his ambitions, his future with her mother, had been crushed by his own clash with Reuben; it was almost as if there had been a pattern destined to be repeated. Their lives in Australia had been so far removed from all they had encountered in England. There were moments when she felt those incidents long ago were part of another family's history. It would all end with her.

Jem offered to accompany her. They had kept in touch throughout the years, first through Gwen, and later following his marriage. She had been surprised when, after all this time, he volunteered to drive her back to Herefordshire to fulfil this last commitment.

He met her at the airport. Lily barely recognised him. No long Gypsy curls, no discernible trace of her young admirer from all those years ago, but an ordinary man, thicker set, grey-haired, sporting a trimmed moustache, with children, and grandchildren of his own.

They stayed in London that first day. She needed time to adjust being ten hours out of step with the world around her, yet eager to shake off jet-lag, complete her task, and spend the remaining time with her cousin and his family.

Sitting in the window of a café, she watched the young people saunter past with their air of studied nonchalance. It was a kaleidoscope of colour and fashions. Apparently anything went in 1964. Amongst the parade were so many Gypsy styles, gathered blouses, embroidery, layered skirts, and gold hooped earrings. On the road, convoys of hippies in hand painted buses craved the Gypsy life. She could remember the brief flirtation with Romani culture inspired by the artist Augustus John, back when she was a girl, but it never lasted. Five centuries of suspicion were hard to eradicate. The life of a wandering traveller in a horse-drawn painted waggon had become an anachronism. These days a Romani face would be hard to define in a crowd.

Jem had brought a packet of black and white photographs with him.

"You might like to see these, Lily. I've settled in one place, lived in the same house now for years, bought several acres of land around it. With my boys we collect and do up the old vardos, paint and repair them, and such. You'd be surprised how many people want them – even shipped a few to America."

She was interested in his family.

"And your children, have they settled?"

"Two of them work with me. My daughter, though, she married out. Don't see as much of her as I would like."

"Where does she live?"

"Back west. Married a local boy from Ledbury..." He laughed ruefully seeing her expression. "It's a different life these days. My sons tried travelling when they were younger. There are still Romani on the road, but they travel in metal caravans pulled by lorries these days. It becomes harder and harder to find places to stop. There are those who want to carry on as a matter of principle, you understand? Need to hold on to it all. But the day will come when the gaje force us to stop, or we run out of room. They want to fill up every space, it seems to me, thought I'd beat them at their own game."

"You're a long way from Wales now, Jem." She enjoyed the musical lilt in his voice. It took her a while to readjust, retuning her ear to forgotten rhythms, and expressions.

"My wife Gemile is Kent Rom'. I like it there. It's similar to Herefordshire to look at, same sorts of crops. Better for business, from our point of view. And there are many more of us who have an

351

interest in reviving the traditions living thereabouts. Gemile writes about it. We still go to the fairs, try and speak a bit of the old language. To honour the customs, you understand?"

"You should set up a museum."

"We've talked about it. A few have, of course, among the bigger families. Soon they'll be one in each county. One day, it is to be hoped there'll be a revival in the old ways. Look at what's happened with the Welsh language. Remember how it was?"

"Yes, I do." She pulled a wry face. "At school we were punished if we lapsed into Welsh. Yet it was the language of my father, and my mother too. I never heard her speak Romani, though, until I met up with you. But *outside* our home it was always English spoken, especially in South Wales."

"Well nowadays," Jem laughed, "even the road signs are in both languages, and mighty long ones they are too!"

The next day they travelled down, but despite progress during the intervening decades, the journey to the Marches was still slow. There was a relaxed atmosphere between them, and they spoke in Welsh, hesitantly at first, but warming to their enjoyment as old phrases conjured even older memories.

Jem had booked two rooms at The Hopsack, an inn on the banks of the Lugg, not far from her father's village. The river drew her gaze. It seemed the logical place to scatter Harry's ashes, but it was high summer, the water looked too low and clear for her purpose.

They sat in the pub garden drinking local cider.

"If you don't mind, Jem, I'd like to walk through the village and complete this last ceremony by myself."

"No, not at all, it's up to you, love. I'll stretch my legs down by the river, supposed to be good fishing hereabouts. I'll drop you at the end of the by-pass though. It joins the old lane, according to this new map."

Lily recalled the name of the hill, 'the Devil's Lip', one of her parents' special places. She would try to find a suitable spot, and cast Harry's ashes into the wind from up there.

It was a steeper climb that she had anticipated. On reaching the top, she discovered the wild place of yesteryear was now the site of a small car park complete with National Trust signs describing its history; how many counties could be seen from the vantage point; the height of the hill, and much other information. She felt oddly disappointed. Her parents' trysting place had disappeared under encroaching tourism.

Behind a new wooden fence, broom thickets, old, straggling, blackened with a myriad seed pods, rattled and swayed as each gust caught them. Occasionally the buffeting stopped, and in the silence Lily could hear the remaining late pods crackle as they twisted open, dispersing their minute seeds.

She climbed over the stile and followed the footpath along the ridge. Here the broom rose higher affording her enough protection to remove the lid from the plastic urn she had chosen. It had seemed the more practical solution, lighter, and more portable than the usual ornate plaster.

Beneath the arching branches the earth was bare. There were hollows large enough to sit in comfort. She imagined her mother and Harry sitting there, and paused to look over the landscape, trying to see it through their eyes. There was no hint of their presence.

Stop being fanciful.

She sighed aloud and the wind rose again echoing her sentiment. Her mother's spirit had gone, joined with her Dada's back when Lily was little more than a girl. There could be no trace of it here. That brief love affair had been long before their settled happy marriage. The young Howell Pritchard, once blessed with the face of an angel, was unrecognisable as the damaged man she knew.

Her mother had made a different choice, married Eli, and enjoyed a life far removed from this tiny village. And brief though her years had been, they were filled with love. She doubted that even in death, and beyond, where ever that might be, her mother's spirit would wait for Harry. But she had made him a promise that his remains would rest in the country of his birth, and now she must honour it.

She shook out the heavier ashes over the roots. In spite of her efforts, an ounce or two of pale grey dust remained in the bottom of the container. When she righted herself, the wind caught in the wide neck, filling the vessel with its own life force, and snatched it from her hands. She tried to grab it, but the exterior had become coated in ash. Her fingers slipped on the surface.

The urn bowled down from the ridge, across the meadows, casting out traces of her ancestry each time it hit the ground. Faster and faster it bounced, higher, arching through the air as it gathered momentum urged on by the following breeze. She could no longer see any dust, only the bronze plastic container bounding down to

354

where bullocks grazed oblivious by the river. It clattered between them, and landed in the water. The animals backed away and ducked their heads, wide-set eyes rolling in alarm. She could see the urn bobbing on the surface, and hurried down after it.

Despite her desire for solemnity, Lily smiled. She watched as the container began to spin. Within seconds it capsized, filled with water, and sank. How appropriate that it should all end here, back where her own history began – on her Dada's farm. And as the current swirled before her, breaking every reflection into wavering bands of colour, she knew that both her real father, and the man everyone had called 'Old Eli', wouldn't mind.

GLOSSARY

Atch	*Stop or wait*
Beebi	*Aunt*
Beng	*Devil*
Bitti	*Little*
Bokt	*Luck*
Boro Puro Dai	*Great grandmother*
Chi	*Girl (child)*
Chal	*Boy (child)*
Chavi, chavo, chavvies	*Child, children*
Churi	*Knife*
Dai	*Mother*
Dadus	*Father*
Dikka	*Look*
Dikalo	*Neckerchief*
Dinilo	*Idiot, fool*
Dir	*Dear*
Dordi!	*Commonly used exclamation*
Drom	*Road*
Dukkering	*Fortune telling*
Familia	*Family (includes extended family)*
Folkendi	*Folk (as in their own people)*

*Gajo, gaje**	*Non Gypsy (singular)* *(plural) *Welsh usage*
Gav	*Village*
Gavvers	*Villagers, can sometimes* *mean policemen*
Grai	*Horse*
Jal, jallin'	*Go, going*
Jukel	*Dog*
Juval	*Girl (young woman)*
Kek	*No*
Kushti	*Good*
Kusi	*Little*
Miro	*My*
Mort	*Woman*
Mush	*Man*
Patrin	*Wayside markers*
Pen, penna	*Sister, sister (affectionate)*
Prala	*Brother*
Puro	*Old (Puro Dai –* *grandmother)*
Rakkli	*Non Gypsy woman*
Rawni	*Lady*

Ratti	*Blood*
Rokra	*Tell, speak*
Rom	*Romany man*
Romipen	*Marriage*
Rommed	*Married*
Sar shan?	*How are you?*
Swiggler	*Pipe (for smoking)*
Tikni	*Baby*
Vardo	*Waggon*
Wafado	*'Bad', a strong curse*
Wonga	*Money*
Yog	*Fire*

ACKNOWLEDGEMENTS

Special thanks to:

Bose Wales of the Romani Cymru Project for help and advice about the Romani way of life and language(and generosity in allowing me to explore his restored 'Jones of Hereford' Burton show waggon). The kind staff at Swansea Museum. Pauline and Will Crawford of the Weekeroo Station, SA, Australia for their warm welcome. Kelvin Jones for his editorial advice. The members of our local literary group in Aylsham for their constructive criticism and support; Gloria, Jemma, Joy, Patricia, Jack and especially Grizelda for her hospitality. My friends Liliane, Penny, and Sheree for reading my early scribblings and encouraging me to continue. Fellow writer Roy Jenner in New Zealand for his interest and enthusiasm. Finally, Maggie for designing this book with professional skill, and love.

Lightning Source UK Ltd.
Milton Keynes UK
21 February 2011

167912UK00001B/1/P